SWEET DREAMS

"Wake up, long rider. It's time to die," Folliard growled through his swollen jaw. He pulled the Colt's trigger and sent a streak of fire blazing down through the blanket. As soon as he'd pulled the trigger, he swung the Colt toward the second blanket on the other side of the campfire, cocked it and braced to fire again. He stood waiting for a second. When no movement came from the other blanket, he looked back down.

"What the hell?" he said. He swung around toward Crane. But instead of seeing his partner standing fifteen feet away where he'd left him, he saw the shadowy outline of a man drawing back the butt stock of a Winchester rifle. "Oh no," he managed to say just as the rifle butt jabbed forward with a fierce blow and nailed him squarely across his forehead.

The Colt in Folliard's hand fired wildly as he fell backward to the ground. . . .

LAWLESS TRAIL

Ralph Cotton

BERKLEY
New York

BERKLEY
An imprint of Penguin Random House LLC
penguinrandomhouse.com

Copyright © 2013 by Ralph Cotton
Excerpt from *Twisted Hills* copyright © 2013 by Ralph Cotton
Penguin Random House supports copyright. Copyright fuels creativity, encourages
diverse voices, promotes free speech, and creates a vibrant culture. Thank you for buying
an authorized edition of this book and for complying with copyright laws by not
reproducing, scanning, or distributing any part of it in any form without permission.
You are supporting writers and allowing Penguin Random House to continue to
publish books for every reader.

BERKLEY and the BERKLEY & B colophon are registered trademarks of
Penguin Random House LLC.

ISBN: 9780451240231

Signet mass-market edition / October 2013
Berkley mass-market edition / March 2023

Printed in the United States of America
7   9   11   13   15   14   12   10   8   6

For Mary Lynn, of course . . .

PART 1

PART 1

Chapter 1

———◆———

Twisted Hills, the Mexican Badlands

The wide dirt street of Paso Alto lay beneath a veil of dry wavering heat as Arizona Ranger Samuel Burrack rode the black-speckled barb at a walk past the Gatos Malos Cantina. From under the brim of his sweat-stained sombrero, he eyed three men seated along a blanket-cushioned swing on the cantina's front porch. Each man held a rifle; each man wore a bandolier of ammunition hanging from his shoulder across his chest.

The three men returned the Ranger's stare, keeping the porch swing moving slowly back and forth with the slightest effort of their scuffed boots.

"That's right, gringo. You just keep moving on along," the man in the middle growled under his breath, more to his two *compañeros* than to the Ranger.

On the man's right, a broad-shouldered Mexican gunman known only as Pesado gave a single grunt of a laugh, finding irony in Ross McCloud calling the stranger a *gringo*. McCloud was from Missouri, after all—less than three months in Paso Alto, where he'd taken refuge from Missouri law.

"You are one *loco bastardo*, Ross," Pesado said with a sharp grin, his dark eyes following the Ranger for a few yards before turning away.

Ross McCloud stared straight ahead and spoke to the gunman on his left, an on-the-run murderer called Little Richard Fitts.

"Did he just call me a *crazy bastard*, Little Richard?" McCloud asked quietly, yet in a menacing voice.

"Yes, I believe he did," Little Richard replied, eyeing a busty young British woman stepping out of the cantina and lighting herself a thin black cigar.

Ross McCloud nodded.

"Good," he said, also watching the woman draw deep on the cigar and let out a stream of smoke. "For a minute there I thought he was insulting me."

Ten feet away the British woman untied the strings holding her blouse shut across her breasts.

"I hope you fellows don't mind," she said with only the trace of a British accent. "It's hotter than Hades at high noon." She fanned the blouse, then retied it loosely, and left it hanging partly agape, her pale freckled breasts half-exposed in the white-hot sunlight.

"We *don't* mind, do we, Little Richard?" McCloud said without taking his eyes off the woman.

"Not too awful much," Little Richard replied, staring at her, his lips hanging slightly agape. "It is high noon," he added.

"And this is hell," McCloud said to her. "Leastwise it was, until it got so hot the devil moved out." Without taking his eyes from the woman, he stood up and held his rifle out sidelong to the Mexican beside him. "Pesado, hold this for me. I'm going to go count this young lady's freckles."

"Oh, are you, now, luv?" the woman said. She turned to face them, a hand cupped at the center of her half-naked breasts. "And what might I be *counting* whilst you amuse yourself?" She turned her cupped hand enough to rub her fingers and thumb together in the universal sign of greed, then clasped it back over herself as if overcome by modesty.

"I can't stand this," said Fitts, leaning his rifle against the end of the swing, stepping forward. "I'll give you something to count," he said to the woman.

"Easy, luv, your fangs are showing," the woman said to Fitts.

"Wait a minute, Little Richard," said McCloud. "Who invited you?"

"When she turned them puppies loose, that's all the inviting I needed," said Fitts. He started forward.

McCloud hurried alongside him, shoving him away.

"We've been pards awhile, Little Richard," he warned. "But I swear to God—"

Behind them, Pesado stood laughing under his breath. But something in the corner of his eye caused him to turn suddenly toward the empty street. When he did, he found himself staring at the Ranger, who stood less than two feet from him, his big Colt cocked and aimed at the Mexican's broad belly.

"Buenos días, Pesado," the Ranger said quietly.

In reflex the Mexican started to swing his Spencer

rifle around, having to drop McCloud's Winchester to do so. But before he could complete his move, the Ranger poked him with the gun barrel, just hard enough to make himself understood.

"If I wanted to kill you, you'd already be dead," the Ranger said menacingly. "Drop it."

McCloud and Fitts both turned at hearing the Winchester hit the ground. Now they saw Pesado's Spencer rifle fall from his hands. They saw the Ranger standing with his Colt jammed into the Mexican gunman's belly.

They started to make a play for the revolvers holstered on their hips.

Pesado saw the look in the Ranger's eyes.

"Don't!" he shouted at the other two gunmen. "This one will kill me. I know he will!"

"Who are you, mister?" McCloud asked, his and Fitts' hands rising chest high in a show of peace. "What the hell is your game here?"

"I'm here to see Fatch Hardaway," Sam said flatly.

"Huh-uh. We can't let you do that," said McCloud, in spite of the Ranger's catching the three by surprise and getting the drop on them. He and Fitts took a cautious step sidelong toward the cantina door as if to block it. The British woman stood back, cigar in hand, watching intently.

"Sure you can," said Sam. "He knows I'm coming."

As he spoke he pulled the cocked Colt's barrel back an inch from the Mexican's belly and pulled the trigger. All three men braced themselves, their eyes widened— especially Pesado's. But the Ranger caught the gun hammer with his thumb at a split second and eased it down. Pesado let out a deep sigh and cursed the Ranger under his breath.

"You dirty, rotten, gringo . . ." He let his words trail.

The Ranger, his Colt hanging in his hand, slipped the Mexican's revolver from its holster, pitched it down beside the rifles and stepped away from Pesado toward the door.

"I already said we can't let you do that," McCloud said in a stronger tone, his and Fitts' gun hands dropping down, poised beside their holstered revolvers.

The Ranger's thumb cocked the big Colt again. He stopped and raised the barrel calmly, smoothly, before either man made their move.

Damn it! McCloud raged silently. Again this stranger had the drop on them. *Damn it to hell!*

The British woman shook her lowered head. She let out a stream of smoke, dropped the thin cigar and crushed it out under her foot.

"By my stars . . . ," she said. "Aren't the three of you just *the berries . . .* "

Her words fell away as a tall man in a black sweat-stained suit coat stepped into the doorway and looked back and forth. He held a sleek long-barreled Remington Army revolver hanging in his right hand. He raised his free hand and removed a long, thick cigar from his mouth.

"Well, well, Ranger Samuel Burrack," he said. "Here you are, just as I'd hoped."

"I said I'd be here, Hardaway," the Ranger replied.

"So you did," said Hardaway. "And you've strolled through my bodyguards without so much as a shot fired, I see." He gave each of his three gunmen a scorching look. "I can't tell you how pleased that makes me, as much as I'm paying these gun monkeys."

Ranger? McCloud, Fitts and Pesado looked at each other as if dumbstruck. McCloud stepped forward, embarrassed, and gestured a hand toward Sam.

"Boss, it's lucky for him you showed up just now," he said. "We come very near killing this fool. Not sure you was expecting him, that is."

"Yes, lucky him," said Hardaway with a searing stare at Ross McCloud. "All of you *bodyguards* best pick your guns up before someone carries them off."

The British woman gave a short, playful chuckle; Hardaway shot her a hard glance too. Seeing her loosely exposed breasts, he took a deep, patient breath.

"Edy, put those away before somebody walks into a post and knocks their damn teeth out," he said seriously.

"I certainly wouldn't want that, now, would I?" she said, closing her blouse front a little better, but not all the way.

"There you are, Ranger," said Hardaway. "See why I want to go back to Texas without getting hanged? Life gets awfully trying around this bunch."

"I bet," Sam said. "You need to remember that the next time before you shoot a man and burn his saloon with him inside it."

"I realize that I may have acted a little rash and hastily, both in killing him and in burning his saloon down," said Hardaway. "But what has become of forgiveness these days?"

Sam just stared at him.

"At any rate . . ." Hardaway looked the Ranger up and down, then motioned him inside out of the sun. "Welcome to the Bad Cats Cantina," he said.

The Ranger stepped inside and looked around the cantina's dingy, dark interior.

"This is your place?" he asked Hardaway.

"Let's just say I've acquired a substantial interest in it," he said, guiding the Ranger across the dirt floor toward tables standing beneath rings of circling flies. "I do hope you've got some good news for me."

On the front porch, the Englishwoman, Edith "Edy the Hand" Casings, tightened her blouse shut and gave the gunmen a disgusted look as they stooped and picked up their rifles, looking them over good. Seeing her adjust her bosom and straighten the blouse as if preparing to leave, Ross McCloud stepped closer to her.

"Don't rush off, little darling," he said with a wide grin. "I haven't lost interest in counting those freckles."

"Nor have I," Fitts cut in, stepping closer himself.

But Edy the Hand was having none of it. She side-stepped the two, moved past them and started toward an alleyway around the side of the cantina.

"I've got an errand to run, luvs. You can go count the nits on each other's arses, as far as I'm concerned," she said, a hand patting her breasts. "These puppies are trained to sniff out *live* game, and live game *only*."

"Wait! I'm live game! I've got money here," McCloud called out after her. He shoved a hand down deep in his pocket and jingled some coins.

"Sorry, but I prefer money that folds instead of rattles. Anyway, money's not everything, is it, now, luv?" she said over her shoulder as she hurried away down the narrow alleyway.

"The hell did she mean by that?" Fitts said, looking confounded.

Behind the two, Pesado stood watching, a mocking grin on his broad face.

"She means that being seen with you two will only make her look bad," he said in a superior tone. "I have to admit, I do not disagree," he added with a dark grin.

"Oh yeah?" said Little Richard, levering a round up into his rifle chamber. "How bad will it make *you* look if I clipped off an ear or two for you—"

"Both of you shut up!" McCloud demanded. He turned to the big Mexican. "How come the Ranger knows your name?"

"Because in some places I am known as a bad hombre," Pesado said, his face taking on a more serious expression, staring at Fitts' rifle pointed toward him. Fitts lowered the rifle barrel a little and took a deep breath.

"So what?" Fitts grumbled. "If I had a dollar for every ragged-assed lawman who knows my name—"

"*Sí*, but this is not just any lawman," said Pesado. "This is Sam Burrack, the Ranger some call *Big Iron*."

"Big Iron, huh?" said McCloud. He and Little Richard looked at each other. "Meaning he's one hell of a gunman, I suppose?" he asked.

"A hell of a gunman, *sí*." Pesado shrugged. "He is a hell of a gunman, for sure. It was he who killed the gringo Junior Lake and his whole gang."

"Say, I remember hearing about that," said Little Richard. "One of the Lake Gang killed the old outrider Sazes, so this fellow killed every damn one of them."

"*Sí*, that's the story," said Pesado. "But that is not all this man they call Big Iron has done." He raised a long finger for emphasis. "It was he who tracked the Red Sleeve Wilson Orez into the Blood Mountains and killed him in a knife fight."

"Whoa, Wilson Orez, the half-breed?" said McCloud.

"*Sí*," said Pesado.

"Yeah," McCloud said, all of a sudden impressed. "I did hear about that." He gazed off at the Blood Mountain line standing in the distance above the upreaching Twisted Hills. "Orez was some kind of high mucky-muck among the old Apache Red Sleeves . . . a real demon when it come to wielding a blade."

"*Sí*, and this is the man who killed him in a knife fight," Pesado said proudly, as if he himself had taken part in the knife fight. His voice lowered a little. "They say this Ranger cut him open like a steer—cut off his head, his hands, his ears, his feet."

The two gunmen stared in rapt silence. Pesado's whisper lowered even more.

"They say he sliced open his belly from here to here," he continued. His hand traveled from his chest to his crotch and he squeezed himself.

"Jesus . . . ," Fitts murmured.

"He sliced open Orez's *escroto*," said Pescado.

"His nut sack . . ." McCloud winced. "My God . . ."

"*Sí*, and now he carries Orez's *cajones* in a leather pouch inside his saddlebags," Pesado said.

"No," said Fitts. He gripped his crotch. The three stared up the street, where the Ranger's black-speckled barb stood hitched to an iron rail, the Ranger's saddlebags hanging behind its saddle.

"*Sí*, and there they are, right before our eyes," Pesado whispered in awe. "I have heard that he carries Orez's very own knife, and at night in the campfire light, he takes Orez's *cajones* out and rolls them slowly back and forth on the knife's blade—"

"All right, that's enough," said McCloud, cutting the Mexican short. He looked away from the saddlebags and shook his head. "You had me for a minute."

"*Sí*, I had you!" Pesado clapped his hands together and chuckled out loud. *These gringo imbeciles.*

Fitts tore himself away from staring at the saddlebags and swallowed a dry knot in his throat.

"Yeah, me too . . . for a minute, that is," he said, his hand still hanging deftly near his crotch.

Chapter 2

At a corner table inside the dingy Gatos Malos or Bad Cats Cantina, Fatch Hardaway looked down at three Mexicans and gave a jerk of his head toward another table. The three hurriedly picked up their drinks and cards and moved away. Fatch gestured the Ranger toward an empty chair and walked around to where a stack of gold coins and gold dust pouches rested on the table.

Taking a seat, Hardaway poured tequila from a jug into a wooden cup and motioned toward the bar for the bartender to bring a fresh cup for the Ranger.

"No, thanks," said Sam.

"It beats the water around here," Hardaway said. He turned up a drink of tequila and slammed the cup down. Stifling a cough, he said, "The town well draws its water from a spring running under the graveyard." He gave a sour expression. "Makes me think I'm drinking somebody's rotted feet." His expression soured even more. "All the more reason why I miss ol' San Antoine."

"I understand," the Ranger said.

"All right, then," said Hardaway. "I can't stand waiting another minute. What's my situation? Am I still marked for a Texas hanging party, or do I remain forever stuck here in *Infierno mexicano eterno*?"

"*Hell eternal* is putting it a little strong, Hardaway," the Ranger said, looking around appraisingly.

"Spend a week here, Ranger," said Hardaway. "You'll see what I mean."

"Obliged, but no, thanks," the Ranger replied. "Anyway, you're free to do as you please, Hardaway. It turns out the man you killed was wanted for murdering three people in Ohio a couple years back."

"No fooling?" said Hardaway, surprised. "So that gets me off the hook?"

"In this case, yes," Sam said. "The folks he killed come from a respectable family in Cleveland."

"*Respectable* meaning rich?" Hardaway grinned.

"That would be my guess," said Sam, continuing. "There was some scandal to it. The family would just as soon let everything settle down as quick as possible. So Texas is saying one dead murderer is no great concern."

Hardaway kept his grin. "How is that for a stroke of luck? A *murderer*, you say." He paused, considering everything for a moment, then said, "Let me ask you, was there any reward money on ol' Lonnie Lyngrid?"

Sam just looked at him for a moment.

"No harm in me asking, is there," said Hardaway, "him being a craven murderer and all?"

"No harm," said Sam. "As it turns out there is a reward. There's a five-thousand-dollar reward posted by members of the deceased's family through the city of Cincinnati." As he spoke he took out a folded reward notice and spread it on the table.

"*Ha!* I can't believe it," said Hardaway, reading the reward notice and amount to himself. He shook his head, grinning, his lips moving quietly across the printed word.

"Don't forget you would have to travel all the way to Cincinnati to collect the five thousand dollars." Sam studied the expression on Hardaway's face.

"So?" said Hardaway. "I've gone a lot farther for a lot less money. Besides, as fast as traveling is these modern days, I could go get my reward money in Cleveland and ride out on the next train to Texas—whole trip wouldn't take over two or three weeks, four at the most."

"You've got a point there." The Ranger nodded. "You might want to walk a little quiet if you go on back to Texas afterward," he warned him. "You could still face charges for murder and arson if you made somebody mad. The man you killed was a wanted murderer, but that doesn't make you a saint in anybody's eyes."

"Yeah, yeah, I got it," Hardaway said, dismissing the Ranger's warning. "I am damn obliged to you for bringing me this news," he added.

"Don't forget," said the Ranger, seeing Hardaway appeared ready to bolt and start packing his belongings, "you agreed to tell me where to find your pards Ty and Wes Traybo."

"You mean my *ex*-partners," said Hardaway, settling back down into his chair. He gave a wince. "I nearly forgot that this was a trade we agreed to."

"I didn't," Sam said flatly. "Don't start tightening up

on me now, Hardaway," he cautioned. "I did what I said I'd do for you. Now pay it up."

"Dang, you just don't know how bad it feels, double-crossing your pards, even if they're a couple of crazy sons a' bitches like the Traybos."

"We made a deal, Hardaway," the Ranger reminded him, rising slightly in his chair.

"All right, I know, I know," Hardaway said, fanning Sam back down. "I agreed to tell you, and I'm trying to. I'm nothing if not a man of my word—most times anyway . . . well, sometimes that is, provided everything—"

"Stop stalling around and tell me where they lie low," Sam said, cutting him off. "The law has looked everywhere."

Hardaway struggled with it for a moment, then let out a long sigh and slumped in his chair.

"I can't do it, Ranger," he said. "I hate to crawfish on a deal, but I've got to." He paused, then said, "I almost wish you hadn't told me I'm free and clear and have some reward money waiting." He held back a crooked little smile. "I fear it might have taken away any incentive for telling you about the Traybos."

The Ranger just stared at him.

"I expect you'll make some threats now, act like you're going to kill me, or shoot me in the foot . . . stuff like that," Hardaway said. "But I'm prepared to call your bluff. See, I don't think you'll shoot a man over something like this."

The Ranger raised his gun hand away from his holstered Colt and placed it on the tabletop.

"It looks like you've got me there, Hardaway," Sam said. "I warned myself you might do something like this—"

"Awww. Don't feel too bad, Ranger," Hardaway cut in. "You're young, still learning. Let this be a good lesson—"

"That's why I went ahead and had your reward money for Lonnie Lyngrid deposited in an Arizona Territory bank before I came looking for you," Sam continued. He raised a folded paper from his hip pocket and pitched it over in front of Hardaway beside the reward poster. "I figured it would save you a trip to Cincinnati, and keep me from putting a bullet through your foot."

"You did what?" said Hardaway, unfolding the paper, seeing the heading *First Bank of Cottonwood Arizona* across the top.

"That's a promissory note for your five thousand dollars, Hardaway," Sam said. "It requires you showing up in person in Cottonwood, and me—a duly sworn officer of Arizona Territory—signing an affidavit attesting that you did indeed kill Lonnie Lyngrid."

"Damn my breaking heart," Hardaway said sadly, shaking his head. "What has this world turned into, when a man can't kill a murdering son of a bitch like Lonnie Lyngrid and get the reward without all this rigmarole?"

"You didn't know he was a murderer at the time, Hardaway," Sam said, trying to keep him on track. "You had no idea there was reward money coming."

Hardaway didn't seem to hear him.

"It was starting that damn fire," he said. "I knew arson was a bad idea—that it would come back on me someday." He rapped a fist down on the tabletop. "And I never should have trusted a lawman," he added, giving the Ranger a cold stare. "You jackpotted me, Burrack. That's all you can call this."

Sam just stared at him for a moment.

"Listen to me, Hardaway," he said finally, rising from the table, picking up the promissory banknote. "I'm going to water and grain my horse, let him rest out awhile before I turn back. You take a few minutes and decide if you want to go along with me, show me where the Traybo brothers hole up." He paused, then added, "On our way to Cottonwood."

"Damn, I *hate* Cottonwood," said Hardaway. "And I've got my interest in this place I need to keep watch on."

"Five thousand dollars is a lot of money. Figure it out and do what suits you," the Ranger said, turning, walking toward the front door. "I've told you how it's going to be. Now I'm through fooling with you." He let Hardaway see him shove the folded note down into his hip pocket. Then he walked out the front door, through the three leering gunmen, toward the hitch rail up the dirt street.

On the front porch of the Gatos Malos Cantina, the three gunmen stepped back as the Ranger walked between them. They stood watching as he walked away in the wavering heat.

"Big Iron. Ha!" said Ross McCloud. "Gun or knife, he don't show me nothing." He spat in disgust as they watched the Ranger step over to his speckled barb at the iron hitch rail. "If he needs to learn himself some manners about not sneaking up on folks, I'd be more than happy to teach him a thing or—"

"Noooo! Wait!" shouted Fatch Hardaway, charging headlong out of the cantina doorway, knocking McCloud down as he ran into the street flailing his arms, his Colt swinging wildly in his hand. "Don't kill him! *Don't kill him!*" He raced toward the Ranger shouting at the top of his lungs, staring toward an empty store across the street.

Quick on his reflexes, the Ranger saw what was happening and dropped into a crouch, spinning fast, raising his Colt from its holster, cocking it on the upswing.

"Don't kill that Ranger!" Hardaway bellowed toward the empty storefront. He skidded to a halt, firing round after round toward the storefront.

Sam saw two figures through the large, dusty display window; he saw bullet holes appear, forming large spiderweb cracks on the wavy glass. Gunfire erupted from within the plank and adobe building. A bullet whistled past his head; he fired twice into the spiderwebs of cracked glass, then moved a step to the side and started to fire again. But before he got the shot off, a body fell forward, crashed through the glass, frame and all, and spilled onto the plank boardwalk.

The Ranger stood tense, crouched, waiting, fanning his Colt back and forth between the abandoned store and Fatch Hardaway, who stood with his hands above his head, holding his smoking Colt pointed at the sky.

"Don't shoot, Ranger!" he shouted. "See? I come to warn you—to save your life! Clifford Spears and Rodney Gaines are in there laying for you!" He held his gun hand to the side and dropped his smoking Colt to the dirt street. "There, you see? I'm on your side, all the way!"

The reward money, Sam told himself.

"You had me all set up for them, Hardaway," he said. But as he spoke he had to turn quickly toward the creaking door opening on the empty storefront. He saw a tall, broad-shouldered gunman stagger out and stop, his gun hanging from one hand, his other hand clutching his bloody stomach. A battered Stetson sat lopsided on his head; blood dribbled down from his lip and dripped from his chin.

"Fatch . . . you son of a bitch . . . ," the man muttered, his words failing. He stumbled forward, trying to raise his revolver. But he couldn't gather the strength.

The Ranger turned his Colt toward the wounded gunman, but only in time to see him buckle down onto his knees, then pitch face-forward onto the street.

"There, then. I suppose that about settles it," said Hardaway. He stooped to pick up his gun from the dirt. But Sam turned back toward him, his Colt pointed at him.

"Leave it lie," he demanded. As he spoke he saw the three gunmen from the cantina running up the street, their rifles in their hands.

"Leave it lie?" Hardaway said as if in disbelief. "Ranger, I just saved your life here. No two ways about it."

"Yep," said the Ranger. "After you found out you won't draw the reward money without me signing for it. Before that you had me jackpotted for these two." He gestured a nod toward the two dead gunmen lying in the street.

"That's an ugly, hateful thing to say," said Hardaway.

He continued to stoop and reach out for his gun, paying no regard to the Ranger's words.

The sound of the Ranger cocking his Colt stopped him.

"You're ahead of the game right now, Hardaway. Don't end it with me putting a bullet in you."

Hardaway heard the seriousness in the Ranger's voice. He straightened and rubbed his palms on his trouser legs.

"All right, Ranger," Hardaway said. "I'll forgo your lack of gratitude for now."

"Tell your men to drop their rifles," the Ranger said.

"All right, men, you heard the voice of authority here," Hardaway said with sarcasm. "Lower those rifles."

"I said *drop them*," the Ranger demanded.

"Very well, then, *drop* your rifles," Hardaway said to his men, sounding put out by the Ranger's persistence.

Sam stepped in closer to Hardaway as the bodyguards let their rifles fall.

"You and I have a lot of ground to cover, Hardaway," Sam said quietly. "If this ride is not worth the money to you, let me know right now, before I waste any more time on you."

"All right, Ranger, it's true I knew Clifford and Rodney were waiting there for you. They hit town yesterday. Said they'd spotted you on the trail headed this way. Like every gunman on these badlands, they wanted to kill you." He shrugged. "What was I to do? It was none of my business."

"But the money changed everything," Sam said.

"Well, hell yes, it changed things," Hardaway said. "Doesn't it always?"

"You're some piece of work, Fatch Hardaway."

"Be that as it may, in the course of things, I did come running to your defense, didn't I?" Hardaway reasoned.

"Yes, you did," the Ranger said. He eased a little, realizing there was no point in discussing the matter any further. Hardaway would do whatever he needed to keep him alive so long as there was money involved. "Obliged," he said.

Hardaway smiled and nodded as if to say *you're welcome*.

Sam took another step and picked up Hardaway's pistol from the dirt, shook it free of dust and handed it to him, butt first. He looked at the three gunmen staring at him and gave them a nod toward their rifles. "Pick them up," he told the three.

"*Gracias*, Ranger," Hardaway said, taking his Remington and holstering it. He gave a nod toward the dead men in the dirt street as a few townsfolk ventured forward from behind closed doors. "I'm wondering now. Do you suppose Clifford and Rodney has any reward on them anywhere? This bounty business might be a good thing to look into."

The Ranger turned and started toward the speckled barb.

"Get ready to ride, Hardaway," he said over his shoulder. "The sooner we're done with this, the better."

Chapter 3

Maley, Arizona Territory

Two strangers dressed in black linen suits stood at the customer service counter in the middle of the Cattleman's Bank. Over their business clothes, they both wore tan trail dusters that hung down to their scuffed bootheels. One wore a stylish but battered bowler hat cocked at a rake above his right eye. The other wore a black wide-brimmed Stetson. Both stood filling out deposit receipts. They looked up at each other as the sound and feel of rumbling hooves began to swell underfoot.

"Vot is dis?" questioned a Swedish shopkeeper who turned on his heel at the teller cage, cash in hand, and looked off in the direction of the deep, powerful rumbling.

"Goodness *gracious*! It sounds like a stampede," said a townswoman in a long black gingham dress, standing behind the shopkeeper. "My poor Albert was in one once—said it was terrible."

"Stampede indeed, Widow Jenson," said the bank manager, a short, hefty man who unlocked the thick wooden door at the far end of the barred teller counter and hurried around toward the front door. "I prefer to think Maley is a good deal more civilized these days than to have a stampede in our streets."

The two men in dusters gave him a dubious look. So did the shopkeeper.

"It is coming from the rail pens, Mr. Bird," Widow Jenson offered.

"Yes, I know," the manager, Phillip Bird, said in a patient but condescending tone.

Behind the long teller counter a serious-looking man wearing a full beard and a green clerk's visor stood staring down at an ink pen as the floor trembled with the low-rumbling vibration.

"Mr. Bird, sir," the man said calmly.

Phillip Bird didn't reply. Instead he smiled confidently at the two strangers.

"No cause for concern, gentlemen," he said over his shoulder. He set a heavy bolt across the front door, locking it. "I'll lock this just in case. We've had reports of the Traybo Gang being in this area. "But I assure you, this is nothing."

"The Traybos! Really?" the man in the bowler hat said, looking worried.

"I should not have mentioned it," said Phillip Bird. He waved the matter away as he turned back toward the door. "At any rate, to be on the safe side, we have armed railroad detectives and town volunteer guards positioned everywhere. If those craven cowards were to show their faces here, I daresay—"

His words came to a halt as he saw the men's trail

dusters part down the front and guns come out pointed at him. The man in the bowler raised a double-barrel sawed-off shotgun and cocked both hammers. The man in the Stetson held a long, sleek Remington .45 conversion leveled at his chest.

Bird's eyes widened in terror as the one with the shotgun took a step forward.

"Craven cowards, huh?" he said to the trembling bank manager. Without taking his eyes off Phillip Bird, he spoke to the man in the Stetson. "Want me to butt-smack him, brother Wesley?" he asked.

"Only if he doesn't do what we tell him, Tyrone," the man in the Stetson replied. He looked at the shopkeeper and the woman. "You two get behind the counter with us. Come on, let's go!" He wagged them toward the open door with the barrel of his big Remington.

"You're them—the Traybo brothers, that is," said the banker, having turned pale in the face. "You're not even wearing masks!"

Wes Traybo touched his stubbled cheeks as if in surprise and said, "I knew we forgot something."

"Look, Mr. Traybo," said Bird. "I meant nothing saying what I said. It's simply one of those cases where—"

"Maybe you will have to butt-smack him, Ty," said Wes Traybo, stepping forward, shoving the banker toward the open door in the long counter.

"I'm going to cooperate with you fellows," Bird said in a shaky voice, "I swear I am."

"That's a good attitude, Bird," said Wes. "Now fly your ass back there and open that big ol' safe for us," he said to the banker.

The clerk, unseen, dropped down on all fours behind the counter and crawled away to a small stockroom as the two outlaws walked through the open door behind Phillip Bird and shoved him to the front of the large vault. The shopkeeper and the woman stood back out of the way, watching intently, their hands half raised.

"Whoa, look at this!" said Wes with a smile, seeing the door to the safe standing open a few inches. "This safe was just standing here waiting to be robbed."

Ty Traybo swung the big safe door wide open and quickly stepped inside.

"My, my, look at all this handsome cattle money," he said.

"Better hurry it up some, Ty," said Wes. "The cattle will be storming through here any minute." He took two folded unmarked canvas sacks from under his duster and tossed them into the vault at his brother's feet. He looked Widow Jenkins up and down.

"Ma'am, you can lower your hands," he said quietly to her.

"Thank you, young man," said the widow, lowering her hands and folding them in front of her.

Wes Traybo kept his big Remington pointed at Bird and the frightened bank manager. "So," he said calmly to the two men, "how's the fishing been around here?"

"The fi-fishing?" said Bird, visibly shaking.

"Iz not so bad," the shopkeeper cut in. "I do good in spring, higher up." He pointed northeast toward a rugged mountain range. "But not so good down here. Iz too hot, too dry."

"Too bad," said Wes, with a shrug. He stood in

silence for a moment, then looked toward the open vault where his brother, Ty, hurriedly stuffed money into both canvas sacks. "How's it going in there?" he said, hearing the rumble of hooves draw closer, the sound of pistol fire exploding above it. "We're not spending the day here."

"Oh . . . ?" said Ty, stepping out of the big vault, pitching the two stuffed sacks at his feet. "In that case, brother, we're all done in here."

"Just in time," said Wes, stooping, picking up one money-filled canvas sack, hefting it over his shoulder. "Sounds like our cattle's coming."

"Good," said Ty, hefting up the other sack of money.

The two started to step out the thick door from behind the teller counter. But Ty stopped and looked all around.

"Wait a minute," he said. "Where's that clerk who was back here a while ago?"

Wes looked all around too. Their eyes went to the open door of a stockroom, the only plausible spot for the man to have gone. A dark wariness swept over Wes like a chill.

"It doesn't matter. Let's go!" he said quickly.

"Like hell it doesn't matter," said Ty, taking a step toward the small stockroom. "I don't want us getting shot in the back while we're leaving—"

His words stopped short when the bearded man stepped out of the stockroom with a short double-barreled shotgun and stood braced, his feet spread shoulder-width apart.

"Detective Ted Ore, railroad security!" he called

out. "Drop your guns! You're under arrest!" Yet, even as he shouted, the shotgun bucked in his hands.

The first blast of the shotgun slammed Ty Traybo in his shoulder and hurled him backward. Wes, seeing his brother fall, wasted no time. Dropping the sacks of money, he swung his Remington up and blasted the young detective with three shots. Each shot sent the detective staggering backward into the stockroom in a thick red mist.

"Oh God!" shouted the bank manager, falling to his knees, scrambling across the floor into the open vault.

As the detective staggered his last backward step into the stockroom, his shotgun hit the doorframe and fired the second barrel.

The wild shot hit Widow Jenkins squarely in her face and blew her backward against the shopkeeper, who had ducked down instinctively. Brains and blood flew. The woman's body lay limp and faceless, sprawled atop the bloody shopkeeper.

His smoking Remington in his hand, Wes hurried to his wounded brother and raised him to his feet. Blood ran braided and thick from the tips of Ty's fingers and formed into a puddle and spread onto the plank floor.

"You're going to be all right, Ty," Wes said, trying to sound convincing. He looped Ty's bloody arm over his shoulder and led him out through the big wooden door from behind the counter, dragging his canvas sack beside him.

"He . . . shot the hell . . . out of me," Ty murmured in stunned disbelief, looking at all the blood. His good hand held on to his canvas money sack. "This is bull—"

"Shut up, Ty. Let's get you out of here," said Wes.

Halfway across the floor, they saw the front door fly open and a man jump inside with a Winchester up and cocked. He fanned the rifle back and forth, ready to fire.

Wes Traybo lowered his cocked Remington at the sight of the rifleman.

"Help me with him, Carter," he called out to the gunman who'd stood on the boardwalk to guard the front door. "He took a bad blast in his shoulder."

"I'm there," said Carter. He hurried forward, seeing Wes struggling with his wounded brother and the stuffed canvas sacks through a cloud of gun smoke.

On the wide main street of Maley, townsfolk had at first frozen in place and listened as the rumble below their feet drew nearer. But they suddenly came back to life and bolted for cover when three hundred head of wild-eyed, bawling cattle thundered up into sight from the direction of the rail pins. The freed cattle pounded along in a swirl of dust; a sea of long cattle horns pitched, bobbed and swayed like a scene of hell set loose and rising.

Out in front of the store overhangs, roofs collapsed and were hastily broken up and devoured beneath the pounding hooves. Empty wagons, durables, barrels and wooden cargo crates rose and fell and flattened to the dirt. A black-hooded street buggy rose, broken free from its dead and trampled horse. The buggy appeared to roll along for a moment atop the sea of horns until at length its broken black hood folded within itself; its spine and frame twisted and snapped like the brittle bones of some winged creature in the hands of a mindless monster.

Behind the herd, gunfire streaked orange-blue straight up through the curtain of dust, keeping the bawling animals at a full run. Only a few yards ahead of the herd, three horses raced along abreast as if leading the frightened cattle. Broken lengths of hitch rail still tied with their reins bounced alongside the fleeing horses. Townsmen and young boys appeared like apparitions on rooftops and looked down helplessly on the spectacle through the thickening curtain of dust.

As the cattle neared the bank, Wes Traybo and Carter Claypool made it off the boardwalk into an alley just in time—the wounded Ty Traybo hanging between them, the sacks of money slung over their shoulders. As the two shoved Ty up into his saddle, broken planks and slats from the boardwalk flew into the air and fell around them.

"Look out, Wes!" shouted Claypool.

Wes turned and fired at a steer that had cut away from the stampede and made a run for the alley. His shot only grazed the steer on the hard rise between its horns, but that was enough to send the animal spinning wildly, racing back toward the passing herd.

"This was a railroad setup! Let's go before we get ourselves killed here," Wes shouted, firing again, this time just to keep the steers racing past them instead of into the alleyway.

"Get your brother out of here! I'll keep them back!" Claypool shouted above the rumble. He slung one of the sacks up over his cantle, jumped into his saddle and put his horse between the Traybos and the stampede. He fired his rifle straight up and levered another round.

"I don't need nobody . . . nursemaiding me," Ty Traybo said weakly, swaying in his saddle.

"The hell you don't," shouted Wes, pitching the other sack atop his horse in the same manner as Claypool. "Sit still and hang on to your horse," he demanded.

"Bull . . . I don't need it," Ty said, his voice sounding weaker still. He tried to pull his reins free from his brother's hands as Wes turned their horses toward the far end of the alleyway.

Watching, firing and relevering until the Traybos rode away and rounded the far end of the alley, Carter Claypool backed his horse a step and jerked it around to follow them. But just as he batted his bootheels to its sides, a shot sliced through the heavy billowing dust and nailed him in his shoulder from behind.

Damn it! Not now!

Claypool flew sidelong off the horse's back as the animal bolted forward and raced away in the same direction of the two fleeing outlaws. As he hit the ground facedown, he felt the air explode from his lungs. He struggled to get up onto his feet, but he couldn't do it. Through a watery veil he saw his rifle lying in the dirt a few feet in front of him and tried to push himself toward it.

No good, he told himself. He shook his head to clear it of whatever had crept down around him. But his head wouldn't clear. Instead it seemed to get worse. A darkness had him; it wasn't letting him go. He fought against it like a man struggling to keep from falling asleep.

The warm blood oozing wider and wider all across the back on his shoulders seemed to press him down, keep him pinned in place, like a heavy boot clamped down on him.

Hell, you've had it, son, he told himself. This was how it felt being dead.

He relaxed, gave in to the darkness, watching a dirt beetle crawling along in the dirt only an inch from his face. The beetle had no interest in anything that had just gone on in the world of man. This *damn bug* . . . Behind him the rumble of the herd lessened and passed. In another moment it fell away along the far end of the wide dirt street. He hoped his horse, Charlie Smith, had gotten away all right—a good horse, Charlie Smith. . . .

Here it is, he thought, closing his eyes, knowing he was dead, knowing that when he opened them again he'd be in hell—find himself facing the devil. Well, that was how he'd played out his string, he thought, feeling smaller, going away.

Chapter 4

As the last of the freed cattle trampled along the main street of Maley, two outlaws, one older and one young, ducked their horses away into an alley and left town at a run. They didn't stop and look back until they had reached a wide stand of cottonwood trees on a rocky hillside. There the two men stopped their horses alongside a thin stream. While the dusty sweat-streaked horse drank, the two men pulled bandannas down from their faces and sat staring back toward the thick cloud of dust engulfing the town. The herd had spilled out the other end of town and begun spreading out and slowing down. Mounted horsemen rode among them, trying to calm and gather the spooked animals.

Baylor Rubens, the older outlaw, had only pulled the grimy bandanna down below his chin, but the younger outlaw, Hatton "Bugs" Trent, had untied his and jerked it from around his neck and shook it vigorously. Dust billowed.

"Cattle have never brought me nothing but bad luck," said Baylor Rubens. He spat and ran a hand across his dry lips. "I should say until today, that is. I expect to make myself a strike today."

"The day I run off from home, I swore I'd never spend a minute more of my life chasing a cow's stinking ass," said Trent. "Now look at me." He shook the bandanna again, twirled it between his hands, draped it around his neck and tied it. "You know I nearly went under back there. If I had been trampled to death, I'd have been known forever for dying while rustling a herd of stinking cattle."

"No, you wouldn't have, Bugs," said Rubens. "I'd've seen to it you were known to be killed participating in a bank robbery." He gave a thin wisp of a grin.

Trent smiled himself and nodded.

"I'd have been obliged to you for it," he said. He hawked up dust from deep in his throat and spat it out on the ground. "Blasted damn cattle," he growled.

The two looked off at two streams of dust approaching them in a wide half circle from the far end of Maley.

"This ain't good," Rubens said sidelong to the young outlaw. "It looks like somebody didn't make it." He noted how the two riders at the head of the streams of dust rode closely together. "No, sir, it ain't good at all," he added.

Bugs Trent squinted into the sunlight and dirt.

"It's Wes and Ty," he said. "They both made it. But Carter's not with them." He paused, then said, "No surprise, I reckon. If we lose a man, it won't be one of these two, huh?"

"Watch your mouth, Bugs," cautioned Rubens. "You don't know what the hell you're talking about."

"I know that kin stick together no matter what," Trent said as the two riders drew nearer. "That's just the way it is."

"Did you just hear me tell you to shut up?" Rubens asked, his tone turning sharper.

The two stared hard at each other for a moment while the Traybos came up the narrow stretch of trail on the hillside toward them. Finally Bugs Trent gestured a nod toward the two.

"Look," he said quietly to Rubens. "Ty's bloodier than a stuck hog."

"Jesus," growled Rubens, jerking his dun's head up from watering. He batted his boots to the dun's sides and splashed across the stream toward the Traybos. Trent booted his horse along behind him.

"What the hell, Wes?" said Rubens, cutting his horse sidelong and sidling up beside Ty, who sat slumped and bloody on his saddle. He noted the single canvas sack of money lying over Wes' saddle cantle.

"Shotgun," said Wes. "He took a load close up. I should have seen it coming, but I didn't." He continued forward, leading Ty's horse close beside him toward the stream's edge.

"He means . . . I should have . . . ," Ty said in a weak voice without raising his lowered head.

"If I meant that I would have said so," Wes said to his brother, stepping down from his saddle beside the stream. He pitched the money sack on the ground. Rubens helped Ty down from his saddle, seated him on the gravelly bank and leaned him back against a large rock beside the stream. Bugs Trent stepped down, took the reins to the Traybos' horses and held them while the animals drank.

"Where's Claypool?" Bugs asked, watching Wes open his brother's bloody trail duster and pull it off carefully.

"Carter didn't make it," Wes said over his shoulder. "This whole deal was a railroad ambush." He said to Ty, "We've got to get a doctor for this wound."

"I'm not going to no damn doctor, Wes," Ty said, his voice getting weaker.

"I never said you're going to one," said Wes. "I'm going to have a doctor come to you."

Ty shook his head and gave a halfhearted chuckle.

"That's good. You do that, brother," he said. "Be sure and bring me some whiskey and a dark-eyed *señorita* while you're at it."

"I'll do that," Wes said. He adjusted the blood-soaked bandanna he had pressed against his brother's gruesome wound earlier. He gave a dark, thin smile. "I'll bring you a new shirt and a hat too."

"Now you're talking," Ty said weakly, his voice strained under the pain in his chewed-up shoulder.

"What do you mean he didn't make it?" Bugs asked Wes, still thinking about Carter Claypool. "How come he didn't make it?"

Wes turned facing him, his brother's blood on his hands and his trail duster.

"I'll tell you more as soon as I know more myself," he said in a flat tone. "Meanwhile, you and Rubens take care of my brother while I go find out."

"Whoa, hang on, Wes," said Ruben. "You don't aim to ride back to Maley, not after all this?"

"Yes, I do," said Wes. "I intend to get a doctor for Ty, and I need to find out what happened to Claypool so I can come back and tell Bugs here." He gave Trent a hard stare. "Right, Bugs?"

Bugs relented, not knowing what to make of the look in Wes Traybo's eyes.

"Aw, come on, Wes, I didn't mean nothing," he said. "I should have kept my mouth shut."

"It's not too late to start," Rubens cut in. He turned back to Wes and said, "You don't need to go back, Wes. This is a hard game of ours. Claypool knows how it's played. He wouldn't ask you to come back for him."

"He stayed back to cover for Ty and me," said Wes. "That's what he does." He gave Rubens a firm look. "Anything more you want to say on the matter?"

"Damn it," Rubens said. "Go on, then. We'll take care of Ty until you get back."

"Well, thank you, sir," Wes said, giving Rubens a look. He turned to his horse and took the reins from Bugs' hand. The young outlaw stepped in close.

"Wes, I didn't mean nothing. I swear I didn't," he said. "I've got no damn sense sometimes."

"I didn't think you meant it, Bugs," said Wes. "If I did, one of us would be dead right now."

"I'm going with you," Bugs said suddenly, wanting to make up for what he'd said. "There could be a bunch of guns waiting for you there."

"Do like I said, Bugs," Wes said. "Stay here with Rubens and watch my brother."

Trent and Rubens stood staring as Wes climbed atop his horse and gathered his reins.

"Stay alive for me, brother Ty," he said. He spun his horse sharply and booted it back toward Maley.

Turning to Rubens, Bugs saw the condemning look on the older gunman's face.

"What?" he said, giving a shrug. "You heard me tell him I don't have any sense sometimes."

"Yeah, I heard you," said Rubens. He spat and ran a hand across his lips. "I expect we all know you weren't lying to him."

Bugs' expression turned sour.

"What do you mean by that?" he said. He opened and closed his gun hand intently.

"Every damn thing you think I mean," said Rubens. He turned away from the young gunman with disregard.

Bugs pointed at him, frustrated at not being taken seriously.

"Listen, Rubens, I only put up with your grousing ways because I like you," he said.

"Lucky me," Rubens said without looking back at him.

"You don't want to push me too far," Bugs warned.

"Push this," Rubens said, walking away toward Ty Traybo, making a profane gesture over his shoulder toward Bugs Trent.

Bugs fumed but kept his mouth shut. He clenched his teeth and cursed under his breath.

Ty Traybo, even in his pained and weakened condition, managed to chuff and shake his lowered head.

"He got you there, Bugs," he murmured. "That's all you can say about it."

Bugs lightened up and let out a short laugh himself.

"Damn it," he said to Ty. "A smart man don't stand a chance around this bunch." He looked off toward Maley. "I hope Wes gets back here real quick. Something about this place gives me the willies."

In Maley, while the dust still loomed and settled slowly on the streets, buildings and locals, Carter Claypool sat slumped in a straight-backed chair in the town's sheriff office. His arms hung limp at his sides. Two crude wads of cloth had been stuffed into his shirt, staying the flow of blood from his left shoulder. The wound was clean, not deep, the bullet having skewered through his shoulder muscle and out without hitting bone. His face was reddened and puffed, turning the color of fruit gone bad from the beating he'd taken at the hands of an ill-tempered railroad detective named Artimus Folliard.

"You might think you're a tough nut," Folliard said. "But I'll get you softened up soon enough."

"You're going to kill him is what you're going to do," a stocky cattle broker named Don Stout said to Folliard. "Then he's going to tell us nothing."

Folliard stood back rubbing a bloody handkerchief across his big rawboned knuckles.

"So what?" he said. "Are you saying that's a bad thing? These dogs have robbed your bank here. Did you have money in it?"

"Yes, it so happens I did," said the broker. Unrelenting under the big detective's cold stare, he continued. "But look at him. This is murder," he said, pointing at the badly beaten outlaw. "I'll have no hand in murder. If we hang him, that's a whole other thing. He deserves a lynching. But not this. This is inhumane. If we had a sheriff, he'd stop this."

"But you've got no sheriff. What you've got is us, compliments of West Southwestern Security, so you'd best shut up," Folliard warned. He cut a glance to the tall figure standing in the shadow of a battered gun case. The dark figure nodded his approval above a glowing cigar.

Stout backed a step and looked around for support from the other gathered townsmen.

Claypool sat with his bloody head lowered, his eyes almost swollen shut.

"Bless your kind bones, mister," he chuckled darkly under his breath.

"Shut up, thief," said Folliard, stepping closer to Claypool, doubling his big raw fist. "I've still got some for you."

"Then give it . . . to me," Claypool said, weak but defiant. "Nothing I like more . . . than a bad hard beating, properly delivered."

"Why, you turd," said Folliard, grabbing Claypool by his hair and pulling his face up into fist range. He drew back for a hard punch, but stopped himself as the front door opened and three dusty figures carried a limp, mangled body into the small office and threw it to the plank floor.

One of the three men, Earl Prew, swiped his derby hat from his head and slapped it against his leg. Dust billowed.

"There's a dead one for you, Mr. Garand," he said. "This one is none other than Ty Traybo himself." He stared straight past the gathered townsmen at the tall figure in the shadows.

Oh no. . . . Claypool turned his swollen eyes enough to take a look at the badly trampled corpse, its clothes and skin hanging shredded and torn, an eye hanging from its socket, a leg ripped away from the knee down.

The gathered men parted to let Dallas Garand step forward and stand over the mangled body. He gave the man a harsh glare from under his hat brim.

"This is not Traybo, you damn fool!" he growled. "This is Hubert Staley."

"Staley?" Prew said. He and the other two men looked at each other. "But, Mr. Garand, how can you—"

"Damn it, I can tell it's Staley by his nuts," Garand said, pointing down. "Look at them," he demanded, nodding down at the shredded, half-naked corpse. "I'd recognize them anywhere."

But instead of looking down, the three men winced and stared at each other.

"His *nuts*, sir?" said Prew, turning to Garand. "I have to say, I have never had either cause or desire to look at Staley's—"

"Damn it, not *those* nuts, you fool!" shouted Garand, cutting him off. He leaned and jerked up a pair of small brass acorns hanging from the corpse's tattered vest pocket. "*These* nuts!" He held the small watch fob ornaments out on his palm for the men to see.

Prew and the others let out a sigh of relief.

"Mr. Garand, I completely misunderstood," Prew said, shaking his bowed head.

"Yes, you ignoramus *son of a bitch*," said Garand.

"You certainly did." He pitched the little brass acorns onto the dead man's bloody-crusted chest and dusted his hands together. "I ought to pistol-whip you all the way to Missouri!"

Listening, watching, Claypool had also breathed a sigh of relief. Even in his battered condition, he had to stifle a laugh. He held his head lowered to this bloody chest. He would have hated to think he'd gone through all this just to have Ty Traybo trampled to death making a getaway.

All right, he resolved, taking another deep breath. In all likelihood, he would hang here today. The most he could hope to do for himself would be to answer whatever questions they asked about the Traybos. *But you know what?* he said to himself. *To hell with them.* He wasn't telling them anything. That wasn't his style. He could take a beating; he didn't care. If he was going to die anyway, what difference did it make? As he considered his situation, he glanced down at the dust-covered butt of the Colt standing in the dead man's holster. There was a whole other way to die.

"Whoa, what have we here?" said Folliard, stepping forward, noting Claypool's interest in Staley's holstered Colt. He stooped and picked up the Colt and wagged it in Claypool's face. "I believe you would like to grab this and shoot holes in all of us," he said, taunting the helpless outlaw.

"Good observation, Detective Folliard," said Garand, stepping in beside him. "You've been showing me something this whole expedition. I expect I'll be putting a longer title behind your name when we get these rowdy boys stuck under the dirt."

"Obliged, Mr. Garand. And it will be my pleasure to stick them there," Folliard said, staring hard down at Claypool.

Claypool tilted his bowed head and squinted up through purple, swollen eyes.

"Folliard," he said in a pained and gravelly voice, "your face reminds me . . . of the red wet end of a donkey's—" His words stopped short as the big detective backhanded him across his already battered face.

Even the onlooking townsmen winced as Claypool's face flew sideways, then bobbed and fell to his chest.

"I dare you to . . . do it again," he mumbled defiantly.

"Don't mind if I do," said Folliard, drawing back for another swing. "I predict we'll see some teeth spilled here today."

But he stopped as a hush fell over the townsmen with the slow creak of the opening front door.

"Holy God," Don Stout said in a whisper.

In the doorway stood the young town doctor, Dayton Bernard, a rope tied around his neck, the tip of a shotgun stuck against the back of his head. Behind him was Wes Traybo, his right hand steadying the shotgun and holding the bight of rope.

Chapter 5

A tense silence fell over the small office. The townsmen and detectives froze in place. Folliard swallowed a tight knot in his throat, standing beside the wooden chair where Claypool sat, battered and bloody. Garand stood with his fists clenched at his sides, fighting the urge to yank a long-barreled Colt from behind his duster and start firing. Wes Traybo gained the edge on everybody, but he also knew how quick he could lose it if he wasn't careful how he played it.

"Everybody who wants this doctor to *live* raise your hands," he said, taking a consensus. As hands were raised, he looked all around counting, then said, "Looks like the hands have it, Doc. Good thing you haven't overcharged anybody lately."

"I—I don't overcharge, sir," the doctor said in a frightened but indignant voice.

"Of course you don't," Wes said, pushing the doctor forward a step. To the others he said, "Everybody stand tight and nobody will have to die here. I come to get my man." He gestured toward Claypool.

"You're one of the Traybos," Garand said in a scornful tone.

"I already knew that," Wes said sharply. He saw Carter Claypool reach out and lift a big Starr conversion revolver from Folliard's holster. The badly beaten outlaw stood up on wobbly legs beside the detective, raising the Starr to Folliard's chest as he steadied himself on his feet.

"My, oh my, *Detective*," he whispered to Folliard through swollen lips. "Look at what a spot you're in."

Folliard clenched his teeth and stared down woodenly at the dusty plank floor.

"I expect you'll kill me now, with my own damn gun," he murmured in a shaky voice.

"Good guess," Claypool said, cocking the hammer on the big, heavy Starr.

Wes Traybo looked at the wound in Claypool's left shoulder. "Are you able to ride out of here, amigo?"

"More than able, and *ready*," Claypool managed to say, keeping his swollen eyes on Folliard's lowered face. "I just need to kill this skunk first."

"Then kill him. Let's get going," said Traybo. He looked around at the frozen, frightened faces. "Nobody move," he demanded.

"On your knees, *rail bull*," Claypool said to Folliard, jamming him with his own pistol barrel.

"Oh no, oh my God, no," Folliard said as realization set in. Even as he sank slowly to his knees, he said to Claypool in a trembling voice, "Please, mister, I was only doing my job."

"I know," said Claypool. "So am I." He put the tip of the barrel against the detective's trembling forehead. "So long, turd," he said.

Folliard's eyes flew open wide in terror as he watched the battered outlaw pull the Starr's trigger. The whole room gasped as the hammer fell. But Claypool, even with his senses and reflexes dulled from the beating, caught the falling gun hammer with his thumb at the last split second. A wicked smile drew across his swollen lips. He saw urine crawl down the detective's trouser leg in a widening dark stream. Folliard shuddered in relief and closed his eyes.

Wes Traybo and Claypool gave each other a look. Then Claypool swung the Starr wide and laid a vicious swipe across the detective's jaw. Folliard flew backward onto the plank floor and didn't move. A puff of breath sent two broken, bloody teeth rolling from inside his mouth.

Claypool said to the knocked-out detective, "There's those teeth you predicted."

Traybo watched as Claypool stepped over to where his gun belt lay coiled like some strange metal and leather reptile. His short-barreled Colt stood in a cutdown slim-jim holster. Beside the gun belt sat the canvas sack of bank money he'd been carrying. He looped the gun belt over his wounded shoulder, hefted the money sack over it, revealing no sign of the pain it caused him, and carried Folliard's Starr cocked and ready toward the door. On his way to the door, with his gun in his hand, he grabbed a battered bowler hat from a townsman's head and put it on.

"You'll not get away with this," Garand said in a tight, angry voice. He gestured a nod toward the doctor. "If anything happens to that poor wretch, we'll hunt you down and hang you on the spot."

Traybo gave a tug on the rope and shotgun in his hand.

"Come on, *poor wretch*," he said to Dr. Bernard. "The quicker we get where we're going, the sooner we'll set you free." He looked at Claypool. "About ready, pard?" he asked, ignoring Claypool's wound and his battered condition.

"Waiting on you," Claypool said through his swollen lips.

Traybo looked at the faces as he backed out the door with the doctor, Claypool covering him.

"We get a half hour start," he called out. "Anybody comes out this door before that, you'll be playing fast and loose with this doctor's life."

Claypool backed out onto the dusty boardwalk behind his leader, dust still looming heavily in the air.

"What are you doing here?" he asked Traybo over his shoulder, checking both ways along the street of the disheveled town.

"I came back for the money," said Traybo. "Why else?"

"I wouldn't have come back for you," Claypool said, stepping down to the hitch rail and swinging the sack of money up over his horse's damp, mud-streaked withers. He stopped for a second, recognizing the horse to be his own sweat-streaked dun. "It's Charlie Smith!" he said to the dun, looking the horse over quickly. "And no worse for the wear." The horse sawed its head and chuffed a hot breath in his face.

"I come across him a mile out," said Wes Traybo. "Figured you'd be glad to see him."

"I don't know what to say," Claypool said earnestly, climbing up into his saddle. He patted the dun's damp withers. "Still," he said, catching himself, "I wouldn't have come back for you. I mean it."

"I know you wouldn't, you stingy bastard," said Traybo, shoving the young doctor up into a buckboard wagon he'd acquired on his way into town. He'd reined his horse to the rear of the wagon. "I'm trying to set a good example here."

"A good example. Hear that, Charlie Smith?" Claypool said to his horse through swollen lips. He leveled the stolen bowler atop his head, backing the dun into the street. "How's Ty?" he asked Wes, turning the horse as Traybo swung the wagon around beside him.

"He'll do," said Wes, "if this doctor's any good." He slapped the reins to the buckboard horse's back and put the wagon forward, eyes watching from inside the sheriff's office as they rode away. "*Are* you any good, Doc?"

"I'm the best," the young doctor said, confident, but not cocky.

"That's good to hear," said Wes Traybo. "You better not be lying to me."

Claypool, looking back over his shoulder toward the sheriff's office, saw stray cattle milling here and there; a long-horned steer licked a wet tongue on its reflection in a storefront window. Along the street townsfolk stared at them from behind cover, not sure what to do, seeing the shotgun to the side of their young doctor's head.

"We're stopping by the saloon on our way out," Wes said sidelong to Claypool. "The mercantile too."

Claypool turned to him in his saddle.

"You come here to *shop*?" he asked, bemused, holding his eyes open as far as his swollen purple lids would allow.

Traybo loosened the rope in his hand and lowered the shotgun an inch, resting the barrel on Dr. Bernard's shoulder. He gave the guarded trace of a grin, staring ahead along the dusty street.

"Sort of," he said.

Rubens stood up from his guard spot behind a stand of rock when he spotted Wes Traybo and the young doctor on the buckboard, Carter Claypool riding along beside them. On the other side of the buckboard, he spotted Wes' horse, a dark-haired young woman in the saddle, her skirt drawn up over her thighs to accommodate herself.

"Looks like your brother has brought half the damn town back with him," he said to Ty Traybo, who sat slumped back against the rock, Bugs Trent sitting beside him, keeping a close eye on him.

"Hear that, Ty?" said Bugs. "Wes is back, and he's brought half the town with him."

"That's . . . my brother for you," Ty said, weak, sweating, drifting in and out of consciousness. He sat up straighter with Bugs' help and looked out toward the approaching riders.

Bugs raised the blood-soaked bandanna from the nasty shoulder wound, eyed the wound, then lowered the cloth back into place.

"Everything's going to be all right now," he said quietly. But his voice didn't sound convincing.

"Damn right it will, Ty," Rubens said, stepping over to them as the wagon rolled up closer. He gave Bugs a doubtful look and shook his head.

"I know," Bugs said, returning the look.

Rubens turned and stepped forward as the buckboard rolled up and slid to a halt a few yards away.

Claypool and the young woman stopped their horses and stepped down from their saddles. Seeing the doctor stand up in the buckboard and pick up a black medicine satchel and loop its strap over his shoulder, Rubens chuckled and shook his head.

"You sure did bring back a doctor," he said, reaching a hand up to help the doctor down. But the doctor ignored his hand and jumped to the ground and walked straight over to Ty Traybo.

Rubens looked Claypool up and down. "Afternoon, Carter," he said to the battered outlaw. "Looks like somebody caught you stealing chickens again."

"While I was there, I figured I might just as well bring Carter back too," said Wes, stepping down and gathering an armful of goods from the wagon bed. He turned and pitched a bottle of rye to Rubens.

Rubens caught the bottle, clasped it to his chest and rolled his eyes to heaven.

"Thank you, *Jesus*," he said.

Wes directed the dark-haired young woman toward

his wounded brother and walked alongside her. All eyes followed the woman, who went to where the doctor had stooped down beside Ty and began stripping away the bloody bandanna and shirt.

"Brother Ty," Wes said. "Meet Rosetta—the young woman you asked for."

"*Buenos tardes*, Ty," the woman said, her dark eyes full of suggestion. "Your brother asked me to help you get well. When you do, I can sit on your lap and show you how I learned to ride a pony."

Ty shook his head slowly and offered a weak smile.

"Wes, you beat all," Ty murmured.

"Everybody stand back and give us some room," the doctor demanded, waving an arm. "This man is in a bad way."

"Sure thing, Doc," said Wes. Yet instead of backing away, he pitched a new hat and a new folded shirt down at Ty's side.

"Here's that new hat and shirt you asked for," he said. "Rosetta here will help you get bathed and dressed soon as the doctor's done with you."

The doctor turned his eyes up to Wes.

"This is not a trivial matter," he said. "Look at this wound." He held back a bloody cloth he'd pressed to Ty's mangled shoulder. Blood pooled from the large gaping center of the wound. "Does this look like something to take lightly?"

"Hey, Doc," Claypool snapped, stepping forward in a threatening manner. "Don't go forgetting who's the captive and who's holding the guns here."

"To hell with your guns," the young doctor countered.

"Let's not forget who's the doctor and who's the patient. If you want this man to stay alive, you'll do as you're told." He eyed the bloody left shoulder of Claypool's shirt. "You're going to need some tending too," he added.

Claypool drew the big Starr from his waist and cocked it toward the doctor.

"I tend myself," he said.

"Suit yourself," said the doctor. "I still have a patient here to look after."

Wes noted how quickly the young doctor had taken charge once he'd seen Ty's condition.

"Carter, lower that smoker. He's right," said Wes, looking closer at his brother's mangled shoulder. "Ty needs to get rested and bandaged up before we head out of here." He reached over and pulled the young woman away from Ty's side. "Let it simmer awhile, darling, until he's better able to—"

"I'm . . . able right now," Ty cut in, sounding weaker.

"*Sí*, I understand," the young woman said quietly to Wes as she looked down at the doctor's bloody fingers probing the gaping shoulder wound.

"I'll pay you," said Wes. "Let you get on back to town with the doctor."

She pressed a hand against Wes' vest pocket as he reached for some gold coins. "No," she replied in the same quiet tone, "I will ride along until your brother is well. He may need some help."

Wes just looked at her for a moment. Finally he let his hand drop from his vest pocket.

"*Gracias*, ma'am," he said.

The doctor turned his eyes from the wound and looked up at the two of them.

"It's for sure he's going to need some help for a few days," he said. "But if you think he's able to mount a horse and ride away from here today, you're dead wrong. Riding will kill him."

"Doctor," said Wes, "those detectives are forming a posse, biding their time right now. In an hour we'll see them coming this way. We've got no choice but to keep moving."

"That will be your decision, not mine," the young doctor said firmly. "I can only tell you what will happen. He's lost lots of blood, and he's still losing it. I'll sew up what I can, but there's a lot of flesh lost here. Stick him on a horse, he'll bleed the rest of the way out before nightfall."

"You heard him, brother Ty," Wes said down to his brother's lowered head. "Are you able to ride or not?"

"Hell . . . yes, I am," Ty murmured, half-conscious.

But Wes judged his brother's weakened voice and looked back at the doctor.

The doctor said quickly, "I know a place where you can hide him, for overnight anyway."

Wes gave him a look. The others stepped in closer.

"It'll be risky," the doctor warned them. "But if you'll trust me to take you there, it's a place where the posse will never look for you."

Wes looked from face to face.

Rubens held the open bottle of rye in his right hand. Corking the bottle, he grinned, rye trickling down his stubble, and handed the fiery liquor to Claypool.

"Hell, *risky* never bothered me," he said. "I'm riskier than a wolf in a meat house."

Wes looked at Claypool, who had to tip his head to look back at him through his swollen purple eyes.

"I've never been in a *risky* situation," he said. "But I'm willing to give it a try." He jerked the cork from the bottle, sloshed the rye around and took a drink.

Quiet laughter rippled across the men.

Bugs took a deep breath and let it out slowly.

"I'll go along with whatever you decide, Wes," he said. Then turning to the doctor, he said, "If you try to jackpot us, Doc, you best understand we'll every one of us kill you."

"I believe that goes without saying," the young doctor said calmly. Then he turned his eyes and his bloody fingers back to Ty Traybo.

"It's settled, then," Wes said to the others. "Soon as the doc is ready, he's leading us out of here."

Chapter 6

It was turning dark evening when Wes Traybo and Dr. Bernard had led the riders around the long hill trail, keeping the town of Maley to their left across the wide stretch of flatlands. Before taking the trail they were on, the group had made their tracks hard to follow by riding west a half mile across a bare rock shelf. When the doctor and Wes both felt they had gone far enough to throw off the detective posse, they circled back through thick brush and rock and picked up the trail the doctor would have them follow.

Dr. Bernard rode bareback on the wagon horse they'd unhitched from the buckboard once they'd driven the rig a long ways on their false trail and left it sitting in plain sight. With their tracks covered, difficult to find in the coming night, Wes and the rest of the men had followed the doctor's lead without question. Yet, after two hours of backtracking, the riders began to grow suspicious of how close they'd traveled back toward town.

No one mentioned it until Wes himself saw the glow of torchlight appear, bobbing toward them across the flatlands floor. Still, the outlaw leader held his peace until he saw that the trail lying before them only wound down to the flatlands.

"Hold it, Doc," he said to Bernard, drawing his horse to a halt on a ridge at the top of the winding trail. "It looks like we're headed right smack back to Maley." He raised his Colt from across his lap and cocked it. "You better tell me I'm wrong," he warned, waiting for the doctor's reply.

"You're not wrong," the young doctor said firmly, stopping his horse beside him, not the least put off by the cocked gun pointed at him. "This trail is the quickest way down to the flatlands, back to Maley."

Hearing him, the men drew their horses closer in around him and Wes.

"What the hell's he talking about 'back to Maley'?" Rubens asked Wes.

The doctor sat braced, tense, like a man anticipating an oncoming storm.

"Yeah, Doc," said Wes, "what are you talking about?"

"Maley is the safest place to spend the night," the doctor said firmly. "That's where I'm taking us."

"Like hell you are!" Bugs said, kicking his horse forward toward the doctor.

"Shut up, Bugs," said Wes, grabbing his horse by its bridle and holding the young gunman back. Wes turned his eyes and gun back to the doctor. "Start talking, Doc," said Wes, already making sense of the doctor's words.

Dr. Bernard nodded at the row of torchlights bobbing across the darkened flatlands below.

"Look at them," he said. "Every able-bodied man in Maley is riding with Garand's detectives tonight. They're coming to kill all of you and save me. My house is sitting empty. Inside, I have all the instruments and medicine and bandaging I need to prepare your brother for the trip to Mexico." He paused, then added, "Which, I can assure you, will be much easier once the posse has given up and pulled back off your trail."

Wes considered it. His gun lowered an inch.

"Who says we're going to Mexico?" he asked.

"Everything about you says you're going to Mexico," the doctor replied. "You need to get your brother in better shape first. Otherwise, he's dead already."

Behind the doctor, Ty sat slumped in his saddle, Rosetta riding double with him resting back on her bosom. She led the spare wagon horse behind her, managing Ty's horse with skill. She looked at Wes and nodded slowly, agreeing with the doctor.

"Doc, you misled us. You should have told me to begin with we were headed back to Maley," said Wes. "Not wait until we're at a spot like this."

The doctor gave a slight shrug.

"Had I told you where I was taking you, you wouldn't have come, now, would you?" he reasoned.

Wes and the men looked at each other.

"That's what I thought," the doctor said. "As it is, you've got from here down to the flatlands to think it over. If you don't agree with what I'm saying, you can ride straight west to the border. You will still have thrown off the posse." He paused to let it sink in, then said, "If you're wise, you'll follow me across the flatlands to my house." He sat staring at Wes. "What say you?"

Wes chuffed and shook his head.

"Doc, I bet you keep all the poker players in Maley ragged and broke," he said.

"I don't gamble," Dr. Bernard said. "I never seem to find the time."

Wes looked at the other faces for comment. Rubens took a deep breath and let it out. He looked back along the trail they'd ridden thus far.

"I figure if we started back now, we'd run into that posse head-on, about where we started from," he said. "I've got a feeling the doc here timed everything— worked it all out in his head."

Wes looked at the doctor.

"Is that true, Doc?" he asked.

The doctor only stared at him blankly.

Taking the doctor's silence to be an admission, Wes looked away from him, at Carter Claypool. The battered outlaw sat with his wrists crossed on his saddle horn, the blood dried back on his shoulder, his swollen purple face looking shadowy and sinister in the failing evening light.

"He warned us it would be *risky*," Claypool said on Dr. Bernard's behalf.

"But he never said it would be plumb *loco*," Bugs Trent cut in, still staring coldly at the doctor.

Wes uncocked his Colt and lowered it down across his lap. He took the conversation back.

"What's loco is sitting here wondering which way to go on a trail that only goes one way," he said. He turned to the doctor. "You'll need light to change Ty's bandages. What will the town make of a light being on in your house?"

"I have a convalescent room in the middle of the house," the doctor said. "We'll close the doors around it. Nobody will have to see a light burning." He raised his reins and gathered the bareback horse beneath him. "It's the safest place for your brother to spend the night, you'll see."

"It better be, Doc," Wes warned him. He motioned the doctor forward with a gesture of his hand. "I hope you've got something to eat in your cupboard."

"I'm certain we'll find something there," the doctor said, riding his horse forward.

"Carter," Wes said over his shoulder, "lag behind us, keep this trail open. If we need it in a hurry, I don't want those torches bobbing right down on us."

"You got it, Wes," said Claypool. "I'll give you warning shots if they come this way." He pulled his horse back, turned it off the edge of the trail and rode back the way they had come through brush and rocky ground.

On the horse in front of Rosetta, Ty sat leaning back, his face lolling back on her bosom.

"What's . . . the holdup?" he murmured in a weak, mindless voice.

"Shh, you must sit still, *mi querido*." She smoothed his hair back with her hand, reached her face down and kissed his forehead. "I have you taken care of," she whispered.

"That . . . you do," Ty whispered, trailing back to sleep. "I'm right as rain here. . . ."

It had been a four-day ride out of Mexico, back across the rocky badlands hills. When the Ranger spotted the

half-fallen adobe and plank shack standing on a cliff at
an abandoned mining project, he and Fatch Hardaway
rode to the spot and stepped down from their saddles as
the sun sank below the horizon.

"How much farther to Cottonwood from here,
Ranger?" Hardaway asked, his voice sounding aching
and tight from the long day in the saddle.

"That depends," Sam replied. He loosened the black-
speckled barb's saddle, pulling it off the horse's sweaty
back onto his tired shoulder.

"Depends on what?" said Hardaway. He slumped
onto a hitch rail as he tied his horse's reins to an iron
loop.

"On how far we are from Cottonwood when you show
me where the Traybos holed up," Sam said patiently.
"Have you already forgotten our deal *again*?"

Hardaway let out a breath and turned back to his
horse.

"It's not so much that I forgot as it is that it's not the
foremost thing on my mind," he said. He loosened his
horse's saddle and pulled it off onto the shoulder. "The
foremost thing on my mind is how bad Wes Traybo is
going to want to kill me stone dead when he finds out I
led you there."

"I don't believe you, Hardaway," Sam said, walking
past him to the remaining two standing walls of the
adobe shack.

"Don't believe me *how*?" Hardaway said, walking
along beside him.

"I don't believe you spook this easily." As he spoke,
Sam stooped and gathered some dried brush for kindling

and some broken, weathered boards for a fire. Hardaway did the same.

"Oh?" said Hardaway. "What makes you say so?"

"You've been a rounder and a tough gunman all your life," Sam said, walking through a low tangle of brush surrounding the shack. "This is not the first time you've done something to make somebody come looking to kill you." He stepped across a short stone foundation, looked all around and dropped his saddle and an arm-load of firewood on the dirt floor. "I don't think you fear the Traybos as much as you're letting on."

"Well," said Hardaway, dropping his saddle and more broken boards and dried brush on the ground. "I expect you're right. I fear no man that much. I've had my scrapes and spills, same as any man who set out to do his own bidding. But fearwise, I'd spit in the devil's eye."

"What is it about the Traybos, then?" Sam asked, turning, facing him.

Hardaway stooped and piled some wood and brush inside a circle of soot-smudged rocks surrounding an old and blackened campfire site.

"To be honest, Ranger," he said, taking out matches from his shirt pocket, "I hate letting the Traybos down. I kind of admire them ol' boys. Not just the Traybo brothers. Hell, everybody that rides with them."

"*Admire* them?" Sam said to keep him talking.

"Maybe that's not the right word," said Hardaway. "Maybe I mean I respect them?" He looked up from the ground, a match burning between his fingers, fire starting to dance among the brittle brush and kindling.

"All right, you respect them," Sam said.

"Damn it, I hate to say it," Hardaway said. "I know we're every one of us a bunch of no-good sons a' bitches out here, top to bottom. But the Traybos are . . . well, they're different. They're the kind of hombres you want to ride with—old Baylor Rubens . . . Carter Claypool. You don't find those kinds of men long-riding these days."

"Then why'd you stop riding with them?" Sam asked quietly. He stooped and took a canteen of tepid water from his saddle, uncapped it and took a sip. A small fire began to flicker and glow.

"Hell if I know," said Hardaway, reaching around, taking his own canteen from his saddle horn, opening it, sloshing it around. He contemplated the matter further for a moment, watching the fire grow, then said, "For some reason I expect I knew I wasn't good enough to ride with them . . . the truth be told."

Sam wiped a hand across his lips and just looked at Hardaway for a moment.

"All right, I know that sounds crazy," Hardaway said, under the Ranger's gaze. "There's a lot of no-good bastards you wouldn't have to pay me a Mexican peso to jackpot. I'd give them to you, just to watch them die over a foaming mug of beer." He paused; his voice lowered, softened. He tipped his canteen almost in a toast. "I'm just saying, the Traybos and their men? They *ain't them.*"

Sam watched him toss back a drink of canteen water. When Hardaway had wiped his mouth, he continued.

"I remember once when we robbed a bank in Texas—" He caught himself and stopped with a wary look on his face. "I didn't mean to say *we*. I meant to say *they*," he corrected himself quickly. "I heard *they* robbed a bank in Texas and on the way outta town, Wes stopped and helped an elderly woman who had fallen in the street in front of us—in front of *them*, that is," he corrected himself again.

"Wait a minute," Sam said, stopping him. "Don't try telling me this story if you have to keep stopping to cover your tracks," he said. "It's hard enough to believe you without you stopping—"

"Old habits don't die easy, Ranger," Hardaway said, cutting him off. "But the thing is, Wes was always doing stuff like that—giving outlawry a classy turn, if you know what I mean."

"And that favorably impressed you," Sam said flatly.

"Yes, it did," said Hardaway. "Leastwise, enough to make me feel bad about jackpotting them this way. All the time I rode with them, they never hurt anybody— maybe cracked a head or two. They only steal from banks and railroads. Let's face it, banks and railroads are the worst thieves in the world. The Traybos haven't killed innocent people. Just the railroad dogs out to kill them."

"It might surprise you to hear this, Hardaway, but not everybody thinks the way you do about banks and railroads," Sam said. "Anyway, the Traybos are out-laws. Let's keep that straight. No matter how well they play their hands, sooner or later something will go wrong and some innocent persons will die. Maybe I can get to them before that happens and take them in alive—" He stopped short and looked off toward the trail they'd ridden up on, hearing a faint but familiar sound.

Hardaway looked at him, knowing something was up.

"What is it?" he asked in a whisper, his hand already closing around his gun butt.

"Horses, coming up the other side," Sam said under his breath.

"Horses . . . ?" Hardaway said. "Are you sure?"

Sam just gave him a look.

"Sorry," Hardaway whispered. "Want me to kill the fire?"

Sam considered it.

"No," he said. He reached over to his saddle and drew his rifle from its scabbard. "Build it up some. Somebody's on this trail, we need to find out who it is and what they're up to."

Chapter 7

Artimus Folliard and another detective, a wiry little Arkansan named Suell Crane, were the first two members of the detective posse to walk their horses up from the trail into the outer edge of the circling firelight. The two stopped and looked all around from behind the cover of a rock, Folliard wearing a blue cloth wrapped beneath his chin and tied at the top of his head to ease the throbbing pain from his broken teeth. On either side of the flickering fire, they saw the outlines of two sleeping figures, each wrapped in a blanket lying back a few feet out of the firelight.

"This is too bloody good to be true," Crane whispered to Folliard.

Folliard's covered jawline still revealed much of the swollen purple flesh left from the blow of his own gun barrel. Dried blood had formed in the corner of his mouth from the broken teeth.

"Yeah, wait here, watch the horses and keep me covered," he whispered to Crane in a stiff and pained voice.

"What?" Crane whispered, surprised, seeing Folliard start to move forward in a crouch.

"I said *wait here*, damn it," said Folliard. "I'm going to wake this bastard with my gun barrel staring him in the eye."

"Garand said wait until everybody gets this camp surrounded," said Crane. "You best do as we're told."

"I'm Garand's huckleberry. I can do no wrong," Folliard whispered confidently. "I'm not waiting—not after what that outlaw did to me." He started to move forward again. Crane grabbed his arm.

"You're not thinking straight, Artimus," said Crane. "You don't even know it's them."

Folliard stared down at the wiry little detective's hand clasped around his forearm. Crane turned him loose quickly.

"It's them all right," Folliard whispered. "Who else would be on this trail this close to where we found the wagon?"

"I don't know. But Garand said wait," Crane insisted. "If this is them, where're the doctor and the woman?"

But Folliard would have none of it.

"I'll find out from one after I've killed the other," Folliard whispered. He turned and moved away silently in a crouch toward the firelight.

"He's lost his mind . . . ," Crane murmured to himself, moving forward a few steps to keep Folliard covered. He watched Folliard move slowly until he stood over the nearest blanket on the ground. As Folliard held a borrowed Colt out at arm's length, cocked and aimed down at the blanket, Crane cursed under his breath, even as he started to step closer.

But before he could take his next step, he recognized the feel of a cold rifle barrel against the back of his neck. He froze, staring straight ahead where Folliard stood ready to pull the trigger on the big Colt.

Oh no! He had a sinking feeling deep down in his stomach as he watched Folliard reach out with his boot and kick it sidelong against the sleeper on the ground.

"Wake up, long rider. It's time to die," Folliard growled through his swollen jaw. He pulled the Colt's trigger and sent a streak of fire blazing down through the blanket. As soon as he'd pulled the trigger, he swung the Colt toward the second blanket on the other side of the campfire, cocked it and braced to fire again. He stood waiting for a second. When no movement came from the other blanket, he looked back down.

"What the hell?" he said. He swung around toward Crane. But instead of seeing his partner standing fifteen feet away where he'd left him, he saw the shadowy outline of a man drawing back the butt stock of Winchester rifle. "Oh no," he managed to say just as the rifle butt jabbed forward with a fierce blow and nailed him squarely across his forehead.

The Colt in Folliard's hand fired wildly as he fell backward to the ground. The Ranger ducked to one side instinctively as the bullet whistled past him, past Hardaway, toward the detectives' waiting horses.

"Ho—*ly!*" shouted Hardaway, he and Crane both flinching, turning toward the horses, seeing the bullet had stricken Folliard's saddle horn and shattered it into pieces. The exploding saddle horn sent Folliard's terrified horse into a wild, rearing, bucking frenzy. Crane's horse, also badly spooked, charged across the campsite. But Sam caught its reins and held on, letting the animal spin in a full circle until it settled and drew to a halt. Folliard's horse went racing away in the dark, whinnying loud and long in the otherwise quiet night. Bits of the shattered saddle horn sprinkled down like raindrops.

"All right, *ambusher*, start talking," Hardaway said to the other detective as Sam led the horse over to them. He kept his face hidden beneath his lowered hat brim from force of habit. "How many more *ambushers* are out there?" He gave the man a poke with his gun barrel for good measure.

"There's a whole posse of us coming, mister," the wiry little detective said. "If you know what's good for you, you'll lower the rifle and give yourselves up to me."

"Now, why on earth would we do that?" Hardaway asked as the Ranger walked over to them leading Crane's horse, Folliard's smoking Colt dangling in his hand.

"To keep us from hanging you on the spot," Crane said, growing more confident.

"Hear that, Ranger?" said Hardaway. "These *ambushers* will hang us on the spot if we don't roll over and show them our bellies."

"Ranger?" said Crane, taking on a peculiar expression.

"Yep, Ranger Samuel Burrack," said Hardaway, suddenly liking the idea of having a lawman riding with him. "What does that do for you, *ambusher*?"

"Ranger, you've got us all wrong," Crane said, speaking rapidly, seeing the badge on Sam's chest in the flicker of firelight. "We're not ambushers. Me and Folliard there are both railroad detectives, riding posse with Dallas Garand. We're after a band of robbers—the Traybo Gang. We got word they were hitting our bank and we tried to catch them red-handed."

"How'd that go?" said Hardaway beneath his lowered hat brim.

"Not good, not good at all," said the detective. "That's why we're tracking them."

Sam only stared at the detective for a moment, hearing more hooves moving along the trail leading up to them. The riders had given up on staying quiet now that they'd heard gunfire erupt ahead of them.

"Your posse will be here any minute," the Ranger said. "I expect Dallas Garand will be leading it?" As he spoke he shoved Folliard's Colt down behind his gun belt.

"Yes, he is, Ranger," said Crane, his hands still chest high. "He won't stand for nothing ugly happening to Folliard and me."

"Good for Dallas Garand," said Hardaway, gigging the detective again with the gun barrel. "Don't do nothing *ugly* and nothing *ugly* will happen to you." He grinned. "Right, Ranger?"

Sam didn't answer. He reached behind the detective's coat lapel and pulled a long Smith & Wesson Schofield from a cross-draw belly rig. He turned the pistol in his hand, looked it over and shoved it down beside Folliard's borrowed Colt.

"Sit down. Make yourself comfortable," he said to the worried detective. "We'll talk it all out when Garand gets here."

"Garand *is here*, Ranger," said a booming voice from the darkness surrounding the campsite.

Hardaway spun around in surprise, his rifle ready to fire.

"No, Hardaway, stand down," the Ranger ordered him in a lowered voice. "Running into these fellows might be a good break for you and me both."

"Throw your guns down, Ranger," Dallas Garand said. "I'm bringing my men in."

"In case you've forgotten, here's how it works, Garand," Sam replied, unmoved by the posse leader's demanding tone. "You only throw your guns down when you're caught sneaking into camp trying to kill somebody in their sleep." He paused, then said, "That would be your two men here."

Hardaway and the Ranger heard the posse leader curse and growl under his breath.

"I didn't tell them to do that, Ranger," Garand said. "Detective Folliard has been acting strange from a gun barrel lick he took earlier today."

"He might be acting strange a little longer," said the Ranger. He looked over at Folliard, who still lay knocked flat on his back, babbling like a drunkard. His right boot wagged back and forth slowly in the dirt.

"We're on the hunt, Ranger," said Garand. "Either let's talk law talk or we'll be on our way. I don't have all night."

"Come on in, Garand," Sam called out. "Wake your man up and tell him where he's at."

"Oh, I'll tell him where he's at," Garand said in a threatening tone, stepping his horse forward into the firelight. "You can bet on it."

The Ranger and Hardaway stood watching, guns hanging in their hands, as Dallas Garand and his posse pulled Artimus Folliard to his feet. Water dripped from Folliard's face where Crane had emptied a canteen of tepid water on him to bring him around.

"Serves him right, the son of a bitch," Hardaway whispered sidelong to the Ranger. "Sneaking in here like he did."

"Walk easy around these men," Sam warned him in a lowered voice, keeping his eyes on the detectives and townsmen who had laid their torches in a burning pile on the ground.

"Obliged, Ranger, but you can't tell me a thing about these buzzards," said Hardaway. "They've had my bones on a spick for a long time."

"For good reason?" the Ranger asked under his breath.

Hardaway stalled a moment, then said, "I'm probably not the best person to ask about that. But the fact is, I paid my time in Mexico, sitting things out awhile. I'm clean—just like you found out."

"Relax, Hardaway," Sam said, seeing how tense the detectives were making him. "You've got the law standing beside you."

As the posse turned, Crane and two of the townsmen led Folliard away toward their horses while the other men followed Dallas Garand to where the Ranger and Hardaway stood.

"Well, well," Garand said, finally recognizing Hardaway, "if it's not Fatcharack Hardaway himself."

Fatcharack? The Ranger gave Hardaway a curious look.

"What are you doing riding with Fatcharack Hardaway?" Garand asked.

"Nobody calls me Fatcharack anymore, Garand," Hardaway said in a tight, threatening tone. "Not for long anyway." His hand gripped the rifle tight. "Maybe you wouldn't realize that, having only seen my name on old railroad posters and such. But it's *Fatch*. And you'll want to remember that in the future."

"I wouldn't be putting lots of stock in the future if I were you, *Fatch*," said Garand. He turned dismissingly from Hardaway to the Ranger. "Ranger Burrack," he said, "let me introduce you to the finest crew of detectives ever brought together." He gestured from his left to his right at the hard, grim faces of his men.

"This is Earl Prew, Fain Elliot, L. C. McGuire, Huey Drambite and Rio DeSpain—or *Spanish Rivers* as some have called him."

Spanish Rivers, the rotten son of a bitch, Hardaway thought to himself, gazing at DeSpain, recognizing him less by sight than by name and bad reputation.

Sam nodded at each of the six men in turn, recognizing the names Fain Elliot and Rio DeSpain. He stopped at DeSpain and looked him up and down, seeing the gunman's fingers open and close restlessly around the butt of a Mason-Richards Navy Colt conversion.

"Spanish Rivers," Sam said. "Last picture I saw of you, they had you tied to a board out front of the sheriff's office in Waco."

Spanish Rivers gave a sharp little grin that was more like some strange wolf showing a gold-capped fang. A round gold earring dangled from his left ear. The top third of the same ear was missing.

"Yeah, they all thought I was dead that day," he said. "But they found out otherwise. The photographer got close enough, I head-butted him—broke his damn nose like an eggshell. When they cut me loose, I wanted to light flash powder up his—"

"So you see, Ranger," Garand said, cutting DeSpain off, "I have all the right men to go after anybody foolish enough to rob our trains or bank holdings."

"Does that include your man over there?" Sam asked, nodding toward Folliard, who leaned against a horse, two men steadying him.

"Hard to believe, but that idiot *was* one of my best men until he had his jaw creased with a gun barrel." He shook his head. "Good gunmen are as unpredictable as they are hard to find," he said.

"Your man Crane there told us the Traybo Gang hit the bank in Maley," Sam said. He took Folliard's Colt and Crane's Schofield from behind his belt and gave them to Garand. The detective leader accepted them with an embarrassed expression.

"Yeah, they did," he said grudgingly. "They emptied the rail pens, sent a stampede down the middle of town—killed a rail pen worker, one of my detectives and some innocent widow, never harmed a living soul in her life."

The Ranger looked at Hardaway with a grim expression.

"There goes the part about the Traybo Gang not killing innocent people," he said. "I expect taking them in alive is out of the question now."

"Take them in alive? *Ha!*" said Garand. "I'll take in their heads on the end of sticks. Don't kid yourself, Ranger. This bunch is as bad as they come. Try taking them alive, all it will get a man is a hard fall and an early grave."

"It was just a thought, Garand," Sam said. "I'm always sorry to hear about innocent people dying. Who identified the Traybos?"

Garand stalled for a second, then said, "The thing is, this was a setup. We got word to the Traybos through a source I won't reveal. We knew it was them coming in."

"Let me get this straight," Sam said. "You knew they were coming? Still they did all that to you?"

"Don't judge me, Ranger!" Garand raised a gloved finger. "You had to be there to see how bad it went. We weren't prepared for a cattle stampede. One of my detectives shotgunned one of them in the bank. I expect that one's dead. We caught one of them making their getaway. Had him ready to break—about to tell us everything about where the gang's headed!"

"What happened?" Sam asked.

Garand stared hard at him, but then he let out a tight breath and continued.

"All right," he said. "Wes Traybo rode back, freed him at gunpoint, kidnapped the town doctor and a young Mexican dove and rode away in a buckboard." He jerked a nod toward the dark trail behind them. "We found the buckboard back there. That's what made us think this might be their campfire."

"You think they would build a fire, a posse on their trail?" Sam asked flatly.

Hardaway chuffed and shook his head.

"That'd be as stupid as tracking them with torches," he cut in before Sam could stop him.

"You son of a bitch!" shouted Garand. "No long-riding, four-flushing trash tells me how to do my job!"

Sam stepped between the two men as they both lurched toward each other.

"Wait a minute, both of you," Sam said, holding out a hand in each direction. "Save your fighting for the Traybos, Garand," he said to the posse leader. To Hardaway he said, "This is law talk. Keep your opinions to yourself."

Garand settled, as did Hardaway.

"What are you doing riding with this known felon, Ranger?" Garand asked again.

"The fact is, he's no felon," Sam said. "The only charge he had against him has been dropped. The man he killed was wanted dead or alive by the state of Ohio. He acted as bounty hunter. I'm accompanying him to see to it he draws his reward without some lawman blowing his head off."

"If you're thinking about changing your plans and going after the Traybos, forget it," said Garand. "I've got them cold."

The Ranger didn't reply.

Garand turned a cold stare to Hardaway.

"Bounty hunter, my dead uncle's ass." He sneered at Hardaway. "Sam, you'll be lucky if this one doesn't murder you in your sleep. I won't have you riding the trail ahead of me, not with him in tow. He'll warn the Traybos if you get close to them."

"You don't tell us what to do—" Hardaway tried to cut in.

Sam stopped him with a cold look. Hardaway shut up, giving a resolved shrug.

"The trail's all yours, Garand," Sam said. "I won't step in front of a man's hunt."

Garand studied his face for a moment, deciding if he believed him. Then he nodded and said, "That's fair of you, Ranger." He turned and walked to his horse. "Does that mean you won't be coming after them at all?"

"I've got to think about it some," Sam called over to him. "Make sure I don't ride off half-cocked."

"Yes, you go think about it some, Ranger," Garand said haughtily. He collected his reins. His detectives and posse men mounted and gathered around him. "Meanwhile, we'll go skin these thieves, bag their heads up and throw them at your feet. Right, men?" he called out to the riders around him. The men rallied a reply.

The Ranger and Hardaway stood watching as they turned their horses and rode away, their torches bobbing above their heads.

Chapter 8

The Ranger and Fatch Hardaway stood in the circle of the campfire, watching until the last glow of torchlight turned black along the trail. Hardaway let out a tense breath, shouldered his rifle and pushed his hat up on his forehead.

"What an asshole," he said toward the darkened trail. "If you were going after the Traybo Gang, would you let him muscle ahead of you this way?"

"You saw his bunch," Sam said. "Where would you rather have them riding, in front of you, or behind you?"

"Good point," Hardaway said.

"But the fact is, I am going after the Traybos," the Ranger said quietly.

"What? Right now? You're joshing," said Hardaway.

"Yep, right now," said the Ranger. "And it's no joshing matter." As he spoke, he turned and walked over, picked up his blanket from atop a bundle of brush he'd laid there and shook it out, seeing the fresh bullet hole through it. "Call it fate or call it coincidence," he said, draping the blanket over his shoulder, "but when you find yourself this close to the men you're after, you go after them, straightaway."

With a curious expression, Hardaway followed Sam as he picked up his saddle and walked to the horses.

"Where does that put you and me?" he said. "Showing you where the Traybos hideout is one thing. Dogging their trail with you is a whole other."

"You're free to ride away," Sam said, pitching his saddle up atop the speckled barb. "I'm not holding you to nothing."

"Not *holding me*—?" Hardaway cut himself short. "Well, that's mighty damn decent of you," he said. "I am nothing but obliged!" he said sarcastically.

"Don't mention it," Sam said flatly, drawing the saddle cinch and testing the saddle with a hand.

"We've got an agreement," said Hardaway. "If I don't go with you, what about my reward money?"

"What about it?" Sam asked sharply. He turned, leading the barb, and walked to the campfire. Hardaway hurried alongside him.

"*Specifically*," said Hardaway, "if you go after the Traybos, when do I get it?"

"When I meet you in Cottonwood," the Ranger said.

Exasperated, Hardaway said, "Oh, and what if you catch up with the Traybos, say you stop a bullet or two with your forehead?" He firmly tapped his forehead as an example.

"Then I won't meet you," Sam said matter-of-factly. He reached out and rubbed out the campfire with the sole of his boot.

"Damn it!" Hardaway cursed. "In other words, if I hope to ever get my money, I best go with you."

"That's one thought," Sam said in the same quiet tone. "You know me, and you know the Traybos. You do the odds."

"Damn it, damn it, damn it!" Hardaway said loudly, pacing back and forth.

"Easy," Sam cautioned him. "Don't spook the horses."

Hardaway stood watching as the Ranger stepped up into his saddle and turned the barb onto the Traybos' back trail.

"Hey, which way are you going?" he called out as Sam nudged the barb into a walk. "Aren't you following Garand's posse?"

"Nope," Sam said over his shoulder. "They're wasting their time and horsepower."

What the hell? Hardaway looked back and forth in the dark, seeing the silhouette of the Ranger and the barb against the purple starlit sky.

"You heard Garand," he called out. "They tracked him this way from where they found an empty buckboard."

"Yep, I heard him," the Ranger said beneath the slow clop of the barb's hooves. "They might have tracked them this way, but this is not the way they're going." The Ranger rode on at a slow clip, leaving Hardaway stopped in his tracks.

A half mile down the trail, he heard Hardaway's line-back buckskin clopping along behind him.

"Don't shoot, Ranger. It's me," Hardaway called out as he drew closer.

Without slowing the barb, Sam rode on at the same pace until Hardaway caught up and slowed his buckskin beside him.

"What makes you say that?" the gunman asked, taking up the conversation right where they'd left off.

"Say what?" Sam replied.

Hardaway drew a patient breath.

"Say that the Traybos aren't headed the way Garand is tracking them?" he said.

"Because they're not," Sam said.

"All right, I'm riding with you," said Hardaway. "How long are you going to keep giving these tight-lipped, one-word answers?"

Sam gave himself a faint grin in the darkness. He didn't say so, but even though he would be tracking a fresh trail, if he lost the Traybos, he'd still need Hardaway to lead them to their lair the way they had planned.

Without answering Hardaway, he said, "I don't know which way the Traybos are headed, but it makes no sense they would stay on this trail knowing the detectives would be riding down their shirts." He looked sidelong at Hardaway. "You know them. Does this sound like something they'd do?"

"No, it doesn't, come to think of it," Hardaway said.

"Wes rode back to town and freed his man from the detectives," Sam said.

"He's that kind of fellow," Hardaway cut in. "I told you he's not like most of these saddle bums posing as long riders. He's the real kind, to the core."

"And while he's there, he takes the town doctor hostage," Sam continued. "So it's reasonable that whoever the detective shotgunned in the bank is alive—badly wounded, I make it."

Hardaway considered it.

"Usually the brothers themselves go inside," he said. "Carter Claypool guards the front door along the board-walk. Rubens and any others hang close out front for backup, just in case some snooping bystander comes along sticking their—" He stopped himself and stared at the Ranger. "I mean, so *I've heard.*"

"I understand," Sam said. He nudged the barb up into a safe but quicker pace. Hardaway rode alongside beside him.

"I hope I haven't said anything that might implicate me in any kind of illegal or untoward behavior," Hard-away said pointedly. "Have I?"

"You can relax from here on," Sam said. "Anything you say to implicate yourself, most likely you've already said it."

The two rode on in silence through the quiet night until they reached the spot where the buckboard sat at the edge of the trail. They both stepped down and the Ranger took a small tin oil lantern from his saddlebags and lit it with a long wooden match. Hitching their horses to the side of the wagon, they walked along the trail a few feet, the Ranger in a crouch, holding the lantern down closer to the hoofprint-covered ground.

"You'll never make nothing out of this mess, Ranger," Hardaway said. But Sam continued on, cutting across the trail to the inner side beneath an upreaching hillside.

"I already have," Sam said, stopping, stooping down and holding the lantern out at arm's length. "Look along here." He gestured toward a single set of tracks running along the lowest edge of the hill, just off the trail from all the others. Layered atop the prints, they saw a single set of prints running back the other way.

"I see them. What about them?" Hardaway asked.

"These belong to a single rider," Sam said. "Someone traveling alone, staying off the trail, keeping out of sight."

"Yeah?" Hardaway looked on in interest.

"I call them scouting tracks," Sam said quietly, as if the owner of the tracks might hear his words. "Whoever made them went that way, looked things over, then backtracked, the way he come. That's the way a trail scout does."

"How do you know it's the Traybos?" Hardaway asked. "Could be one of the posse."

"You met their two scouts," Sam said. "This wasn't them." He stood and walked back to the wagon and held the lantern over into the empty bed.

"No sign of blood," Hardaway remarked in the lantern glow.

"Whoever's wounded wasn't in the wagon," Sam said, looking around in the purple darkness. He snuffed out the tin lantern. "Wes Traybo only brought the wagon along to make his hostages easier to handle." He stepped back from the wagon bed. "You think the wounded man is his brother, Ty?"

"That would be my first pick," Hardaway said. "Like I said, the two always go inside, take the money themselves."

"Who's the most likely one to be scouting their trail?"

Sam asked, still looking around at the jagged edges of black hillside silhouetted against the starlit night.

"That would be Carter Claypool, no question," Hardaway said without having to consider it. "You've heard of all-around cowboys? Claypool is your all-around long rider. Anything risky and bold the Traybos need done, they look to Claypool. He keeps them covered, back trail and front alike."

"So these would be his tracks?" Sam said, already walking to his speckled barb.

"That's my call," Hardaway said, walking alongside him. "Where we headed now?"

"We're going to track him as far as these prints will take us," said Sam. "You've got me curious to meet the man." He put the tin trail lantern away and stepped atop the barb. Hardaway followed suit.

As the two rode away in the darkness, higher up the hillside, Carter Claypool let the hammer down on his rifle and rode his horse quietly across the trail. He'd taken close aim on the Ranger only moments ago and been ready to drop the hammer on him. But then the lantern had gone out. He shook his head.

"You got lucky tonight, Ranger . . . ," he whispered aloud toward the dark trail. Nudging his horse forward, he climbed down through brush and rock to the same trail winding lower down the hill. He had a hard ride to make back to Maley. But he had to let the gang know the Ranger was on their trail. More importantly, he had to let them know that their former pard Fatch Hardaway was riding beside him.

In the small empty barn behind the doctor's large clapboard-sided house at the edge of town, Bugs Trent listened closely, hearing the first sounds of men's muffled voices and footsteps moving along the empty street from the far end of town. Without hesitation, he slipped out of the barn across a short path, up onto the back porch and in through the back door of the large darkened house.

Wes Traybo, the doctor and Rosetta heard his footsteps coming toward the room in the center of the house where they stood watch over the wounded, sleeping outlaw. Wes drew his Colt and stood with it pointed and cocked. Bugs burst through the door and closed it quickly behind him to keep the dim lamplight from seeping outside the room.

"Townsmen coming!" Bugs whispered, drawing his holstered Colt as he spoke. "They'll be here any second!"

"Get to the front window," said Wes. "You and Rubens hold them off while I get my brother to the horses." He hurried to the cot where his brother lay sleeping and reached down to scoop him up in his arms.

"Wait!" Dr. Bernard said. He looked Bugs up and down quickly, as if sizing him for a suit. "Most of the town knows I have a secret friend who sometimes arrives here late at night. They've never seen him up close, but the barber knows his name is Burle . . . Burle Minton."

Wes and Trent turned to each other; then they gave the doctor a curious look.

"A *secret friend*?" said Wes.

The doctor didn't respond to Wes' question.

"Listen to me," he said to Bugs. "Burle is about your size."

Bugs stared at the doctor as he turned to Wes Traybo.

"Wes, what's this sumbitch asking me to do?" he said in an almost shaky voice.

Wes nodded at the doctor, getting it right away.

"Get your gun belt off, get yourself out front, *Burle*," he demanded. "You're going to get yourself caught."

"Caught? Then what?" Bugs said, unbuckling his belt even as he asked. He shoved his Colt inside his shirt behind his trouser waist.

Wes opened the door and gave him a push toward the front room. Rubens was already on his way back through the hall to warn them.

"Make it up as you go, *Burle*," Wes said. He gave a short dark chuckle in spite of the tight spot they were on. "Just don't accept no gifts from them," he added. He reached down and turned the door handle.

"Son of a bitch! Wait!" said Bugs as Wes pushed him out the door. Bugs tried to shove the door open, but Wes had already closed it firmly from the inside.

From the street, a voice called out, "Hold it right there, fellow!"

Bugs turned on the porch, facing four townsmen armed with rifles. He heard what sounded like steel crickets as rifle hammers cocked on the street.

"Oh my God!" he said in a terrified voice, his hands raised high above his head. "What did I do?"

"Step down here where we can see you good," said

an older townsman named Barnes Coomer. "Who are you and what're you doing here?"

Bugs took a breath and stepped forward and down the porch steps as the four men moved forward in a half circle around him.

"I'm—I'm a friend of Dayton's—*Dr. Bernard*, that is," Bugs corrected himself quickly. "I came to see if he was home and maybe wanted to play some two-handed Parcheesi. . . ."

From the inside of the front door, Rubens stood listening closely. He grinned at Wes and whispered in surprise, "Ol' Bugs is good at this—"

"Keep quiet," Wes warned in a whisper, him and the doctor leaning against the wall bedside the doorframe.

Out front the townsmen gave each other a knowing look.

"Two-handed Parcheesi, I bet," one townsman whispered to the others.

"Oh? What's your name, then, young man?" the barber, Lyle Medford, asked shrewdly.

"Burle," Bugs said tight-lipped. He stopped there.

"Your last name, Burle?" a townsman asked.

"I'd rather not say," Bugs said.

"You better say," a townsman threatened, raising his rifle.

"It's—it's Minton, sir," said Bugs in a frightened voice. "I live over near—"

"Never mind where you live, young man," the barber cut in, feeling sorry for him. "You've answered enough." To the others he said under his breath, "He's

telling us the truth. The doc told me his name a while
back."

The townsmen gave him a curious look.

"We barbers hear a lot," Medford reminded them.

"All right," said a townsman named Albert Hasp. He
bounded up onto the porch. "I'll take a little look-see
while we're here, make sure everything's up-and-up."

As Bugs heard the front door open, he almost made
a grab for the gun from under his shirt and started
blasting. But he kept himself cool and waited.

Hasp stepped back outside after looking all around
inside the house from the open doorway.

"Everything looks all right," he said. He stepped
down off the porch and noted the bulge behind Bugs'
shirt. "Wait! What have we here?"

"It's a gun, sir," Bugs said meekly. "I—I arrived here
earlier and saw loose cattle milling everywhere, the
town looking like it had been attacked by savages. I
was frightened. I took this gun from Dayton's desk and
loaded it. It was foolish, I suppose."

"Yes, it was," said the townsman, moving away from
him with a slight mocking grin. "You might have shot
a toe off."

The townsmen chuckled, but began losing interest.
Their rifles were lowered and uncocked.

"In a sense, we were hit by savages, Burle," the barber said. "But these were white savages." He stepped
forward and laid a hand on Bugs' shoulder. "I'm afraid
we have some bad news for you, Burle. Dr. Bernard has
been kidnapped. We're all hoping he'll be returned
safely, of course."

"Oh no, oh *no!*" said Bugs, clamping a hand over his mouth. He swooned sidelong; Medford caught him and steadied him. The townsmen looked on with strange expressions. A couple of them stifled a quiet laugh.

Medford slipped his arm up around Bugs' shoulder and told the other townsmen, "Go on home, fellows. I'll look after young Burle."

As the townsmen turned and drifted away, Bugs said sidelong to the sympathetic barber, "You can go too, mister. I'll be all right now." He moved a little to the side to get out of the barber's arm. But the barber kept it across Bugs' shoulders.

"Nonsense, Burle," Medford said softly, leaning a little too close to Bugs' ear. "I'm not about to leave you all alone in that big dark empty house. I'll stay right here with you."

Bugs pulled his head sideways away from Medford, and slipped a hand around his side to a hideout knife he carried sheathed beneath his shirt. He stood silent for a moment until the other townsmen were out of sight. "Mister," he said, "you'd better get your arm off me just as fast as you can, you ever want to cut hair with it again."

Chapter 9

———

Once inside the big clapboard house, Bugs fell back against the closed door and let out a long tense breath. Ruben, the doctor and Wes Traybo stood watching him recollect himself and push his hat up on his forehead.

"I ain't never doing nothing like that again," said Bugs, pulling his Colt out from behind his shirt. "Somebody'll just have to shoot me, send me straight on to hell." He looked back and forth at the three faces in the darkened room.

"Dang, Bugs," said Rubens with a dark grin. "Don't act like that. You did it so well."

"Don't say another word, Rubens," Bugs warned. "I won't be joshed and kidded about this."

Rubens saw the young gunman was serious and he quickly dropped his grin.

"I'm just saying you did a good job, is all," he said.

Bugs just stared at him.

"Yeah, good job, Bugs. I mean it," said Wes, seeing it to be the way to settle the young man. "You managed to save all of us without firing a shot." He held Bugs' gun belt out to him.

Bugs only nodded, took the gun belt, pushed himself away from against the door, threw the belt around his waist and buckled it. He shoved the Colt down loosely into its holster.

"I'll go and check on my patient now," the doctor said. "The townsmen won't be back tonight, but we'll need to get out of here as soon as we can—no later than first light, I'd say."

"Hey, Doc," said Wes, stopping the doctor, his Colt cocked and pointed loosely at him. "You're full of surprises, aren't you?"

Dr. Bernard only stared at him without replying.

"Yeah," Rubens cut in. "Want to tell us all about this *secret friend* of yours?"

"There's nothing to tell," the doctor said firmly. He started to leave again. Rubens stepped over in front of him.

"We have a discreet relationship that accommodates our mutual needs," the doctor said.

"Good Lord," Bugs said under his breath, listening. He brushed his shoulder where the barber's arm had been.

"I'm betting it does," Rubens said, blocking the doctor's way. "Just what kind of *secret friends* are you?"

The young doctor stared coldly at him.

"That's none of your damn business, sir," he said boldly, his fists clenched at his sides.

"I'll make it our damn business," said Rubens.

"Both of you, stop it," Wes said, pushing the two apart as Rubens advanced. He looked at the doctor and said, "You're right—it's none of our business, Doc. You're saving my brother's life. That's all I want from you." He looked at Rubens and said, "Have a drink, settle down. You're letting things rub you the wrong way. Hell, we're outlaws. What do we care?"

Rubens mumbled under his breath and walked away to where a bottle of rye stood on a lamp table.

Wes turned back to the doctor and let out a breath.

"You've done right by us so far, Doc. Get us through the night—that's all I'm asking. Come morning, if you say Ty's rested some and able to ride, we'll be out of your hair for good."

"He brings me cadavers," the doctor said quietly as he turned again toward the hallway.

"What?" said Wes.

"My special friend, Burle Minton," said the doctor, stopping without looking back at him. "In addition to my practice, I do research in the discipline of pathological anatomy—morbid anatomy if you will. Mr. Minton provides me with cadavers to dissect."

Wes Traybo stood considering it for a moment, letting it sink in. "You mean you and he—"

"No," the young doctor said firmly. "Burle is an undertaker establishing himself over in Frey—married with three children. To make ends meet he sells me cadavers of drifters and derelicts. He delivers them at night while the town sleeps because many look down on medical research. When the barber got too nosy, I concocted a ruse, one I knew he'd let out, but that would be discussed in whispers—"

Wes' sudden outburst of laughter cut the doctor short. Bugs stiffened in place with a look of both rage and confusion.

"We thought that you're . . ." Wes said, letting his statement trail.

"I saw what you thought," the doctor said. "With the townsmen coming, I had no time to tell you otherwise." He looked at Bugs, then back to Wes. "I don't know why your first conclusion was of such a nature. I strive to understand the human body, not the mind."

"Why, you *son of a bitch*! That's it! *I'm killing him!*" Bugs shouted. He leaped at the doctor's throat with both hands out, fingers spread like talons. Wes caught him in midair. The doctor stood rigid, staring.

"No, Bugs!" Wes shouted, holding the young gunman back while trying to stop laughing. "He didn't lie to us. We took it wrong. Settle down before we crack your head. We can't have this."

Rubens stepped over with his Colt out, the butt raised for a hard swipe if Wes gave him the word.

Seeing the big gun butt looming, Bugs calmed down. He wiped a hand over his mouth and breathed deep.

"All right, I'm done with it," he said. But he still stared hard and cold at the doctor.

Wes turned Bugs loose, holding up a warning finger toward him. Then he faced the doctor.

"Doctor, I hope you're not thinking that my brother might end up being one of your research cadavers," he said, the laughter gone, a grim look on his face.

"I'm not thinking it," the doctor said. "But that's exactly the sort of attitude I'd have to contend with if knowledge of my research were made public."

The others looked at him with blank expressions.

"I understand," Wes said, easing back as the doctor

walked away down the hall toward the room where Ty lay sleeping.

Rubens walked over and handed Wes the bottle of rye. Wes took a drink and passed it to Bugs. The two outlaws watched as Bugs took a long deep drink of rye and let out a whiskey hiss. He sloshed the rye around in the bottle, ready for another swig.

"Feeling better, Bugs?" Wes asked.

"Yeah, a hell of a lot," Bugs replied, raising the bottle halfway to his mouth.

Wes and Rubens looked him up and down.

"What?" Bugs asked, seeing something was on their minds.

"Two-handed *Parcheesi*?" Wes asked.

The rye was calming him, and instead of flying off angry, Bugs just chuffed grudgingly, then took another swig and finally laughed with them.

"What the hell else could I say?" he offered.

Before either man could answer, the rear door creaked open and the three looked down the hallway, guns out and cocked as a black silhouette stepped in through the rear door.

"It's me, Carter," said Claypool in a lowered voice. "This would be an easy place to rob."

The three relaxed, their guns lowered as Claypool walked down the hallway to them. Seeing the bottle, he held out a hand.

"I'll have a shot, unless this is a private party," he said, taking the bottle. "I saw nobody standing guard out back, I heard you laughing, I eased on in. What's so funny?" he asked.

"You had to be here and see it," Wes said.

"I saw it from an alley across the street," said Claypool. "I come looking from one end of town to the next for the doctor's house. I saw Bugs out there with his hands in the air. Lucky I didn't start shooting." He took a drink and passed the bottle to Bugs.

"For a minute there I wish you had," Bugs said.

"How's the trail?" Wes asked.

"Not good," said Claypool. "That's why I'm here. The posse went on just like we thought they would. But we've got a lawman on us." He paused, then added, "Fatch Hardaway is riding with him."

"Hardaway? Damn him!" Rubens cursed.

"Did you recognize the lawman?" Wes asked.

"Ranger Burrack, out of Nogales, unless I'm mistaken," said Claypool. "I recognized him in a lantern light—mostly I recognized his sombrero." He looked at Wes closely. "How's Ty coming along?" he asked.

"Let's go see for ourselves," said Wes, turning to the hallway. "The doctor says with any luck we can leave come morning."

"I make the Ranger and Hardaway will follow your tracks and figure we're here in about four hours," Claypool warned. "From everything I've heard, Burrack is good at spotting a false trail when he sees one."

"Damn it," Wes swore quietly. "It looks like we'll be leaving earlier than I planned."

The three men looked at one another as they followed Wes down the hallway, into the room where Ty rested leaning back against a pillow. He gave a weak smile as the men walked in and stood near his cot.

Rosetta gave them a look from where she stood holding a bowl of warm beef broth she'd heated in a glass beaker over a single flame. Dr. Bernard sat on the side of the cot. He turned toward Wes with a stethoscope in his ears and pulled the end of it away from Ty's chest.

"You feel like riding out tonight, brother Ty?" Wes asked, without giving the doctor so much as a glance.

"Ready as I'll ever be," Ty replied. As he spoke he tried to edge up onto the side of his cot.

"Hold it," said the doctor, standing, jerking the stethoscope from his ears and letting the instrument hang from his neck. "We agreed to first thing come morning."

"How's he doing, Doc?" Wes asked.

"He's doing well, but he still needs more rest—at least until morning. The broth is helping replenish his blood. But he's not able to ride yet."

Wes reached around and took the bowl of broth from Rosetta and handed it down to Ty.

"Here, drink this," he said firmly. To the doctor he said, "It can't be helped, Doc. We've got a new problem. There's an Arizona Ranger on our trail. We've got to go."

The doctor shook his head slowly.

"Don't worry. We're leaving you and the girl behind. You've done what we needed you to do." As he spoke he held out a leather pouch full of gold coins to him. "We're paying you for your service."

"Huh-uh," the doctor said, refusing to the take the pouch. "Not until my patient is healed."

"He's riding, Doc," Wes said firmly. "There's no time to argue it."

"Then I'm going with you," the doctor declared in a tight, determined voice. "I won't have a patient die for lack of proper medical treatment."

"Wait," said Wes. He grabbed the doctor's arm, seeing him turn to gather supplies for the trail. "It can get rough, Doc. Maybe you best consider this."

"I thought we didn't have time to argue," the doctor said. He looked at Wes' hand on his arm in a way that prompted the outlaw to turn him loose.

"I'll be damned," said Rubens. "We kidnapped him. Now we can't get rid of him?"

"So it appears," Wes said. He looked at Rosetta and held the leather pouch out to her. "Part of this is for your help with Ty. The rest is to keep your mouth shut for a while until we've had time to clear out of here."

"I go too," she said as she grabbed the pouch and made it disappear beneath her peasant's blouse.

"You too?" Wes said, surprised.

"*Sí*, me too," the young woman said. "I will take care of your brother. I do a good job, no?"

"You've done a fine job, Rosetta, but now . . . ," Wes said, his words trailing. He stared at her, thinking of all the reasons she shouldn't ride with them. He saw the anticipation in her eyes as he searched for the words. Finally he settled on saying, "Why do you want to ride with us?"

Rosetta looked back and forth at the eyes on her. She lowered her head and looked at the floor.

"I don't know," she said quietly. "To not be *here*?" Her answer was a question, yet Wes understood.

"That's a hell of a reason for going somewhere," said Claypool, who stood checking his rifle as he waited. "But I've been using it all my life."

"Let her come," the doctor said. "It beats what she's got here. She's new to Maley, probably brought here by one of the slavers."

Wes looked back at Rosetta.

"Is that true?" he asked. *"Los traficantes de esclavos te trajeron aquí?"*

"Sí, the woman sellers from Durango bring me here and sell me," she said, her eyes still lowered. "But here is not where I want to be."

"Hell, me neither, far as that goes," Rubens said, watching the conversation with a crooked grin. "She's one horse-riding bitch—we've all seen that much."

"Sí, I am one horse-riding *beech,"* Rosetta said with a trace of a smile. "You have seen this much, eh?"

"As good as any horseman I've ever seen," Wes had to admit, nodding.

Seeing Wes considering it, Claypool said in a low-ered voice, "It's not a good idea, Wes." Then, seeing the way Wes was headed on the matter, he added, "But what the hell do I know?"

Wes nodded at the woman and said, "You can ride with us as far as Mexico. Then you're on your own."

"Sí, Méjico," the young woman said, raising her face. "I will take good care of your brother, you'll see."

"Good," the doctor said. He stepped in and nodded

toward a tall white supply cabinet against the wall. "Rosetta, help me gather what we'll need."

As the woman hurried away to help the doctor, Wes looked at Claypool.

"Get on ahead of us, Carter," he said. "Clear the trail out of here."

"You got it," Claypool said, his swollen, dust-streaked face looking tired and haggard. "Want me to check around town first, see if anybody else wants to ride with us?" he said wryly.

"No, I think we're good," Wes said. "Now get going, 'less you want to stick around, cook breakfast for Fatch Hardaway and the Ranger." He gave a slight half grin, but then it went away and he said, "We spilled blood in this town, Carter. That changes everything."

"I know that," Claypool said, his tone more serious. "I'll do whatever needs doing."

PART 2

Chapter 10

The first thin line of buttermilk sunlight streaked along the low, jagged hill line as the Ranger and Fatch Hardaway rode onto the wakening street leading into Maley. A freight wagon pulled to one side and stopped as the two rode by. Three men stopped on a boardwalk and stepped back out of sight into the shelter of morning shadow and stared warily.

"This is an edgy bunch, for sure," Fatch Hardaway said, looking back from his saddle in the grainy morning light.

"They've been hit hard by your amigos," the Ranger said, riding a few feet in front of him.

"*Former* amigos," Hardaway said. He winced and looked all around as if to see who might be listening. "I wish you'd keep that in mind if you're going to keep bringing it up."

"I'll try," the Ranger said, staring ahead.

Three of the last loosened steers still wandering free looked back and forth from the mouth of an alleyway. They back-stepped in unison as the two riders moved past them.

The Ranger led the way toward the scent of coffee and the glow of lamplight in a restaurant window up the wide dirt street. Out in front of the restaurant, two workers stood atop ladders, their hammers already banging against the silence of morning. Two other workers stood steadying a new support post beneath a sagging overhang. All four workers stopped and stared as Sam and Hardaway veered their horses to a repaired hitch rail. They stepped down from their saddles and hitched their tired animals.

A bald head above a black string tie and a long white apron appeared in the open doorway and cocked around toward the workers, the man having noted the halt of work tools.

"I'm not paying for the time you're loafing. I'm only paying you for the time you're working," the restaurant owner called out to the workers. Then he turned, looked the Ranger and Hardaway up and down, noting the badge on the Ranger's chest.

"My goodness, that was fast, Ranger!" he said, stepping back for them to enter. "We just got the pole and broken lines repaired last night."

"I'm not responding to a telegram," Sam said. "I met Dallas Garand and his posse on the trail last night."

The owner looked at them as they walked past, across the floor to a counter, following the aroma of boiling coffee as if drawn to it. Four townsmen who sat huddled in conversation around a corner table straightened and watched as they stopped at the counter.

"Oh? And you didn't ride on with them?" said the restaurateur, slipping deftly around behind the service counter. Sam and Hardaway both caught a critical edge to his voice.

"That's right. I didn't," Sam said bluntly, leaving no promise of further explanation. He nodded toward a row of clean coffee mugs sitting bottoms up along a white cloth on the inside edge of the counter.

The restaurant owner tried to redeem himself as he set two of the mugs upright. A Chinese waiter with watery red-veined eyes reached out with a large steaming coffeepot and filled them.

"Oh well," the restaurant owner offered. "I suppose not everyone should go the same direction at once."

"That's right," Hardaway said almost in a growl. "If they did, the trail would tip over."

The owner gave Hardaway a puzzled look.

"Drink your coffee," the Ranger said sidelong to Hardaway.

Chairs scooted back from the corner table and the Ranger watched as four townsmen rose and walked to the counter, stopping a few feet away.

"Ranger Burrack?" said a strong voice.

Sam and Hardaway both turned, coffee mugs in hand. Sam only nodded in reply at the broad-shouldered townsman.

"You don't know me, Ranger, but I sure know about you," the man said. "If you'll permit me, I'm Walter Nye, Maley's blacksmith." He gestured a wide callused hand toward the other three. "This is Albert Hasp, Barnes Coomer and James Franklin." He explained, "We're sort of the town overseers until we get ourselves a new sheriff."

"Gentlemen," the Ranger said with a nod. He gestured a hand toward Hardaway. "This is Mr. Hardaway. We were on our way to Cottonwood when we ran into Garand's posse."

"Mr. Hardaway, you look familiar," said Albert Hasp, speaking around a thick cigar in the corner of his mouth.

"No, I don't *look familiar*," Hardaway said bluntly. "I've never been in Maley before." He continued to stare at Hasp.

Hasp shrugged and tried to let it go. He took his cigar from between his lips.

"I hope you'll excuse me," he said. "I see lots of faces in the beverage and entertainment business. I often think I recognize faces I've never seen—"

"You're excused," said Hardaway, cutting him off. He raised his coffee mug and sipped through a rising curl of steam.

"Any success to report from the posse, Ranger Burrack?" Walter Nye asked, diverting the conversation away from Hardaway.

"None, I'm sorry to say," the Ranger replied. "Whoever owns the stolen buckboard will find it up the trail—no horses, though. I expect they took them for the young woman and the doctor to ride."

"Yes, of course they did," said Franklin, the town real estate broker. "But that's a relief. Better than those two walking, being dragged along on these hill trails in the dark of night."

"Yeah," said Hasp. "But I'm not nearly as concerned for the young *puta* as I am for our town doctor. Let them drag her along. Mexican whores come a dime a dozen these days." He chuckled under his breath.

"Do they, now?" the Ranger said pointedly, his eyes fixed and locked on the saloon owner.

Hasp's smile vanished.

"Figuratively speaking of course, I should add," he said.

"Tell me about this woman," Sam said, eyes still locked on him.

"Tell you what," Hasp said, his hands spread. "She's about so tall, a hefty gal, but sweet as a plum—big on top, if you know what I mean." He cupped his hands at his chest and jiggled them and laughed. But his laughter wasn't returned.

"Who'd you buy her from, the Durango slavers?" Sam asked flatly.

"Oh no, no! Ranger," Hasp said, wagging a finger, "I'm afraid you mistake me. I don't *buy* Mexican *putas*. They just show up."

"Her name is Rosetta," Nye cut in. "Or so she says."

"Yes, Rosetta is her name," said Hasp. "She showed up out of nowhere less than a month ago." He gave another innocent shrug. "Said she needed work—said she likes whoring, to tell you the truth." He looked back and forth among the townsmen for support. "So . . . I put her to work. Can you blame me?"

The Ranger ignored him.

"What about the doctor?" he asked Walter Nye. "What kind of man is he?"

"Oh, Dr. Bernard is the best, Ranger," Nye said. As he spoke he and the other townsmen gave each other a look. "He may have his peculiarities," he said. "But we're all grateful to have such a talented young physician."

"What's that look?" the Ranger cut in.

"Look? What look?" said the blacksmith.

"The look you just gave each other," Sam said, pressing, turning his gaze from one townsman to the next. "Is there something about the doctor I need to know?"

Franklin, the real estate man, stared to speak, but before he could the front door swung open and the barber, Lyle Medford, hurried in carrying a bloody wad of bandage in his hand.

"Whoa, Medford, slow down!" said Nye as the barber hurried to the counter.

Noticing the Ranger, Medford held the bloody bandage out for all to see and said, "Ranger, I'm glad to see you here. I'm afraid something terrible is going on."

The Ranger and the others looked at the bloody bandage.

"I—I went by the doctor's house a while ago—" He panted, out of breath as he looked at the townsmen. "—you know, just to make certain young Burle Minton was comfortable there alone." He saw the look on the other townsmen's face as he spoke. His hand trembled. "Anyway, Burle Minton is gone! I found this bandage and many more just like it. Something's going on there!"

The Ranger looked at the bandage, then at Hardaway.

"Let's go," he said, already headed for the door.

In the first silvery light of morning, Carter Claypool backed his horse out of the early rays of sunlight into a dark shadowed crevice atop a steep ridge. Stepping down from his saddle, rifle in hand, he listened as the sound of hooves pounded closer along the trail far below him.

Stepping forward in a crouch, he stooped down, laid his Winchester across the top of a rock and aimed down on the shadowy trail. As the riders drew into sight around a turn in the trail, he recognized Wes Traybo in the lead and centered his aim on his chest, adjusting the sights on his rifle with his finger and thumb until the yardage and his adjustment suited him. He waited and watched until Wes rode into a long stretch of sunlit trail.

Perfect . . . He took a breath, let it half out, then held it again, the rifle sights homed on his target.

"Bang," he whispered to himself, his finger only lying loose against the trigger. As soon as he whispered, he simulated jacking a fresh round into the chamber as he swung the rifle sights away from Wes Traybo onto Ty Traybo, who rode double with the woman, lagging back a few feet at his brother's side. "Bang," he whispered again. Then he lay with a half smile as he watched the riders file past his rifle sights, Wes casting a quick glance up along the ridgeline.

When the riders had disappeared out of sight, he lay quietly for a few minutes, his swollen face feeling the lingering coolness of morning. Moments later he stood and looked all around. This was a good spot for a gun-fight, he told himself, dusting his trouser legs. He'd have to get a move on now, get in front of them and scout the trail toward the border. He might have to scour the hill line a long ways before finding another spot this good. *But that's the work,* he told himself. He jacked a real round into his rifle chamber, stepped over and had started to shove the Winchester down into his rifle boot when he caught the distant sound of more hooves on the trail below.

Turning, he slipped back into the same position behind the rock and waited as the sound grew nearer. He watched the trail where the sunlight cut sharply across the shadowy darkness. When the riders came into the slanted sunlight two abreast, he was ready for them.

The first two to ride into his rifle sights were Arti-mus Folliard and Suell Crane, Garand himself having instinctively fallen back when he saw the bright open stretch of trail ahead. Claypool's first shot flipped Crane backward from his saddle and sent him sprawling on the trail in a spray of blood. The sound of the shot fol-lowed a second behind its impact.

From his rocky perch, Claypool jacked a fresh round and swung his smoking rifle to Folliard. In a split sec-ond he centered his sights on Folliard as the stunned detective drew his horse around in a sharp circle. The sights moved from Folliard's chest to the center of his back as the horse finished its turn and bolted away. Claypool started to squeeze the trigger.

No, wait!

He stopped himself, turned down his shot at Folliard and instead swung his rifle at the sound of a pistol shot. He squeezed the trigger without hesitation and lifted Huey Drambite from his saddle, sending him spilling from his saddle behind a spiraling ribbon of blood.

As he levered another round and swung his Winchester, searching for his next target, he heard Dallas Garand shouting at the posse as the riders turned their horses, the animals bunching up on one another, and fell back out of the sunlight in a billowing rise of dust.

Two more quick pistol shots erupted, but Claypool heard them fall short and whine as they ricocheted off the hillside rocks.

Damn it!

"Why'd you do that?" he chastised himself under his breath, wincing. He'd just let Detective Artimus Folliard, the man who had beaten him mercilessly, ride out of his sights when he knew he had him cold. That was crazy!

Claypool tightened his trigger finger, needing to make up for what he'd just done. But he had to ease down as he realized the posse men and their spooked horses were already melting from sight into their shadowy back trail.

It was nothing but stupid! he scolded himself in silence, still smarting inside for letting the detective go. He backed away in a crouch as rifle fire from the shadowy trail began nipping at rock and hillside in retaliation. All right, it was a mistake, but now it was over. *Forget it,* he reconciled with the angry voice inside his head.

Loosening his horse's reins, he led the animal away on a hidden path leading up the side of rocky cliff. Below, rifle fire filled the air. Looking back, he saw a gray looming cloud of burnt powder drifting up the hillside. At the top of the path, he led the horse aside, slipped back down a few steps and watched until he saw a man in a bowler hat and a long duster venture forward, scanning the hillside, a rifle in his hands.

Claypool smiled to himself. It was time he'd signaled Wes Traybo anyway, he decided. Taking an aim on the trail below, he spaced three signal shots close together. The first two shots hit the dirt only inches from the posse man's toes. Before the man could jump back quick enough, the third shot nailed his left foot dead center.

"That'll keep everybody busy for a while," Claypool said to himself, watching the rifleman hurriedly limp away, dragging his bleeding foot back into the shadowed cover of the trail.

As quiet as a ghost, Claypool walked back up to his horse, slipped up into the saddle and put the horse forward behind the cover of the towering cliff.

Chapter 11

The Ranger had spotted Dallas Garand and his posse an hour earlier in the grainy morning light, as the Ranger and Hardaway rode up off the flatlands and stopped on an old game trail. Looking out across a deep valley at another trail known for leading onto a winding route to the Mexican border, they saw detectives and townsmen alike moving along at a fast pace, their duster tails flapping out behind them.

"Garand reasoned things out and turned back quicker than I expected he would," the Ranger said, backing his speckled barb into a lingering slice of morning trail shadow.

"We could still beat them to the Mexico trail fork if you want to push it," Hardaway offered.

The Ranger looked at him.

"I don't want to push it," the Ranger replied. "It's going to be a long day for them if one of their horses comes up lame or, worse, runs off the side of a hill."

"I've done it more than once," said Hardaway. "It's risky, but it's better than—" He caught himself and stopped.

"You did it because you had to," Sam said. "There's nobody chasing us, Hardaway. You keep forgetting we're not the ones on the run."

Hardaway looked embarrassed. "I'm just saying, we can get on the Traybos' trail before they do—if we want to, that is."

"I understand," said Sam. "We'll make up time once we've got some better light. He watched the posse men move out of sight around a turn in the distant trail. Then he put the barb forward, Hardaway right beside him.

"I'm just trying to get us ahead of the game, Ranger," Hardaway said, trying to sound restless. "The quicker we catch up to the Traybos, the quicker I can get my money in Cottonwood and put all this behind me."

"We both know this is the same trail we'd be riding to the border whether we'd come across the Traybos' robbery or not," said Sam.

Hardaway fell silent for a second.

"Does it make any difference if it is?" he asked after a thoughtful pause.

"Not a bit," the Ranger replied. "Right now I've got the Traybos' trail. But if I lose it, I'll still need you to take me to their hideout. Either way, your money's still coming to you. There's no tricks here. You're just not used to people giving their word and meaning it."

Hardaway relaxed and pushed up his hat brim.

"You're right," he said.

The two rode on in silence for the next half hour until morning sunlight had risen enough to warm and reveal more clearly the rocky hill trails. As they reached the end of the deep canyon and started around it toward the trail the posse men were on, rifle fire erupted in the near distance, causing them to quicken their horses' pace.

"Sounds like Garand just caught up with the Traybos," Hardaway said as they rode along.

"Lucky him," the Ranger said wryly, drawing his rifle from its boot as he urged the barb forward. "From the sound of it, there's only one rifle in the fray. It's not one of Garand's men. I'd say they're in big trouble."

On the trail, Dallas Garand stood out from behind a tree as the Ranger and Hardaway rode into sight and reined their horses down to a halt. They stopped a ways back from where the rest of the men were still taking cover behind rocks alongside the trail. Garand hurried forward in a crouch as they stepped down from their saddles and walked toward him.

"Get your head down, both of you!" Garand ordered. "Unless you want to get it blown off."

Sam and Hardaway ignored him. They stopped and scanned the hill line high above the trail.

"I haven't heard any gunfire the past few minutes," the Ranger said. "My guess is whoever was doing the shooting is gone."

Garand straightened a little, then a little more as he turned and looked up with the Ranger.

"I don't need you riding in to tell me that," Garand growled, reluctantly standing up straight. The rest of the posse men stood up and backed away, looking upward with trepidation along the high ridgeline.

"Unless you've killed the shooter, he's going to be sniping at you the rest of the way into Mexico," Sam offered.

"Oh? You suppose so?" Garand said in a sarcastic tone.

Seeing the detective leader's surly attitude, the Ranger touched his hat brim and said to Garand, "Sorry to have interfered." He looked at Hardaway and said, "Let's ride on up, get on this shooter's trail before he sets up and strikes again."

Dallas Garand watched the two turn back toward their horses. Behind him the townsmen had separated themselves from the detectives and formed a tight frightened-looking group.

"Wait a minute, Ranger," Garand called out. "You mean you're going to ride up there—up this hillside after him?"

The Ranger stopped and looked around at Garand.

"I see no choice. He's not going to come down here to us," he said.

"I know this shooter," Fatch Hardaway cut in. "He won't stop until the lot of you are lying dead."

The Ranger gave Hardaway a silencing frown. But it was too late. The townsmen looked at each with fearful eyes. Garand saw it too and cursed under his breath.

"I am not in the least surprised that the man is a *friend* of yours, *Fatcharack*—" he said, bristling.

"I warned you not to call me that again," Fatch said, cutting him off, taking a step forward. Sam held an arm out, stopping him, seeing Garand's detectives starting to draw into a half circle around them.

"But these men from Maley are not afraid," Garand continued in a grandiose voice. He raised a finger for emphasis. "They are driven to bring these cowards to justice." He looked around at the townsmen. "Isn't that right, men?"

"Hell *no*, it's not right," the cattle broker Don Stout said, emboldened by the Ranger's presence. He stepped forward, rifle in hand, his face crusted with trail dust and sweat. "You've dragged us through these hills and valleys all night—gotten two of us killed and one of us wounded—"

"Let me remind you that only my detectives are the ones lying dead or wounded," said Garand, cutting him off.

"So far it has been your men," said Stout. "So this is a good time for us to go home, while we're still wearing our hide."

"Just like that? You're going to cut and run?" Garand said, hoping to shame the men.

A cattle pens worker named Mose Pullet stepped forward carrying a well-worn Spencer rifle.

"It'd be different if we were making any headway," he said. "The way it looks is all we've done is ride half the night one way, then half the night back." He turned to the Ranger and said, "Where'd you go, Ranger Burrack? How'd you know to pick up this trail?"

Sam wasn't going to lie to defend the detective leader.

"We rode back to Maley," he said. "We believe the Traybos and the doctor went back there, treated the wounded man and rode on. That's what put us on this trail."

"Bull!" Garand shouted. But he looked stunned. "The Traybos would not have dared show their faces back in

Maley! They know we would have killed them!" His face reddened at his foolishness as soon as he finished his words.

"That's why they led you so far up toward the Old Mexico Trail before they circled back, Garand," the Ranger said. "I don't know whose idea it was to go back to Maley. But it was a good one."

Garand stood dumbfounded.

The Ranger turned and looked at the frightened and haggard townsmen.

"You townsmen are volunteers. If you want to leave, nobody's going to stop you," he said, looking at Stout as he spoke to the group. "Get your horse and ride out."

"Just a damn minute, Ranger," said Folliard, eager to get back in good graces with his boss. "You don't waltz in here giving orders to Mr. Garand's posse—"

"Let these cowards go, Detective Folliard," Garand said, cutting him off. "We're better off without them." He turned his eyes to the Ranger and said, "There, they're leaving with no trouble out of me. Satisfied?"

The Ranger didn't answer. He and Hardaway stood watching as the Maley townsmen stepped quickly to the horses and began mounting. But Folliard wasn't through yet. He moved in close and faced the Ranger from only three feet away. He tapped a finger to a welt across his forehead the shape of a rifle butt.

"Ranger, I understand you're the son of a bitch who butt-smacked me across the forehead," he said.

"Whoa! Bad idea," said Hardaway with a dark, thin chuckle. He swung his rifle around toward the other detectives in anticipation.

The Ranger ignored the insult and looked past Folliard to Garand.

"We don't have time for this," he said quietly to Garand. "Are you going to call him off?" As Sam spoke, the Maley townsmen turned their horses and filed past them toward the trail back to town.

Seeing part of his posse leave, Garand gave a slight shrug.

"You did give him quite a nasty whack, Ranger," he said.

Sam stared into Folliard's bloodshot eyes, the cloth gone from around his jawline now, his face showing its bruises and welts.

"Why don't you stop this while you're still on your feet, Detective?" he said quietly, letting Folliard see him brace his rifle in both hands.

"Don't think you're going to catch me off guard with that rifle butt again," Folliard said. He stood in defiance, in a fighting stance, his feet shoulder width apart. He turned his head sideways and spat on the ground in contempt. "I don't get tricked twice," he growled. "I'm no damn fool."

"I can see that," said the Ranger. Yet even as he spoke, he feigned a quick, short jerk on his rifle, just enough to draw Folliard's attention to it. Folliard instinctively flinched and ducked his head away.

Hardaway, Garand and all the gathered detectives winced in unison at the sight and sound of the Ranger's boot toe burying itself up deep into Folliard's crotch.

"Whoa!" Hardaway said again, this time as Folliard lifted high on his tiptoes, jackknifed at the waist and

landed on his side in the dirt, his hands cupping himself. "I felt that all the way over here!" said Hardaway, his rifle covering the detective as the men stared as if in agony at their fallen comrade.

"If you'll keep your men in check, Garand," the Ranger said in an unchanged tone of voice, "Hardaway and I will get up the hillside, see if we can keep the Traybos' shooter from killing any more of you."

Without reply Garand stepped back and gestured a gloved hand toward the rocky hillside. He stood watching as the Ranger and Hardaway led their horses up a steep game path and into the rocks on the hillside.

In the dirt, Folliard groaned and reached a seeking hand up for Rio DeSpain—*Spanish Rivers, the rotten son of a bitch*—to help him to his feet, but DeSpain only gave him a sour look and stepped over him to Garand's side. Fain Elliot and L. C. McGuire stood watching Folliard drawn up and writhing in a ball of pain. Earl Prew stood on his wounded, thickly bandaged foot, using his rifle as a crutch.

"I can't help you, Folliard," said Prew. "Hell, I can't help myself."

Finally Elliot and McGuire looked at each other, stepped in and pulled Folliard to his feet. Folliard stood bowed at the waist.

"We don't have to take this, Mr. Garand," DeSpain said. "Say the word and I'll put a bullet in both their backs before they reach the top of the hill."

"No, no, Rio," said Garand. "Leave them be for now. They'll take us to the Traybos. Let them be our shield between the Traybos' shooter and ourselves. After that, if he hasn't killed them, we will. Either way, they're both graveyard dead." He looked Folliard up and down and said to Elliot and McGuire, "Fain, L.C., straighten this jackass up. I won't have a man bowed over like his guts are on fire."

Folliard let out a painful wail as the two gunmen yanked him upright by his shoulders.

"Let's get ready to move out," said Garand, walking away toward his horse.

Atop the steep path, standing on a bald cliff, the Ranger looked down at the hoof marks and boot prints the two had been following for the past twenty yards. They had first found the lone boot prints at the spot where Carter Claypool had lain against the rock and calmly killed two men from a remarkable distance. Even more remarkable, Claypool had directed a round through a third gunman's foot.

Now, gazing out along the trail atop the cliff in the direction the hoofprints on the ground indicated, the Ranger considered the masterful shooting as he scanned the thin trail ahead.

"We best get off this cliff, Ranger," Hardaway said, also looking around, but doing so in a wary manner. "We're sitting ducks here, as good as Claypool is with rifle."

"As good as this man is, we're sitting ducks from anywhere in his sights," Sam replied. On his gloved palm he bounced an empty cartridge brass he'd found down by the rock. "But a good trail scout never stays too long away from the ones he's protecting. Don't forget he's got the trail in front of them to keep an eye on too." He paused, then added as he closed his hand around the empty cartridge, "And in this case, that trail runs straight into Mexico."

"That doesn't mean he can't stop long enough to send a couple of bullets back our way," Hardaway said.

Staring out at the trail, the Ranger realized the rider had slipped away so easily that he'd been able to take his time, make certain he left no dust looming in the air.

The man was good, he told himself. He had to give him that.

"No, he's gone on," Sam said. "He's cleared their back trail for them. His shots let them know he's finished back here. He's gone on to make sure the trail into Mexico holds no surprises for them."

Hardaway eyed him closely.

"Yeah?" he said. "What if you're wrong? What if he does drop down and fix his sights back in our direction?"

"Then I expect we'll both be dead and gone and won't have to worry about it," the Ranger said. He stepped forward, leading the barb off the hard stone surface onto the dirt trail.

"I find that's one hell of an attitude," Hardaway said, leading his horse alongside him. "I don't like knowing odds are that I'm walking into a gun's sights."

"Neither do I," the Ranger said. "But the job doesn't stop because the odds get narrow." He gave the thin trace of a smile. "It just gets more interesting."

Chapter 12

Carter Claypool pushed himself up from the stream on his palms and swung his wet hair back and forth. On his downstream side only three feet away, his big dun drew water, its hooves six inches deep in the stream, as if to cool them after the long midmorning ride. Giving the dun time to replenish itself, Claypool picked up his canteen from the water, scooted back from the edge of the stream and leaned against a rock stuck in the gravelly cutbank.

His face had begun healing from the beating the detective had given him, but it was going to be a while before the swelling was gone and the purple mask had faded from around his eyes. Other than that and a few closing cuts, a pained jaw and some ribs that dealt him a shooting pain that ached when he moved a certain way, he was mending right along.

Soon be good as new, he told himself, running a hand along his lumpy, beard-stubbled jawline. He gave himself a crooked grin. "Just *capital*!" he said aloud, noting the dun's ears twitch at the sound of his voice.

He chuffed a little to himself, capping the canteen,

and relaxed back against the rock in reflection. The fact that he hadn't killed Artimus Folliard when he had the chance still nagged at him, especially now that blood had been spilled in Maley and killing was in the game. It wasn't like him to forgo vengeance. He had every right to kill the man and he should have. Yet he hadn't, *damn it!*

All right, don't start, he told himself. When the next opportunity came along, he'd kill Folliard and be done with it—all would be well with the world.

He leaned back and closed his eyes for a moment, pleased with how smoothly things were going now that they'd gotten Ty Traybo cared for and gotten out of Maley before daylight. Like clockwork. *Smoother than a Cincinnati timepiece.*

He smiled to himself and caught himself drifting off, until the sound of the dun grumbling under its breath caused him to open his eyes with a start. In front of him stood two Mexicans, one holding the dun's dripping reins. The other man held a cocked rifle one-handed, pointed at his chest.

"Ah, *señor*, did we wake you?" the one with the pointed rifle said in a sympathetic voice. He jerked his head toward the other man. "This one is so noisy. Always I tell him, 'You can be *noisy*, or you can be a good sneak thief.'" He gave a wide grin and wagged his finger. "But you cannot be both, no, no. Eh, amigo?"

"Sounds right," Claypool said calmly, having frozen in place with his right hand lying on the ground at his side, close enough to his short-barreled Colt to make a play for it. He considered it, asking himself what the sound of his gunfire would signal to the Traybos. He held himself in check.

"I have money," he said.

"Oh, do you?" the rifleman said, feigning pleasantry. "You also have a bloody shirt," he added with a curious expression.

Claypool ignored the short remark. He started to raise his left hand toward his buttoned shirt pocket. "I'm always willing to pay my way through."

The Mexican's hand tightened on the rifle; Claypool's left hand froze at his pocket button.

"Take your hand down, meester, or I will blow your head off," he said, his mask of cordiality gone. "We will take your money when the time comes and you will have no say about it."

So that's how it is. Claypool saw no way to keep from firing the Colt.

"First you tell us what the gunfire was about," the Mexican insisted.

"How would I know?" said Claypool, getting an attitude now that he knew the two had no intention of letting him leave here alive. "I heard it myself." He gave a shrug.

"I get the feeling you know," said the rifleman, eyeing Claypool's bloody shoulder. "Miguel, do you get the feeling he knows?"

Holding the reins to the dun, the other Mexican stood gripping a big battered French revolver down his thigh.

"*Sí*, I get a feeling he does," he said.

"Gunfire could mean anything. What do you care?"

Claypool asked, relaxed but ready to make a move at just the right time.

"What *do we*—?" The Mexican halted, taken aback. He shook his head and continued. "Let me 'splain to you, gringo. You would never guess it, but Miguel and I are *banditos*, eh?" He stepped closer. Claypool stared up at him.

Perfect.

"Because we are *banditos,* it is 'portant to us what we hear along this trail. On this lawless trail, we must be well informed—be prepared to meet *federales,* gringo lawmen, long riders, all that sort of thing." He shook his head as if in regret.

"Lawless trail, huh?" Claypool looked back and forth. The man liked to talk, so he'd keep him talking.

"*Sí,* it is what my people call it. Because it is a *lawless trail*, filled with *lawless men*," the Mexican said. "Men like *us* . . . men like you perhaps?" His rifle barrel sagged, only slightly, but enough for Claypool to take note. "It is a terrible thing, this way that we must live." He shrugged in resignation. "But what can we do?" he sighed. "Now tell us about the shooting so we can kill you and take your—"

His words stopped short beneath the blast of Claypool's short-barreled Colt; the bullet sliced upward in a streak of blue-orange fire, ripped through his chest and left a red streak of blood and matter jetting upward in the air behind him.

Before his accomplice hit the ground, the other Mexican swung the big French pistol up and fired, the gun giving off the strange tinny sound of cheap metal. But even as his bullet struck the rock beside Claypool's shoulder, Claypool's Colt blazed again. The bullet cut through the Mexican's chest and grazed Claypool's dun along its rump.

"Oh no, Charlie Smith!" Claypool shouted as he leaped to his feet.

The dun screamed in pain and jerked its reins free from the second Mexican's hand. The Mexican staggered wildly, backward into the stream before falling with one large and final splash.

Claypool, his short Colt smoking in his hand, made a wild grab for his dun's reins as the spooked horse spun in a wild full circle and bolted away. The Mexicans' horses jerked their reins free from a nearby tangle of scrub juniper where the men had rein-hitched them and fell in with the fleeing dun.

"This is all I need," Claypool said sourly. He gazed out to where the second Mexican's body had bobbed away fifteen yards downstream and draped itself over a rock. In the ringing silence, Claypool looked off through the hilltops, following the direction the gunshots' echo had taken.

There goes the Cincinnati timepiece, he told himself, seeing a flock of birds rise from a stand of pine on a distant hillside and bat away across the white sunny sky. Turning, he ejected the two spent rounds from his Colt. Sighing, he replaced them with fresh rounds from his gun belt and started walking through the dust stirred up by the horses' pounding hooves.

Rubens walked up to Wes Traybo, who stood gazing back along the main trail they'd ridden across the border. They had made a camp on a high, sloping hillside in the shelter of pine and bald grounded boulder. Rubens arrived at Wes' side and looked out across the hills with him, sharing the leader's concern for the whereabouts of Carter Claypool since they'd heard the distant pistol fire.

"He'll show, Wes," said Rubens. "He always does."

Wes cut him a glance, then looked back out in the direction the gunshots had come from, as if some clue would soon reveal itself from that spot.

"I hope so," Wes replied. "We'll give him a while longer. If he hasn't shown, I'm sending the rest of you forward and riding back to see why."

Rubens squinted and scratched his whiskered chin.

"Not to be contrary, Wes," he said. "But ain't the whole idea of having a man like Claypool out there watching our trail, is to allow us to get away while he takes on whatever's coming?"

Wes Traybo turned and looked him up and down.

"I suppose you didn't hear me, did you?" he said, half joking, yet with a look that invited no questions on the matter.

"Yeah, I heard you just fine," said Rubens, seeing Wes turn away and look back out along the winding trail. "I'll have the doc and the woman get Ty up and ready to ride. I'll go ahead and saddle your horse and bring it to you—I figure you're going back."

"Obliged," said Wes. "And, Baylor?" he said as Rubens turned to walk away.

"Yeah?" said Rubens, stopping, looking back at him.

"Things didn't go well for us this time," Wes said quietly, not facing him.

"I sort of noticed that," Rubens said wryly. "But we still got out with the money."

"What I'm saying is," Wes went on, "if you and Bugs want to ride away when I get back, you'll both get your share and nobody'll say anything."

"Damn these ears of mine," Rubens said. "A minute ago I heard you just fine . . . now I can't make out a word you're saying."

Wes Traybo studied the back trail. He nodded slowly.

"Good man," he said under his breath, even though Rubens had already turned and walked away.

Moments later, Wes heard his horse clopping toward him at a walk across the hard ground. But when he turned, instead of seeing Rubens leading the animal, he saw Rosetta smile at him and hold out the reins.

"Where's Rubens?" he asked, staring past the woman toward the campsite where Rubens stood staring and gave an uncertain shrug.

"Don't be angry with him, *por favor*," she said, seeing an irritated look on his face. "I asked him to let me bring your horse to you. I hope that was all right?"

Wes let out a breath and eased his expression.

"It is *now*," he said.

"Your brother says he is well enough to ride on his own now," she said. "I asked the *médico*—I mean, the doctor," she corrected. "He said it is not so. I come to ask you if I have done something wrong that makes your brother not want me to take care of him?"

Wes saw hurt in her eyes as he took the reins to his horse.

"No, Rosetta, you've done nothing wrong," he said. "My brother is a proud man. He wants everybody to know he can take care of himself." As he spoke he instinctively looked his horse over before mounting it and putting it on the trail. "I'll talk to him some when I get back." He looked her up and down. "Meanwhile, I'm sure you can charm him enough to keep him in line."

"In line?" she asked, not familiar with the term.

"Keep him *smiling*," he said, stepping up, swinging his leg over the saddle.

"Ah, *sí*, of course," she said, sounding reassured.

He settled into his saddle and looked at her, seeing she had more on her mind.

"We're in Mexico now," he said, anticipating her thoughts about leaving. "But I'd like to get closer to where we're going before you take off."

"It's all right," she said. "I still have a long ride. It can take me weeks—perhaps months—to get home. It is better I travel with someone as long as I can." She paused and then added, "I am a long way from home."

"What part of Mexico are you from?" Wes asked.

"I am not from Mexico. I am from Guatemala. I live in Tera Paz, a small village near the Mexican border. That is where the slavers stole me."

"*Guatemala . . .* woman, you sure *are* a long way

from home," Wes said. He studied her face. "You speak good English to be from so far away."

"I learn English from the French—from the *religieuses*." Seeing the look on Wes' face, she said, "From the *monjas*."

"The *nuns*," Wes said, understanding now that she'd switched from French to Spanish. He nodded. "You learned your good English from the French. That makes sense, I reckon."

"*Sí.*" She smiled. "So I will ride with you as far as I can, to keep from riding alone. . . . Is all right?"

"Yes, is all right," Wes said, backing his horse a step to turn it to the trail. "Now, if there's nothing else anybody needs to talk about, I'll go find my scout and bring him back."

The Ranger and Hardaway had heard the sound of gunfire and ridden on until they found two worn-out horses standing in the speckled shade of an ironwood tree clinging to the side of a shallow cutbank lining a dry creek bed. One horse's saddle hung below its belly. The other still had part of the juniper bush tangled in its trailing reins.

"Unless these cayuses left home searching for a better life in America, I'd say somebody's in bad trouble," Hardaway said, looking all around as he and the Ranger stopped and stepped down from their saddles. "This is from the gunshots, you suppose?"

Sam just looked at him without replying. Instead of struggling with unfastening the horse's cinch, he raised a knife from the well of his boot, cut the strap and let the saddle fall. Then he slipped the bit from the horse's mouth and tossed the bridle away. As he unfastened the other horse's cinch and dropped its bit, he gazed in the direction of the prints he and Hardaway had followed along the top of the ridgeline.

Hardaway looked appraisingly at the scrawny horses, their battered and worn saddle ware.

"Bandits, you reckon?" he asked as the Ranger came back to the barb and remounted.

"I don't know," he said, turning the barb back to the tracks on the ground. "Their tracks are coming from the direction Claypool's going in."

"Good chance they met but didn't become friends," Hardaway said as they rode on in Claypool's tracks.

They had ridden no more than a mile when they stopped their horses atop a rise and looked down at the stream and found a bandit's body lying sprawled in the gravelly dirt. Out in the rushing current, another body bobbed in place, draped over a rock.

Hardaway shook his head and crossed his wrists on his saddle horn.

"See? I told you," he said, watching the Ranger step back down from his saddle and lead the barb toward the water. "These desert bandits haunt these watering spots like vultures. Claypool is not a man they wanted to catch them lying in wait. He must've picked them off from a hundred yards out. They never knew what hit them."

The Ranger looked all around.

"You can't even see this stream from a hundred yards out, in any direction," he said.

Hardaway shrugged and stepped his horse down to the water without getting out of his saddle.

"He spotted them from somewhere," Hardaway said, "and when he did he put that Winchester of his to work."

The Ranger had been studying the ground. He saw an indented spot where someone had sat leaning back against a rock. He looked from that spot to where the dead Mexican lay. He walked over and closely examined the front of the dead man's shirt.

"This one was shot close up enough that it almost set his shirt afire." He looked at Hardaway. "What kind of sidearm does Claypool carry?"

"He carries a short-barreled gunman's Colt, a four-and-three-quarter-inch barrel," Hardaway said. "Must figure like some that he gets it drawn faster than the five-and-a-half-incher—especially faster than the long cavalry barrel." He eyed the big Colt on the Ranger's hip. "That's not to say you're slow."

"Obliged, that's kind of you," the Ranger said drily. He nodded over toward a narrow dirt path where boot prints and hoofprints led away from the water. "Fast or not, he might have caught a bullet from one of these two. There's blood on the ground in that direction." He walked over and looked closer at the ground and saw the boot prints overlapped the hoofprints.

"Jesus, what else?" said Hardaway.

"His horse left without him," the Ranger said. "My guess is it spooked and cut out. He's off trying to catch it."

"Damn," said Hardaway. "You got all that from staring at the dirt?"

"I got it from paying attention, learning a little more every time I track a man," Sam said. He stepped up into his saddle. "Claypool's on foot, most likely with a bullet wound."

"A bullet wound won't stop him—won't even slow him down," Hardaway said. He turned his horse to the narrow trail behind the Ranger.

"Maybe being afoot will," the Ranger replied, nudging his barb forward.

Chapter 13

When Carter Claypool looked over his shoulder past the dun, he saw twin rises of dust on the distant stretch of sandy flatlands behind him. He led the dun by its reins, detecting only the slightest limp in its walk. The horse's limp was from pain, not serious damage. But it was enough to keep Claypool out of the saddle for a while. He knew Charlie Smith—knew the big dun was all heart. The horse would bust a gut for him, no question. If he'd asked it of him, the dun would carry him until it dropped. But with him already limping, Claypool knew that riding outside his normal gait could worsen the limp and bring on bigger problems.

"I wish you wouldn't look at me like that," he said, seeing Charlie Smith's eyes on him before he turned away from looking at the rising dust.

At the sound of Claypool's voice, the dun chuffed and piqued its ears, then let them relax as the two trudged on toward the hill line ahead of them. A patch of dried mud crusted the long graze along the horse's rump. Dried blood glistened in long black streaks down the hind leg to its hoof.

They walked on.

Overhead, the sun had started its long arc toward the western horizon by the time man and horse reached the rocky slope at the base of the next hill line. Halfway up the nearly bald slope of rock, gravel and short cactus spurs, the meandering trail led him into a wide forest of young pine wrapped around the northern reach of the hill. Thirty yards inside the striped shade, Claypool stopped and looked all around.

This will do, he told himself, eyeing back toward the rise of trail dust, judging how much closer the riders had gotten to him.

He slid his Winchester from his saddle boot, grabbed his canteen and sat down on a low rock. The dun stood watching him as he drank tepid water, its hind leg tilted up onto the tip of its hoof.

"Damn it, Charlie," Claypool said after a moment. "It's not like I did it on purpose." It swished the water around and had started to take another sip when the voice of Wes Traybo spoke out from behind one of the larger pines.

"You act like that horse is going to answer you someday," Traybo said. He stepped his horse into sight from behind the tree cover.

"Jesus, Wes, make yourself known!" said Claypool, letting out a startled breath after dropping his canteen and swinging his rifle around toward Traybo. Grabbing his canteen up from the ground, he capped it and set it aside.

"I just did," Wes said. He stepped his horse over and

looked at the mud and dried blood along the dun's rump. Then he looked down at Claypool.

"So," said Claypool with a short, wry grin, standing and dusting the seat of his trousers, "what brings you out this way?"

Wes crossed his wrists on his saddle horn and gazed out through the pines at the twin rises of dust.

"I thought I better get started finding myself a good trail scout," he said. "Know of any?"

Claypool let out a breath as if considering it.

"None that I honestly feel I can give high reference to," he said. "Most of the good ones have been hung, else they're just waiting to be."

"You know this is the second time I've had to come back for you in as many days?"

"It's been two *days*?" Claypool said, looking surprised. "Where does the time go?"

Wes chuffed and shook his head a little.

"Who've you got out there?" he asked, gazing through the pines toward the rising dust.

"Beats me," said Claypool, stepping over to Charlie Smith and hanging his canteen from his saddle horn.

"Trail scout, you say?" Wes said with a skeptical look.

Claypool gestured at the Winchester in his right hand.

"I was just getting ready to knock on their door," he said.

"Save it for now," said Traybo. "I spotted a *federale* patrol less than three miles back."

"This'll make twice I've had the Ranger and Fatch Hardaway in my sights and had to let them go," Claypool said. "I'd just as well ride back and make friends with them."

"What makes you think it's them?" Wes asked.

"I waylaid Garand and his detectives on the lower trail," said Claypool. "They wasn't about to climb that hillside. But the Ranger would. I looked back later and saw him and Hardaway riding a long way behind me. I figure this is them."

"How hard did you hit Garand's posse?" Wes asked.

"Killed two of them," Claypool said. "Shot one through the foot." Seeing the look on Wes' face, he added, "It wasn't something I wanted to do. But this is where we are now. They keep coming, we've got no choice."

Wes Traybo nodded, understanding.

"You've had a busy day," he remarked.

"There's more," Claypool said. "I had a couple of Mexican bandits try to upend me. I had to kill them too."

Wes shook his head again.

"*Federales*, posses, detectives, bandits, lawmen," he said. "I've never seen this trail so busy. We ought to open a saloon."

"Weather's good," said Claypool. "I guess nobody wants to stay indoors."

"That must be it," said Wes. He reached a hand down for Claypool to take. "The bandits shot Charlie Smith?" he asked.

"No, I shot him," Claypool said grimly. He took

Wes' hand and swung up behind his saddle, the dun's reins in his free hand.

"Why? What'd he do?" Wes asked.

"He was about to be led off by one of the bandits," said Claypool.

"So you shot him?" Wes said.

"I shot the bandit. The bullet came out wrong and grazed Charlie Smith. The way he's acted, you'd think I did it on purpose."

"You patched him up, I see," said Wes. "That ought to be worth something to him."

"Let's not talk about it right now, Wes," Claypool said in a lowered voice. "He's acting salty enough about it as it is."

Wes gave a slight chuckle; he tapped his boots to his horse's sides and put it forward up the sloping, treed hillside at a walk.

"I heard three pistol shots," Wes said over his shoulder. "Only two of them come from your short-barreled Colt."

"You've a keen ear for my gun," remarked Claypool. "One of the bandits carried a big old French pistol. He only got one shot off. It sounded like a rock hitting a tin roof."

"Yep, I heard that," said Wes.

"How's Ty?" Claypool asked.

"Coming along well enough, it appears," said Wes. "We might have some problems with the doctor and the girl, though."

"How's that?" Claypool asked.

"They neither one act like they want to leave," Wes said. "I've never seen anything like it."

"I can't blame them," said Claypool. "You have to admit we live some *fine and dandy* lives."

"I'd be the first to say so," Wes agreed wryly.

In the afternoon, the five riders stopped at a turn in the switchback of the upward-reaching trail. In the cooling shade of massive boulders stuck deep into the gravelly hillside, they relaxed in their saddles and looked back in the direction Wes had taken earlier.

"He should have been back by now, with or without Carter," Rubens muttered. "That's all I'm saying."

"Yeah, we hear you," said Ty, sitting atop his own horse, the woman's horse sidling close to him. "You've been saying it every five minutes since he was gone an hour." He gave a weak grin beneath his new hat brim. One of the sacks stuffed with bank money hung across his horse's rump. Behind Bugs Trent's saddle was the other sack.

"I don't like us being broke up like this," said Rubens. "Especially not along this trail. This Old Mexico Trail is fast. You can get in trouble here, if you're not careful—so much trouble that you never get out of it," he added.

As Rubens spoke, Dr. Bernard stepped down from his saddle and started to lead his horse off the trail and around behind one of the boulders.

"Hey, now! Hold it there, Doc," Rubens said. "Just where do you think you're going?" He raised his rifle from across his lap and swung the tip of the barrel toward the young doctor.

Bernard stopped and turned and looked Rubens up and down.

"With everyone's permission, I'm going into the brush," he said calmly. He gave a collective nod to the four faces looking at him.

"Into the brush?" said Rubens, looking nervous and uncertain.

"Jesus, Baylor," Bugs chuckled. "He's going to relieve himself. You need to settle down some."

Rubens let out a breath.

"What I need is a drink," he said, wiping a trembling palm across his forehead.

Without saying a word, the doctor opened the medical satchel hanging from his shoulder, took out a silver flask and pitched it to him. Rubens unscrewed the cap with nervous fingertips.

"Obliged, Doc," he said. As he took a swallow, Dr. Bernard led his horse away quietly into the brush.

"Still," Rubens said. "Shouldn't somebody go with him?"

"He knows how to do it," Bugs cut in, with a slim grin.

"I mean to make sure he comes back, damn it," said Rubens. But he relaxed, feeling the warm surge of whiskey in his chest.

"He'll be back," Ty said confidently. "He likes riding with us, I can tell it." He looked at Rosetta. "So does she. Don't you?" he asked her.

"*Sí*, I do," Rosetta said. Recalling what Wes Traybo had said, she added, "I like to keep you smiling."

"Oh? Well, *gracias*," said Ty with a curt nod to her. To Rubens he said, "Besides, where's the doc going to go out here?"

"I don't know." Rubens shrugged. "Maybe I needed that drink worse than I thought. Hell, if you trust him, I expect he goes off suiting me."

"I trust him," Ty reassured Rubens as the silver flask was raised to the older gunman's lips again. "I would say I'd trust him with my life, except that I already have."

"Yeah, well, like I said," said Rubens, "if he suits you he damn sure suits me—"

His words stopped short as eight *federale* riflemen sprang to their feet in the brush surrounding the trail. Two more stood with pistols pointed and cocked.

"Nobody move, you *sons-of-beeches gringos*!" shouted a tall, lean Mexican in a tan, sweat-damped tunic. He held a nickel-plated revolver raised and cocked.

The four riders froze under the sight of the Mexican soldiers' big French rifles cocked and aimed at them from close range.

"If they move, blow away their damn gringo heads," the tall Mexican officer bellowed. "If any of them look like they are even thinking of making a move, shoot them so many times—"

"Hey, we're not moving, hoss," Ty said, cutting him off. "You've got us cold. Congratulations." He glanced around, his hands chest high. Bugs sat in his saddle with his Colt lying on his lap, his rifle in its boot. Rubens sat staring, the silver flask in his hand, its cap hanging by a thin chain. His rifle lay across his lap, but Ty could see that any sudden move they made right then would only get them and Rosetta killed where they sat.

"Good, you do not want to die," the officer said, stepping forward, the big nickel-plated revolver held out and aimed at arm's length. He wagged the gun barrel toward the sack of money lying behind Ty's saddle. "Juan," he called out to one of the pistol men, "untie the sack from behind his saddle and pull it to the ground." He gave Ty a gold-toothed grin and said with a gleam of greed shining in his dark eyes, "It is full of money, no?"

"You mean this sack?" Ty said, giving a backward nod toward the sack as the rifleman stepped forward and untied it. "Why, yes, I believe it is. But it's not mine. It belongs to my brother. I've been watching it for him."

The captain gave a nod. The soldier untied the sack and held it up and open for the captain to see.

"It is much money, *Capitán*," the soldier said, as if in awe.

The captain nodded and looked back at Ty Traybo.

"Is that your brother in the brush behind the boulder?" he asked.

"There's nobody in the brush," Ty said with a shrug of his good shoulder.

"He is armed, no?" said the officer, not buying Ty's lie.

"Armed to the teeth," Ty said, having to give up one false claim but jumping right back with another.

"Heco, go get the other gringo out of the brush," the

officer said to the other pistol man, his grin turned sly. "He is unarmed. Bring him and his horse to me." He looked back at Ty. "I have never been to America," he said, stepping over to the sack on the ground as Juan jerked the other sack from behind Rubens' saddle. "But it must be such a wonderful, joyful place—everybody who comes from there carries such huge sacks of money." He grinned knowingly, wagging his nickel-plated revolver. "But always you are in a hurry, you gringos," he added, "to leave such a wonderful, joyous place behind you."

"It is a peach of a place—that's for sure," said Ty, taking whatever glances he could, weighing the odds, seeing what kind of move to make when the time was right.

Dr. Dayton Bernard had led his bareback horse around behind one of the towering granite boulders and left it standing unreined as he walked off into the brush to relieve himself. He'd finished and started back to his horse when the sound of the Mexican officer's booming voice had caused him to drop down in the cover of brush and venture forward on his belly. He made his way to a place at the edge of the trail where he could see the Mexican officer and the sweat-streaked, tan-uniformed riflemen surrounding the riders.

As he looked, Dr. Bernard heard a soldier call back to the officer from only a few yards away where he had left his horse standing by the boulder.

"He is not down here, *Capitán* Torez," the soldier Heco said. "Only his horse."

The doctor pressed himself down to the dirt in brittle spiky brush and watched and listened.

The captain sat staring at Ty Traybo as he spoke to the soldier.

"Then find him, Heco," Captain Torez called out. "Find him and kill him *quietly*," he added. "You will catch up to us on the trail." He grinned at Ty and said, "Always when there is *americanos*, there is a big sack of money. But always when there is a sack of money, I find there is *more americanos* following it." He gave a laugh at his little joke. "Why this is, eh?" he chuckled.

Ty shrugged and managed to lower his hands just a little.

"I don't know," he said. "We just all love that stuff."

"Ah yes, I think that is it," said Torez, as if having just come to a great realization. He looked at the soldier Juan and gestured toward the place up on the hillside where the soldiers had reined the rest of their horses. "Bring our animals," he said. "Leave Heco's horse beside the trail for him. We will move away from here and go count the money. Sergeant Malero is meeting us at the ruins." He turned in his saddle and scanned back and forth along the trail. Dr. Bernard instinctively inched back in the brush.

He watched through the brush as the soldier called Juan left, and returned within moments with the horses. He watched the men mount, and he lay flat—as still as death as the soldiers and their prisoners filed past him.

No sooner were they out of sight than he turned and looked toward the sound of a machete swinging back and forth through the brush, pitching the reaping of its swath from side to side as it moved closer.

"Chew-mus-*com-out-now.* Chew-mus-*com-out-now*," the soldier Heco taunted, chanting lyrically with each swing of the machete blade. "Chew are unarmed. My machete *will find you*," he added in a singsong voice.

Some deadly child's game, Bernard thought, listening.

Yet he only stared calmly as his hand pressed the lapel of his coat and felt the sheathed surgical blade standing there, like some dutiful servant waiting to be called upon. Then the doctor's calm hand searched the ground around him and closed over a rock the size of a croquet ball.

Just right, he told himself, hefting the rock in his hand as the sound of the chanting and the chop of the machete moved closer, seemingly homed on him through some mystic sense known only to those bound to one another by murderous circumstance. In the stir of such dark and grim thinking, he resolved to sit still—not budge an inch—and wait in the path of the swinging blade.

You've been here before, he told himself. *You have never run from death.*

His left gripped the rock; his right hand reached inside his lapel and drew the surgical blade, flipping the sheath from the blade deftly with the tip of his thumb.

Dr. Dayton Bernard, M.D. Healer of man, he told himself with black irony. He gripped the instrument in his fist, his thumb pressed firmly against the flat back of the blade. He would wait; the taunting chant would continue; the machete would move steadily closer. When it swung so close—close enough he could kiss the passing blade—he would spring up and forward like a panther.

Yes, that's the plan, he told himself. *It's the only plan you've got.*

Chapter 14

Wes and Claypool were riding double, Claypool leading his dun behind them, when they saw the rider approaching them at a fast pace. A saddled paint horse followed on a lead rope behind him. The two horses raised dust along the trail that could be seen for miles in three directions. The rider appeared to have spotted them and kicked up the horse's gait the last two hundred yards. Wes, rifle in hand, turned his horse off the edge of the trail.

"Looks like one more person not wanting to be indoors," Claypool said.

"I believe he's seen us, but he's riding right to us," Wes said studiously. He looked closer. As the rider closed the distance between them, he said, "Hell, it's the doctor."

"Running out on us, you think?" Claypool asked.

"No, I don't think so," Wes said, seeing the dark front of the doctor's white shirt. "Like I said, him and the woman don't seem real eager to leave."

"Something's got him spooked," said Claypool. "I better get up high enough to see if anybody's chasing him." He dropped down from the saddle and handed Wes the reins. Drawing his Winchester from its boot, he climbed quickly up the hillside over broken boulders and jagged rocks until he could see a good distance all around the approaching rider.

Wes sat with his rifle butt propped on his thigh as the doctor slid his horse and the paint to a halt a few feet away. Dust billowed and swirled around the horses. Wes saw the dark dried blood on the doctor's shirtfront. He saw a dusty straw soldier sombrero hanging behind his shoulders on a length of hat cord.

"What are you doing out here, Doc?" he asked, glancing back along the dusty trail behind him. "How's my brother?"

"Soldiers have him," said Bernard. "They captured everybody." He nudged his horse over closer. Wes saw a black flapped military-style holster belted around his waist. A bandolier of ammunition hung from his saddle horn. A battered rifle butt stood from a Mexican saddle boot.

"Everybody except you," Wes pointed out. "You've found a saddle for your horse, I see."

The doctor didn't answer about having switched the Mexican's saddle to his bareback horse.

"I was in the brush when they overtook us," Bernard said, speaking fast. "They left a man behind to get me. I killed him."

Up the hillside, Claypool had looked all around, found the trail clear in both directions and climbed back down. He stood listening, catching up on what he'd missed of the conversation.

"You armed yourself too, and brought along a spare horse, I see," Wes said to the doctor.

"I thought I better," the doctor replied. "I didn't know how far I'd have to ride to find you—if I found you at all."

"And if you didn't, you were going to ride on?" Wes asked.

"I think that goes without saying," Dr. Bernard replied, looking back and forth between the two.

"How many soldiers?" Claypool cut in, already walking around, looking the paint horse over.

"Ten—nine now," Bernard answered, "plus their leader."

"He's wearing one on his shirt," Wes put in.

"I heard it," Claypool said. He stepped over to his dun, loosened its saddle and brought it over and pitched it atop the paint horse.

"They're after the money," Dr. Bernard said. "That's all the leader was interested in."

"I figured as much," said Wes, turning his horse as Claypool finished saddling the paint horse and swung up atop it.

"Ten's not so bad, if we can just get there in time," he said, his mind already at work, calculating what kind of move to make once they caught up with the soldiers.

"We've *got* to get there in time," Wes emphasized. "Once these buzzards get their hands on the money, they've got no reason to leave anybody alive."

"We'll get there, Wes," said Claypool, putting the paint horse forward beside him. Dr. Bernard rode alongside the two, pulling the straw sombrero up atop his head against the glaring sunlight, his medical satchel bouncing on his side. "I figure they'll head for the old ruins," said Claypool.

"That's a big place," said Wes. "It's hard to find anybody in there that doesn't want to be found. You know of any shortcuts there?" Wes asked, nudging his horse up into a faster gallop.

"No," said Claypool, he and the doctor staying up with him. "But these soldiers won't get in any hurry to kill them tonight. They're going to want to try and find out where the money came from—and who might be on the trail looking for it."

"But once they know all that, they *will* kill them," Wes said.

"That's the game," said Claypool.

The two long riders fell grim and silent as the horses' hooves pounded beneath them. Dr. Bernard, who had been listening closely, turned forward and rode on.

As dusk was falling in on them, the captain, his soldiers and their prisoners came to a halt out in front of a roofless and crumbling adobe, which stood in a cluster of ancient two- and three-sided structures of the same condition. Red eyes of coyotes had popped up in the shadowy blackness as the contingent rode into sight. But the ruins stood silent and vacated as the soldiers stepped down from their mounts and hitched the tired animals to a row of pitted iron hitch rings still warm from the day's scorching sun.

Rosetta had been riding double with Ty Traybo leaning on her the whole way. When they came to a halt,

Rosetta stepped down quickly and eased Ty down beside her. She caught him when he almost collapsed to the ground; she leaned him against her, his wrists bound together with strips of binding rawhide.

"Capitán, por favor," she said. "This man is dying. Can you not see it?"

Captain Torez gave a dark chuckle among his men.

"Sí, of course I see it. He *is* dying, I have no doubt of that," he said knowingly.

His men laughed under their breath, all of them realizing their prisoners' lives would soon come to a bloody end.

Stepping down from their saddles, their hands also bound, Bugs Trent and Baylor Rubens hurried over and assisted Rosetta, steadying their barely conscious comrade between them.

"Can she fix him some hot beef broth, Captain?" asked Rubens. "I've got some jerked beef in my saddlebags. It'll gain him back some strength."

"He does not need his *strength* where he is going," the captain said, still enjoying his black humor. "He will need a fan." He laughed and fanned his hand back and forth in front of his face.

Rubens and Bugs gave each other a guarded look.

"You are some funny *sons a' bitches,*" Bugs Trent blurted out, suddenly stepping forward, his bound hands out like claws toward the captain's face. "See how funny you think this is—!"

A soldier stabbed a hard sideward blow to his ribs with a rifle butt. Bugs hit the ground with a painful grunt, but he didn't lie there long.

Rubens winced as he watched Bugs struggle to his feet.

"My," Bugs rasped, "but ain't you some tough turds?" He held up his bound hands. "Cut these off, let's see if any of you has the guts to stand up *uno a uno*—"

The rifle butt stabbed out again; Bugs doubled up and hit the ground.

"Jesus, Bugs, shut the hell up!" said Rubens.

But Bugs would have none of it.

As the Mexicans laughed and jeered, they cheered him on, daring him to stand up again.

"Stay down, damn it, Bugs!" Rubens yelled at him.

The injured young gunman continued to ignore Rubens' pleading. He struggled, this time taking much longer to get to his feet, but finally managing to do so. He staggered in place and took a step forward, watching out of the corner of his eye as the same rifleman stalked alongside him, ready to strike again.

"Try it again, you son of a bitch," he snarled. "You hit as weak as your mother—"

The riflemen jabbed again, seeming to grow bored with his harsh game. But this time when he jabbed the rifle butt, instead of Bugs taking the blow in his ribs, he sidestepped fast, throwing the man off balance. Before the man could withdraw the rifle butt, Bugs caught it with his tied hands, jerked it enough to regrip it at the small of the stock, cocked the hammer and pulled the trigger as the rifleman yanked the rifle way from him. Fire exploded from the barrel; the rifleman jumped away as the bullet sliced past his belly.

The shot went wild, but the soldiers thrust their rifles

up and cocked them quickly. The captain stared at Bugs with fire in his eyes. The silence he'd maintained through-out the ride was gone, shattered far across the night.

Hearing the soldiers cock their weapons, Rubens jumped forward with his hands raised high.

"No! Don't shoot!" he bellowed, turning back and forth. But his words went unheard beneath the bark of the rifles.

Bugs flew backward with the impact of four bullets hitting him at once. Rubens heard Bugs let out a defiant yell, almost a mocking laugh. He even thought he saw a crazy smile on the young long rider's face before the bullets carried him away.

Rosetta screamed and held Ty to her bosom as if he might be next. In the swirl and drift of rifle smoke, Rubens allowed himself a deep breath, knowing the look he'd seen in Bugs' eyes only a moment before.

Loco little bastard. You beat me to it, he said bro-kenly to himself, seeing Bugs Trent's body lying still in the dirt.

The captain's eyes fixed on Rubens curiously as the riflemen turned their rifles on the older long rider. He caught a look of strange satisfaction on Rubens' face.

"Fire at will, *Capitán*," Rubens said. He spat on the ground in contempt.

"Wait! Do not shoot! Torez's voice boomed at his men. "This is what they want, these stupid damn grin-gos." He glared at Rubens in the pale-purple-shaded night.

"Figured that out, did you?" Rubens said. He grinned sadly at Bugs' body, then looked back at the captain, leveling his shoulders, feeling a surge of invincibility. "Then I expect you must be smarter than you look."

In the dark, the three riders had stopped at a place on the trail where the hoofprints they'd been following vanished across a wide ledge of rock. Wes Traybo and the doctor stood holding the horses. Carter Claypool kneeled close to the ground a few yards ahead, one of his last remaining matches burning down to his fingertips. When the single rifle shot caught their attention, he dropped the hot match and stood up. Only a second passed before the sound of the shot drew a sudden volley of return rifle fire.

"There it is, Carter, the ruins—just like you said," Wes called out to Claypool. He and Dr. Bernard turned and stepped back up into their saddles. Claypool ran back toward them. He caught his horse by its saddle horn and swung up into the saddle as the two rode past him.

"How far do you make it?" Wes called out to him above the sound of their horses' hooves across the rock shelf.

"They're damn close," Claypool called out in reply. "Less than three miles, I make it."

Wes looked at the doctor riding on his other side.

"When we get there, Doc, you best stay back—keep down out of sight," he said.

"I'll do whatever I must to stay alive," the young doctor said in a firm tone.

Wes just looked at him as they rode on along the shadowy trail.

"I mean it, Doc," he emphasized.

"So do I," the young doctor replied.

But as they neared a thin path leading up into the ruins, stopped their horses and stepped down from their saddles, Bernard pulled the dead soldier's battered rifle from the boot and checked it.

Wes and Claypool looked at each other. Wes gave a slight shrug and gestured toward a spiky downed oak lying alongside the path. As they stepped over and hitched their horses, Claypool gazed off into the black shadows of countless half-fallen structures, where the glow of a campfire flickered barely visible between breaks in a crumbling adobe wall.

Claypool nudged both the doctor's and Wes' arms, drawing their attention toward the thin firelight.

"What is this, Doc? Give us your opinion," Wes whispered, as if testing Bernard.

The doctor looked back and forth.

"Either we've caught a stroke of good fortune or we're getting ready to walk into a trap," he whispered bluntly.

The two long riders looked taken aback.

"Not bad, Doc," Wes whispered.

"How do we find out?" Dr. Bernard asked in a whisper.

"That's my job," Claypool said. Without another word, he turned and appeared to vanish into the darkness toward the silhouettes of the standing ruins.

"He seems to have lots of jobs," the doctor whispered.

Wes only looked him up and down appraisingly.

"Are you sure you're up for this, Doc?" he asked. "If you're not, now's the time to step away."

The doctor stared at him in stony silence. On their way up the lower trail, he'd shown them the body of the Mexican soldier he'd killed.

"All right, you're up for it," Wes conceded. He looked down at the battered rifle in Bernard's hand. "Did you check the rifle?"

"What do you think?" the doctor whispered with a snap.

Wes nodded. "But you haven't fired it. You're going into a gunfight with an untried weapon."

"That's the game," the doctor whispered, repeating what he'd heard Claypool say earlier.

Wes considered it, liking the doctor's attitude.

"I've got to get in a close position and wait until Carter checks them out," he said in a lowered voice. "How quiet can you be, slipping in there with me?"

"Quiet as death," the doctor whispered in reply.

Chapter 15

The Ranger and Fatch Hardaway had also heard the gunshots on the trail in front of them. Before dark they had been following the trail dust they'd seen rising when the doctor and the two long riders had put their horses forward at a run. They had stopped at the spot where the Mexican soldiers had taken Ty and the others prisoner. Backtracking bloody footprints around the boulder into the brush, they had found the body of Heco in a swath of chopped brush. His machete lay three feet away, its blade unstained by blood.

They saw that the Mexican soldier's throat had been sliced clean and deep, the thrust of cold steel expertly delivered. In looking at the gaping bloody wound, Hardaway rubbed his own throat and stepped back as if wary the same fate might befall him.

"Holy Jake and Ethel," he said. "What do you suppose happened here, Ranger?"

"I have no idea," the Ranger said, letting out a breath. He noted the side of the soldier's head had been caved in at the temple. A bloody rock lay beside the body. "I'd say he never felt the blade, though."

"What?" said Hardaway in mock surprise. "We've finally come upon something you can't expertly *opine* on?"

The Ranger didn't answer. Instead he turned and walked back to where their horses stood beside the trail.

"Now it looks like we've got *federales* sticking their beaks in the trough," Hardaway said. "I don't like that one bit. The things a man has to go through to draw reward money." He shook his head. "No wonder bounty hunters are such dirty sons a' bitches."

As the Ranger lifted his reins and swung up into this saddle, he said, "At least we're all headed in the same direction now. That's worth something to us." He looked back along the trail. "Even Garand and his men will be coming along sometime tonight, unless they stop short and take the night off."

"I hope to hell they do," said Hardaway. "I take no comfort in us all headed the same direction. It's one thing if I take you to the Traybos' hideout. I'd hate to think our trail leads Garand and his band of lousy railroad detectives there."

"I understand," said the Ranger. He stared at Hardaway, waiting for more.

"This trail runs up past the old ruins," Hardaway said. "We need to swing off of it and head southwest to get to where the Traybos hole up." He stepped up into his saddle and pushed his hat brim up. "Sorry to break that bad news to you," he added. "I figure you're getting as saddle-weary as I am."

"I'll get weary when we're finished, Hardaway," Sam said, nudging the barb forward. "We're staying on these tracks. When they turn, we'll turn with them."

Hardaway sighed and nudged his horse forward alongside him.

They'd ridden on as the sun dropped out of sight over the hilltops and their shadows stretched long across the ground and turned black under purple starlight.

Another two hours had passed when they heard the gunshots split the silence on the trail ahead of them. The Ranger looked in the direction of the loud volley of rifle fire and the single shot preceding it.

"They didn't run off. They've gone on to the ruins," Hardaway said, both of them noting how close the gunfire sounded. They put their horses forward into a gallop and watched the black ribbon of trail fall behind them beneath the animals' hooves.

Inside the ruins, Dr. Bernard and Wes Traybo had belly-crawled into position, rifles ready in their hands. They lay watching a clearing from beneath a hanging canopy of thick vines and heavy foliage clinging to the side of a single standing adobe brick wall. In the clearing surrounded by the remnant stands of adobe, stone and timber, a single guard strode back and forth, in and out of the circling glow of campfire light, his rifle cradled in the crook of his arm.

Just out of the circling firelight, the soldiers' horses stood in a row, hitched to a long rope tied between two encroaching pines. Having scrutinized the clearing closely, Wes Traybo looked around at Dr. Bernard lying beside him. The doctor was calm and silent, his hands holding the rifle, cocked and ready.

Steady as an oak, Traybo remarked to himself.

His eyes went back to the clearing. He saw the guard make his turnaround at the edge of the firelight and start back across the clearing. But before the guard had taken two steps, Traybo and the doctor caught a glimpse of Carter Claypool slipping forward in a crouch, like some stalking panther out of the greater darkness. Claypool's right arm went around the soldier's face, muffling his mouth in the crook of his elbow.

The hapless soldier struggled; his rifle fell to the ground. Claypool's left hand came around him gripping a long knife. He buried the glistening blade to the hilt in his chest as the soldier walked backward limply on the tips of his toes. The soldier's arms flailed, then fell and dangled as he disappeared from sight, swallowed by the night.

The two watched Claypool slip back into the flicker of firelight, catlike, pick up the discarded rifle and again fade into the darkness.

In the deafening silence that ensued, Dr. Bernard brought the rifle butt up and seated it to his shoulder. Taking aim down the long barrel, he moved the rifle's sights across the doorless entrances and windows. Beside him, Wes Traybo did the same for a moment. Then he lowered the rifle and looked the clearing over again.

"It's not a trap," he whispered sidelong to Bernard. "Carter's caught them sleeping."

Bernard lowered his rifle, realizing that had it been a trap, had there been soldiers waiting with guns at the doors and windows, Claypool would have sprung it on himself. By now he would be lying dead in the dirt. He didn't understand why, but he found something noble in all this—something strangely heroic in these long riders, these rogues and thieves.

"Cover us from up here, Doc," Wes Traybo whispered beside him, cutting into his thoughts. "Get that six-shooter out and ready, in case the rifle doesn't fire," he offered.

"But I haven't fired the pistol either," Bernard said.

"Give yourself a fifty-fifty chance one of them works," said Traybo under his breath.

"Right," said Bernard. He nodded; he pulled the flap open on the holster, drew out the dead Mexican's pistol and laid it beside his right hand.

Traybo watched as he raised the rifle to his shoulder again. This man had nerves like iron, he told himself.

The doctor looked around as Traybo raised into a crouch, ready to move away in the darkness.

"What are you going to do?" he asked in a whisper.

Traybo reached over and patted his shoulder.

"You did good just now, Doc," he said. "Don't worry. You're going to handle it just fine."

"I know that," Bernard whispered a little testily. "But I need to know what to expect."

"Whatever I'm going to do doesn't matter. I'll figure it out as it comes up," Traybo said. "I'm getting my brother and my men out of there. Sound good to you?" Without waiting for a reply, he moved away in the darkness.

"Yes," Bernard whispered to himself. "It sounds fine to me." He held the rifle steady and waited.

Moments later he caught a grainy glimpse of Claypool circling in the shadows outside the firelight. Claypool moved silently, crouched low, the big knife in his hand, his short-barreled Colt holstered low on his hip. The doctor's eyes followed the catlike figure until Claypool faded from vision, vanishing along the row of partially standing walls of unmortared brick and stone.

Where did he go? How could he possibly just—?

His thoughts were cut short by a loud but muffled grunt resounding from an open doorway. He ducked down, fearing the entire camp would be awakened by the sound. Yet he eased a little, realizing none of the sleeping soldiers had been disturbed by the sound, save for the unsuspecting soul who'd made it.

The young doctor grew restless, waiting, opening and closing his hands on the rifle stock until he consciously reminded himself to stop. Whatever was going on down there, he was part of it. And for now his part was to lie still and wait. . . .

In the shadowed glow of firelight through the open doorway, Claypool dragged the dead Mexican's body out of sight. Bloody knife still in hand, he jerked his blanket from around the dead man's shoulders and the straw sombrero from around his neck. He threw the blanket around his shoulders and the sombrero around his neck and quickly moved back into the doorway. He leaned against the wall, becoming the man he'd killed.

"It's about damn time," Baylor Rubens whispered harshly, watching from a dark corner as Wes Traybo slipped over the edge of a high window in the rear wall and dropped to the dirt floor. Rubens sat with his wrists still bound behind him. Beside him, the woman was in the same predicament. Ty Traybo lay in the dirt next to her, his head almost in her lap, his wrists also bound behind him. A long rope ran between each of their wrists and reached upward, tied on either end to an iron ring in the adobe wall.

Silently, Wes stepped over and sliced the rope with a knife from his boot well. Then he moved from one to the next and sliced through the rawhide stripes holding their wrists.

"I'd kill for a long shot of rye, right here, right now," Rubens whispered, rising, rubbing his numb wrists. He stepped over, stooped beside the dead Mexican and jerked a revolver from behind a loosened holster flap, turning it in his hands. "I've had my eyes on this gun for the longest—"

"Shut up, Baylor," Claypool whispered harshly. "I've got one coming this way." With his bloody knife ready, he looked back out onto the campfire light at the figure walking toward the doorway. *Damn it! Don't come over here,* he silently pleaded.

"Hurry up, over there," he whispered across the darkness to Wes as quietly as he could.

Wes Traybo heard him as he and Rosetta pulled his brother to his feet.

Ty awoke enough to start to say something, but Rosetta's hand clamped across his mouth, stopping him. Ty grew more coherent and saw what was going on. His eyes moved back and forth between his brother and the woman. He nodded and looped his arm over Rosetta's shoulders.

"Es una hermosa noche, eh, soldado raso?" said the soldier approaching the doorway.

Here we go, Wes told himself, helping Rosetta and Ty across the dark room toward the other side of the doorway.

"Sí," Claypool replied to the soldier, *"es una hermosa noche."* As he straightened and kept his knife tucked at his side.

"Quién es usted?" the soldier asked, stopping quickly a few feet away, not recognizing the voice from the dark doorway.

"Soy Ramón," said Claypool with a shrug. He prepared himself to leap forward and make his strike. This was starting to go bad, and it wasn't going to get better.

"I do not know a Ramón," the soldier said in quicker Spanish, his rifle leveled and cocked toward Claypool. "Step forward. Let me see your face!"

Claypool did as he was told. He took a step forward. But as he did so, he drew the blade up from his side and, quick as a whip, sent it whistling forward. Before the soldier could duck away from it, the big blade sank halfway to its hilt in the center of his chest. Claypool moved fast, making a grab for the rifle before the Mexican could get off a dying shot. But he didn't make it. The rifle exploded straight up as the Mexican staggered backward to the dirt.

"Get moving," Wes said to Rosetta, giving them a push toward the doorway. Get horses for yourselves and a couple extra. Shoo the rest of them out of here. We'll meet you along the trail."

"*Sí,*" Rosetta said, hurrying away with Ty hugged against her side, even though Ty appeared to grow stronger with each step.

As Wes spoke, the sound of gathering soldiers had already begun filling the quiet night. Outside the doorway, Claypool had pulled his knife blade from the dead soldier's chest and wiped it back and forth across the tan uniform shirt. He picked up the soldier's smoking rifle and pitched it to Baylor Rubens, who had already started hurrying forward to retrieve it.

"Here, Baylor, shoot somebody," Claypool said.

"Don't mind if I do," Rubens said, levering a round into the rifle's chamber. "They killed Bugs, you know," he said, raising the rifle as he sidled over to Wes Traybo.

"We saw his body," Wes said. "I knew you or him was dead when we heard the rifle fire. What do you want to do about it?"

"I figure on killing every one of these sons a' bitches," Rubens said in a gruff tone.

"Sounds right to me," said Wes. "But do it on the way to getting our money back."

"Right," said Rubens. "The *capitán* has both bags. Follow me," he said.

As the soldiers' boots began pounding from the surrounding adobe structures, a shot from the overgrown hillside hit one of them high in his leg and sent him rolling in the dirt clutching his thigh. Rubens looked questioningly at Wes as he and Claypool started retreating into the shadows of the crumbling walls.

"That's Doc, up there," Wes said. "We found him on our way here. He's covering us."

"Suits the hell out of me," said Rubens. Bullets began slicing through the air.

Chapter 16

—◆—

Stepping out of the roofless adobe where he slept, Captain Torez moved into the firelight with his nickel-plated revolver raised and ready. He looked all around courageously. Two riflemen stood guard over the sacks of money.

"Where is Sergeant Malero?" he asked. "He should be here by my side."

"He was here, but now he has left," said one of the riflemen. "He said he must check on a matter of urgency."

"Damn it!" said Torez. "Here is his urgency." Looking around, he didn't see the prisoners. He only saw two wounded soldiers crawling across the dirt, the body of the dead rifleman lying out in front of the adobe where the prisoners were kept. He heard the pounding of hooves and stood stunned as the last of the soldiers' horses disappeared into the night.

"They are escaping, *Capitán*!" said one of the riflemen flanking him a few steps behind.

"I see that, you *imbécil*!" shouted the captain. As he spoke, he caught a rifle flash in the growth on the hillside. A soldier fell on the ground, yelling. "They are up there!" Torez shouted, turning his revolver and firing on the orange-blue flash of fire. Yet, on the hillside, Dr. Bernard had already backed into the foliage and moved away in a low crouch to his new position.

Torez's soldiers sought whatever cover they could find around the darker edges of the campfire.

"Capitán!" shouted the soldier Juan. "They are everywhere! They ran that way." He gestured his rifle barrel in the direction of the darkness behind the adobe where prisoners had been.

"I don't give a damn which way they ran," shouted Torez. He gestured his gun barrel upward along the hillside. "They are up there in the *sin valor* vines! Charge the hillside! Get up there and kill them. Kill them all!" He stared back and forth and yelled, "Sergeant Malero! Where the hell are you?" But he heard no reply from anywhere around the clearing.

Turning to the two riflemen just as a bullet from Dr. Bernard thumped the ground at his feet, Torez jumped and hurried back into the open doorway of his dark adobe. Stepping away from a revealing shaft of pale moonlight cutting slantwise through a rear window, he stood in his long johns and jerked on one of his boots and spoke.

"You, go catch our horses for us," he said to the rifleman standing at the doorway. "If you see my sergeant, send him to me!"

"Sí, Capitán," said the rifleman. He stepped outside warily and ran in a crouch around the dark fronts of the adobes, leaping over piles of scattered brick.

"You, guard the money with your life!" he bellowed

at the other soldier, gesturing his pistol barrel toward the two sacks lying in a corner. "Nothing must happen to the money!"

When the soldier only wobbled in place and remained silent, the captain straightened rigidly, boot in hand, and stared at him angrily.

"Are you deaf, you fool? Do you not hear me?" he bellowed in the young soldier's face.

Only then did he see the soldier's dead eyes staring in stunned surprise at something far away from the captain, or from anything of any mortal importance. The soldier's body sank to the ground. Shaken, Torez dropped his other boot when he saw Carter Claypool standing behind the fallen soldier, his bloody knife in his hand.

Beside Claypool, Rubens' hand raised his confiscated revolver to the captain's head from three feet away.

"This is for Bugs, you stiff-necked turd," he growled. He started to squeeze the trigger. But Wes Traybo's hand came out of nowhere and clasped tightly over the gun's hammer, stopping him.

"Wait, Baylor," he said. "We're going to have the good captain here go with us to our horses—see if his men like him enough to not shoot holes in him."

"Horses?" said Rubens.

"Yeah, Baylor, our horses," Wes said with a dark little chuckle. "Did you think we walked here?"

"Baylor needs a drink, sure enough," Claypool said as he turned the captain around roughly and gathered a handful of his long johns at the nape of his neck.

"Thank you, Carter, for noticing," Rubens said wryly.

He looked back around at Wes. "Tell me what you want, before I get too damn sober to do it."

"Get on the other side of the window with me," said Wes. "Carter, shove the captain to us," he said to Claypool.

Outside they heard the sound of soldiers breaking through foliage and vines as they climbed the dark overgrown hillside.

"I—I have no clothes, no boot," the captain pleaded. "Let me dress. It will only take a—"

"You might not be *needing* any," Claypool said, pressing the blade of his knife along the captain's throat. "Now keep your mouth shut and keep reminding yourself how bad we all want to kill you."

He turned the captain toward the rear window as Wes pulled himself onto the window ledge and held his hand down to help Rubens get a start. Rubens scrambled up the short distance, climbed over between Wes and the window edge and dropped to the ground on the other side.

From higher up the hillside, above the charging soldiers, they heard two rifle shots fire simultaneously. Wes and Claypool looked at each other.

"Think the doc is all right up there?" Claypool asked.

"I believe the doc is all right no matter where you find him," Wes Traybo said.

He pulled the captain up and dropped him down to Rubens. The older long rider caught him and pinned his back to the wall with the revolver jammed to his chest. Inside, Claypool threw the sacks of money, one after the other, to Wes, who caught them and dropped them at Rubens' side.

As the sacks hit the ground with a solid thump, Rubens grinned close to the scared captain's face.

"You son of a bitch," he said proudly. "You ain't never been robbed by the likes of us."

Dr. Bernard fired his last two shots at the shadowy figures moving up the hillside through a tangle of vines and overgrown adobe ruins. As soon as return fire whipped through the foliage, he abandoned the empty rifle on the ground and moved quickly yet quietly around the hillside and down in the direction of where they had left their horses.

Once he had made his way off the hillside, he looked back at the sudden sound of rifles and saw streaks of gunfire zip through the deep green foliage. He smiled to himself and kept moving, the pistol hanging in his hand, his medical satchel still looped over his shoulder. By the time he reached the hitched animals, he swung his pistol toward the sound of men moving quickly toward him from the direction of the ruins. Dark figures moved into sight against the grainy purple starlight.

"Who's out there?" the gruff voice of Baylor Rubens called out to the other dark figures.

Dr. Bernard crouched and remained silent. Although it was Rubens' voice, he didn't know who might be listening in the darkness.

"Hold it, Baylor," said Wes in a hushed tone. He asked the silent darkness in a whisper, "Is that you, Doc? It's okay, we're all over here."

"It's me," the doctor replied in the same restrained

tone. He straightened some and watched them in the darkness.

The men moved forward, closer, until Dr. Bernard saw the Mexican captain in his underwear, his balance compromised by his uneven footwear and Claypool's prodding from behind.

"Is that you they're shooting at, Doc?" Wes asked as they gathered around him. Rifle shots still zipped wildly on the hillside.

"I think so," the doctor said, all of them turning toward the waiting horses.

"Glad you made it," Wes said sincerely, one of the sacks of money on his shoulder. Rubens was carrying the other sack.

Dr. Bernard looked at the captain as they made their way the few last yards to the horses.

"You got your money and captured their leader too?" he said, sounding impressed.

"Yeah, we cleared accounts," Wes replied. "Thought we'd better bring this one along, just in case."

The captain's hands were pulled behind his back and bound with a belt. Claypool held the long end of the belt like a leash. A bandanna had been drawn around the captain's mouth and tied behind his head.

At the horses they mounted up double, Claypool behind the captain, Rubens behind Dr. Bernard, one arm clamped around the money sack. Wes rode alone, in the lead, a sack of money over his lap. As silent as ghosts, they turned their horses at a walk and slipped away down the path and across the main trail. They followed a shallow ditch alongside the main trail for fifty yards until Claypool spotted the woman's stocky silhouette sitting atop a horse in the shadowy starlight. She held a hastily rigged string of three horses beside her.

"I have to admit I had some doubts," Rubens said quietly to the others as Wes led them closer to the woman.

"I didn't," Wes said, seeing the dark outline of his brother sitting slouched in the saddle in front of Rosetta.

When they stopped, Rubens dropped down from behind the doctor and hurried to the string of horses. The doctor stepped his horse over and sidled up to Ty and the woman.

Ty opened his eyes and gave the doctor a weak smile.

"I never seen a man take so long to relieve himself," he said in a shallow voice.

"I'll try to be quicker next time," the doctor said drily. As he appraised the bloody shoulder wound in the pale moonlight, he swung the satchel around onto his lap and pulled up a roll of medical gauze and a thick cotton pressure pad. Without taking time to remove the old bandage, he had Rosetta hold Ty's arm up. Then he pressed the pad against the blood-soaked bandage and wrapped a firm three layers of gauze around it, unwinding the gauze roll under Ty's arm and around over his shoulder.

"How's he coming along, Doc?" Wes asked. Rubens and Claypool had gathered in close, Claypool with the captain on the leash. Claypool had picked up one of the straw sombreros lying in the adobe and jerked it down over the captain's eyes.

"Not good," the doctor said. "If you don't get him to a

place where he can lie still long enough to let this wound start healing, he's going to die, plain and simple."

"We're headed there now, Doc," said Wes. "We'll be there by midmorning."

"If we're all through with this bastard, can I go ahead and kill him?" Rubens asked, nodding toward the Mexican captain. The captain whined behind his gag.

"Do what suits you," Wes said. "No gunshots, though."

"Suits me," said Rubens. He took the knife and the end of the belt from Claypool and shoved the captain along in front of him to where the edge of the trail cut across a high bluff. There the ground dropped away at a steep angle. The captain whined pitifully, jerking back and forth on his leash as Rubens stood him facing out over the bluff and reached the knife around to slice his throat.

"Hold still, you coward!" said Rubens. "This is for Bugs."

Rubens tried hard to make a deep slice across the captain's throat, but he found he had no stomach for it right then. After a moment of listening to the captain struggling and whining, Rubens cursed his own cowardice under his breath, stepped back and booted him off the edge. Dead was dead, he told himself, no matter how it came about. He heard the sound of thumps, breaking brush and sliding rocks. Then silence.

"There you are, Bugs. We're all square," he murmured.

"Baylor, hurry up, come on," Wes called out in the darkness even as Rubens turned away from the edge and came back out of the darkness at a trot. "Carter says we've got riders coming at a run."

"They rounded up their horse that fast?" Rubens said, climbing up onto one of the stolen horses.

Claypool reached over and took back his knife, noting the blade was clean.

"I don't think it's the soldiers," he said.

"Who else, then?" Rubens asked, turning the horse to the trail along with the others.

"I don't know," Wes said, gigging his boots to his horse's sides. "But we're not sticking around here to find out."

On the trail a mile below the ruins, the Ranger and Hardaway had pulled their horses to the side and sat looking back in the purple night at the sound of horses running toward them. Across the trail from them, a narrow winding path ran southwest off the hill line.

"You can bet it's Garand's posse," Hardaway said. "They heard all the shooting, same as we did."

The Ranger crossed his wrists on his saddle horn and listened ahead toward the ruins. The gunfire had gone silent some minutes earlier. He had a feeling that was the last they would hear of it. Whatever had gone on at the ruins was over and done.

"What do you want to do, Ranger," Hardaway asked, "get ahead of them or let them get there first—arrive unannounced so to speak?"

"We're not going to try to stop them. The way they're riding, we'd be lucky if they didn't run over us," the Ranger said. "Either the Traybos are lying dead in the ruins or else they got the better of it and moved on. Let's sit tight here, see what Garand and his men can tell us once we let them pass."

"Sounds good to me," Hardaway said with a slight grin. "We know Dallas Garand doesn't like anybody getting in his way."

The two eased their horses back out of sight and waited until the hooves of the posse's horses pounded past them in a flurry of dust and disappeared up the trail toward the ruins. As the sound fell away, the Ranger stepped down from his saddle and stretched and took down a canteen and uncapped it. He drank as Hardaway stepped down and stretched and stood beside him.

"I figure a half hour will give them enough time to get into whatever trouble they find up there," Sam said.

"I'd say so." Hardaway grinned and took down his canteen and uncapped it. The two bumped their canteens together. When they finished drinking, they capped their canteens, hung them back on their saddle horns and stood listening to the silent trail lying ahead of them.

Chapter 17

———

Captain Torez awakened at the bottom of the high bluff, having bounced and flopped and grazed the side of the rock wall as he dropped through the darkness and finally skidded to a halt. He had lain unconscious for a time, but when he awakened he realized that in spite of his pain, his cuts, scrapes and bruises, he was alive, and that was all that mattered. With the straw sombrero stuck down even deeper and tighter over his head and face—all the way down to his gagged mouth—he struggled to his feet in the purple darkness.

His hands were still bound behind him, and he tried in vain to remove the hat from his face, and with it the tight bandanna from around his mouth, with his shoulder. Yet neither of his encumbrances would give an inch.

After groaning and struggling and finally falling to his knees, he gave up and stared as best he could through the loose and broken straw weaving of the hat's crown. Standing up again, he began making his way up a path leading back to the trail above him.

An hour later, after several slips, falls and slides, he

lay gasping for breath on the hillside only a few yards beneath the trail. But as exhausted as he was, he felt a sudden surge of strength when he heard the sound of horses rounding the trail from the direction of the ruins and come charging along the dark path toward him.

Rolling onto his raw, bleeding knees, he managed to shove himself up the side of a young pine and finish his haphazard climb. Staggering on one boot and a bare and bloody foot, he limped sidelong out onto the trail in the shadowy moonlight and jumped up and down wildly as the silhouettes of men and horses pounded hard in the night.

"Mmmmmmmph! Mmmmph!" he bellowed as loud as he could through his tight bandanna gag.

The riders heard the strange muffled sound—but only barely—above the pounding of their horses' hooves and the creak, rattle and clink of saddles and tack. Their horses neither slowed nor veered as they came upon the grainy, staggering, stumbling figure that had thrust itself in their midst. The captain banked off the side of one charging animal to the next.

The impact of the blows kept the ill-fated captain suspended on his feet. He spun for a moment from horse to horse like a child's toy top until the outshot rear hooves of the last passing animal launched him in the air. He sailed in a high, weightless arc. Then gravity spat him back down, and he hit the ground like a limp bundle of rags.

"Holy God! What was that?" shouted Dallas Garand, reining his horse to a sliding halt, then turning it in the darkness as the men bunched and slid and turned their

horses, gathering up around him. Garand's horse shivered and chuffed and blew out a breath as he nudged the animal warily toward the dark lump lying in the trail behind them. He raised his rifle from across his lap and cocked it.

"Careful, Mr. Garand," Detective Folliard whispered, riding close beside him, his borrowed rifle also cocked and ready. "If that thing ain't dead it'll come up charging you."

"I dare it to," Garand said. Over his shoulder, he said to the rest of the men, "If it's alive, get ready to put it down."

Hammers cocked, levers snapped back and forth as the men stepped their horses closer with caution.

On the hard ground, broken, bleeding, barely alive, Captain Torez heard the voices. Dazed, he saw the dark figures through woven straw.

"Mmmph . . . mmmmph—!" he bellowed. But his muffled voice was cut short by a cacophony of pistol and rifle fire that lit the trail in an eerie flicker of blue-orange fire.

"That's *enough*!" Garand shouted amid the roar of gunfire surrounding him. The dark form on the trail jumped and bucked in place as the hail of bullets chopped into him.

"Hold your damn fire!" Earl Prew shouted, his thickly bandaged foot sticking forward out of his stirrup.

The gunfire fell away as quickly as it had started.

"Jesus! Do you think you've killed it?" Garand said to the men with sarcasm. He fanned his hand back and forth through the thick brown cloud of burnt gunpowder smoke looming around them. He stepped his horse forward, his own rifle barrel still smoking from the two shots he'd made.

"Want me to check it out, Mr. Garand?" Folliard asked, wanting to do whatever he could to get back in his boss' good graces.

"Yeah," Garand growled sidelong. "You too, DeSpain," he said.

The two men put their horses forward the few remaining feet to the dark lump in the trail, Folliard trying successfully to arrive there first.

"Uh-oh," he said, looking down at the bullet-riddled body.

Arriving beside him, DeSpain looked at the mangled, battered body, its ragged underwear, the straw hat pulled down over its face, the bandanna wrapped tight beneath its ripped and hanging brim.

"What is it there?" Garand called out, his horse moving toward them at a slow walk.

"It's a man, Mr. Garand," Folliard said. "But I don't know how to describe him. He's got a—"

"It's some barefoot fool in his drawers," DeSpain called out, cutting Folliard off. "Either his head's missing or he didn't want to show it."

Folliard gave DeSpain a dark stare.

"Damn it," Garand grumbled. As he sidled up to his two detectives, he examined the body and shook his head, baffled. Folliard looked back and forth between DeSpain and Garand, not wanting to be left out.

"Is it one of the Traybos, Mr. Garand?" he asked.

"How the hell would I know?" Garand barked. "Get

down there and get that hat off him. What the hell was he thinking—" He stopped short and said, "Are his hands tied?"

Jumping down from his saddle, Folliard turned the body a little and saw the belt wrapped around the dead captain's wrists.

"Yes, sir, he's tied," Folliard said.

The rest of the men moved their horses up and half circled the dead man in the trail.

"Good Lord," Garand said, realization beginning to set in.

As Folliard cut the straw sombrero from the dead man's head, DeSpain looked back along the dark trail. He chewed on a wad of tobacco.

"We got riders coming," he said matter-of-factly. "Hell, boss, they're almost here." He levered a fresh round up into his smoking rifle chamber.

The rest of the men did the same and stared toward the sound moving in around the turn in the trail only fifteen yards away.

"Damn it to hell," said Garand. "You cannot fire a weapon in this infernal country. Every son of a bitch must sit around saddled and ready, waiting to hear a gunshot!"

"He's a Mex, Mr. Garand," Folliard said, jerking the sliced sombrero away from the dead man's face.

"Hell, I'm not surprised," Garand replied in disgust. "We *are* in Mexico. You can't avoid the sons a' bitches forever."

As he spoke, he looked at the riders slowing their

horses to a walk and coming toward them from the turn in the trail.

"Hola," said the voice of the man at the head of the riders. "Lay down your weapons. You are being arrested by Sergeant Malero, under the authority of *Generalísimo* Terrero Pablo Juan Duro García."

"Say *what*?" DeSpain chuckled under his breath, itching for a fight, ready to start pulling a trigger for the slightest reason. "Damn greaser's got more names than a dozen Christian white men," he added with a muffled laugh. He spat a long stream of tobacco juice.

"Stand firm, men," Garand whispered sidelong. To the Mexican sergeant he said, "We're Americans here. Stay where you are. This doesn't concern you."

"This does not concern us?" said the sergeant as if in disbelief. Ignoring Garand's order to stay back, he rode his horse forward at the same slow, stalking pace. His men followed close behind him. Four soldiers rode double, owing to the fact that Rosetta and Ty Traybo had made off with their horses from the ruins.

"You heard me right," said Garand. "I'm Dallas Garand with the railroad security. This is *American* business. Unless your chili-sucking *generalísimo* wants to have you stuffed and stood in a corner, you better back the hell off."

"The land you are on is *Mexican land*," the sergeant continued, ignoring the threats and insults. He stopped his horse less than ten feet away.

"Today it's Mexican land, Sergeant Malaria," DeSpain said, deliberately mispronouncing the soldier's name.

"But it's getting away from you beaners awfully fast." He spat another stream.

Again, the sergeant ignored the insults.

"I will have your weapons and hear your reason for being here—" His words stopped short as he drew close enough to look down at the dead face of Captain Torez.

Uh-oh! Garand thought, seeing the sergeant's face in the pale moonlight.

Backing his horse away quickly, the sergeant stared in black rage at Dallas Garand. He raised a hand and shouted commands in Spanish to his soldiers too quickly for Garand and his men, even those well learned in the language to understand.

"The hell is this monkey jabbering about?" DeSpain asked.

The Mexican soldiers raised their big French rifles to their shoulders and took aim.

"Oh, hell!" said Garand, able to make out some of what the sergeant had said. "We've gone and killed their damn leader here."

"Heh-heh-heh," DeSpain chuckled in a dark tone. "That ain't nothing. Watch this."

"No, Rio!" Garand shouted as DeSpain kicked his horse forward a step toward the angry sergeant. But DeSpain wasn't to be stopped. Taking a deep breath, he rolled the wad of tobacco over onto his tongue and with all his strength blew it in a straight wet line. The projectile, spittle and all, splattered the sergeant's horse squarely between its eyes and sent it into a bucking, twisting, whinnying frenzy.

"Now you've done it, you crazy son of a bitch!" Artimus Folliard shouted at Rio DeSpain as the Mexicans' rifles exploded in the grainy darkness.

Already traveling at a quick pace, Hardaway and the Ranger looked at each other and sped their horses up even faster upon hearing the sudden outburst of gunfire farther up along their trail. As they rode on they saw a flashing blue-white glow standing out on the turn in the trail.

Hardaway shouted to the Ranger above the roar of the thunder of their horses' hooves, "I bet that's Garand introducing his detectives to General Terrero García's soldiers."

The Ranger didn't answer. But he had a feeling Hardaway was right, judging from the distinct sound of the French-made rifles. He gave Hardaway a nod, the two of them riding hard for a short distance, then drawing their horses down and veering them off the trail as they neared the turn. Around the turn the blue-white light of battle still flashed in the pale grainy light. On the far eastern sky the first thin silver wreath of light mantled the horizon.

Behind the protection of the massive and deeply creviced boulder standing where the trail curved out and around, the two stopped their horses, and the Ranger handed Hardaway his reins.

"Whatever you do, Ranger," Hardaway said, "I hope you don't get them stirred up and shooting at us."

Sam just looked at him.

"Pay me no mind. I'm just a little nervous, is all," Hardaway said, a little embarrassed by his comment.

The Ranger shoved his rifle into its boot. He lifted his big Colt, checked it and slid it back into his holster.

"I won't be gone a minute," he said quietly.

Hardaway wasn't sure if the Ranger was speaking to him or the barb as he saw him pat the horse's withers.

Sam stood straight up on his saddle and stepped over into the jagged crevice. As if making his way up a crooked ladder, he climbed eighteen feet and pulled himself over onto the boulder's broken rounded surface. He moved to the front of the large boulder, below which the flashing light and the sound of battle stood strong in the fading night. Flattening onto his belly, he inched closer, careful not to be seen and mistaken for a combatant.

On the trail below he saw gun muzzles streaking fire back and forth, ricocheting off rock and whirling and zipping in all directions. In the darkness he caught flashing glimpses of dead men and dead horses. On one side he saw the tan uniforms of the *federales* revealed in quick bursts of flashing gunfire. On the other side he saw glimpses of Garand, his remaining horses and men gathered here and there behind the cover of rock.

"What a waste," he murmured to himself, looking back and forth in the streaking gunfire.

He lay still for a moment longer, realizing the firing had already waned since he and Hardaway first heard it. Below he saw Garand and his remaining men backing away as they fired—preparing to make a fighting run for it.

He backed away a foot and stood in a crouch, making

his way to the crevice in the boulder. By the time he'd climbed down the short distance, he noted the firing had diminished even more.

"It's about time you got back," Hardaway said in a tense whisper. "I was already practicing what to say if you fell off dead from a stray bullet and the soldiers came sniffing around here."

"It's winding down," the Ranger said, dropping easily into his saddle and taking the reins. In the east the sun had begun to rise over the edge of the earth.

"Garand's men and the soldiers, like we figured?" Hardaway asked as the Ranger drew his Winchester back out of its boot.

"Yep," said Sam. "Looks like Garand's posse is ready to pull stakes and hightail it—what's left of them anyway. The soldiers chewed them up pretty good."

"You mean the soldiers have won?" Hardaway asked.

"If you can call it winning," the Ranger said. "While they were all killing each other, the Traybos must've eased away in the night." As the Ranger spoke, he took his bandanna from around his neck and tied it to the tip of his rifle barrel. Morning turned from purple darkness to dim silvery dawn.

"Good for the Traybos," Hardaway said as they reined their horses and started around the boulder toward the trail. The gunfire had fallen silent by the time they rounded the turn and kept their horses at a walk into a low-looming cloud of gun smoke. The animals chuffed and blew and slung their heads at the biting odor of burnt sulfur and charcoal.

"Alto! Alto! Quién va allí?" a weak broken voice called out from behind a rock along the side of the trail.

"Estamos aquí en paz," Sam called out.

"Oh, you are here in peace?" the sergeant said in English, in a bitter tone. "I will show you peace!" He stepped in front of Sam and Hardaway holding a pistol cocked at arm's length. Blood ran down his forehead from a bullet graze. A cloth had been drawn and tied around a wound in his upper arm.

The Ranger let his rifle barrel level down at him.

"Con calma, Sergeant," he said coolly, recognizing the insignia on the man's uniform. "I'm Arizona Territory Ranger Sam Burrack. We heard the fight. We came to help you and your men."

"My men? Ha! My men are dead, as is my *capitán*. I have two men left, and they are bleeding to death in the dirt." He wagged the gun toward the side of the trail. "We were chasing desperadoes my *capitán* had captured. They had escaped from us."

"You had captured them?" Sam asked.

"Sí, my *capitán* captured them while I was scouting the trail. We met here at the ruins. Do you know of these desperadoes?" he asked.

"Yes," the Ranger said. "I'm tracking them myself. They robbed a bank and cut out for the border. They hide out here in Mexico."

"Ha," said the sergeant. "Everybody hides out here in *Méjico*. My poor country is cursed."

"Were they carrying sacks of money?" the Ranger asked, watching his eyes closely to check his reply.

"Sacks of money? No," said the wounded sergeant. "I

saw no sacks of money." He paused for a second, then said, "I only met the *capitán* and the soldiers back there at the ruins. They did not mention any money. I know they would have if there was any." He gave the Ranger a sincere and leveled gaze. "Always I trust my men and my *capitán*," he added. He hung his head and shook it in grief. "And now they are all dead," he ended in a whisper.

"Except for two," Sam said. "So let's not waste time, Sergeant. Let's get the three of you patched up and over to Espenoza to the doctor there."

"*Sí*, step down, Ranger. You are not my enemy," he said, uncocking his gun. He swayed in place and wiped his gun hand, gun and all, across his forehead. The air still smelled heavily of burnt powder beneath a waft of brown-gray smoke.

"Espenoza? It's near thirty miles to Espenoza!" said Hardaway.

Seeing the Ranger step down from his saddle, Hardaway followed suit. He followed alongside him as Sam stepped back to his saddlebags, opened them and reached inside.

"What about catching the Traybos?" Hardaway asked, looking concerned.

"They'll keep," said Sam. "We need to get the sergeant and his men some help." He pulled a roll of gauze and cotton ties from inside his saddlebags. "See if you can round up what horses are still alive."

"What about the deal between you and me?" Hardaway asked. "What about my reward money waiting in Cottonwood?"

"We'll get to it," said the Ranger. "Right now we're going to take these soldiers to Espenoza. I'm going to let both Garand and the Traybos cool down some—they're all too hot to handle right now."

"Too hot to handle?" Hardaway just stared at Sam for a moment. Then he hurried alongside him toward the sergeant, who had sunk to the ground and sat clutching his wounded arm.

PART 3

Chapter 18

It was noon when the Ranger and Hardaway escorted the wounded sergeant and his two soldiers onto the dusty empty street running through the heart of Espenoza. The town lay centered on an ancient Spanish mission standing above the narrow shale banks of Río Blanco, where a life-sized Christ hewn from stone stood suffering on an ironwood cross affixed to the church's steeple.

The Ranger, Hardaway and Sergeant Malero rode abreast, the sergeant sitting slumped in his saddle, head bowed. Hardaway and the Ranger each led a horse that carried the bodies of the other two soldiers, the mortally wounded men having died less than halfway along the rocky trail.

As they rode toward the large open front doors of the whitewashed adobe church, an old stoop-shouldered priest and two tight-faced, middle-aged nuns hurried forward to meet them. Stepping down from their saddles, helping Sergeant Malero off the horse and steadying him between them, the Ranger and Hardaway followed the gesturing sweep of the old padre's arm toward an infirmary beside the church.

"*Bienvenida,*" he said, welcoming them, looking the sergeant up and down as the two led him toward the open door of the infirmary. "Is this yet another of the victims from the gun battle at the Sant Felipe ruins?" he asked. Looking back at the bodies as he spoke, he crossed himself quickly as the nuns summoned the assistance of a worker from the churchyard.

"Yes, it is," the Ranger said. "There's been others?" He looked around instinctively.

"They're still here?" Hardaway asked.

"Ah yes, and like yourselves, they too are *americanos*— lawmen from the railroads. . . ." His words trailed as he looked the Ranger and Hardaway up and down curiously.

Hardaway and the Ranger looked at each other as they helped the sergeant through the infirmary door and sat him on the edge of a thin straw-filled mattress lying atop a gurney in the middle of the clay-tiled floor.

"I'm Arizona Ranger Sam Burrack, Padre," the Ranger said, taking off his sombrero. "This is Fatch Hardaway." He nodded toward Hardaway, who also took off his dusty hat and smoothed back his hair behind his right ear.

"*Hola,*" said Hardaway.

"Where might we find these other *víctimas americanas*?" the Ranger asked.

The old priest's eyes took on a wary look. He raised an arthritic finger in questioning.

"You do not wish to kill them here?" he asked. "This is a holy place."

"We don't want to kill them at all, Padre," Sam said. "We only want to talk to them if we can."

"Ah, then they are *sus amigos*?" he asked with a growing look of relief.

"No, they're not our friends, Padre," said the Ranger. "But they are not our *enemigos* either. We are all riding this lawless trail—all seeking the same men." He gave Sergeant Malero a questioning look.

"I should kill them," said Malero. "Especially the man who spit in my horse's face, if he is still alive." He let out a tight breath. "But I won't," he added. "They didn't know who the captain was." He shrugged his good shoulder. "They only defended themselves against our rifles, as all men will do."

"That's a good way of looking at it," the Ranger said. "You and them were both after the same men. Things just got out of hand."

The priest nodded and looked closer at Sergeant Malero, noting his soiled and blood-splattered uniform.

"También busca usted a los hombres sin ley, en el rastro sin ley?" he asked, posing his question to Malero in Spanish. He then stepped in and removed the sergeant's hand from gripping his wounded arm.

"Yes, Padre," he replied in English. "I too seek lawless men on this lawless trail." He added, "We are all of us seeking these same lawless men."

The old stoop-shouldered priest looked up from examining the blood-crusted gunshot wound.

"If you are all seeking the same lawless men, why is it you kill each other in your pursuit?" he asked coolly.

"I do not know, Padre," said the sergeant, looking at the Ranger as he replied. "For that answer you must ask this man."

The Ranger returned the sergeant's gaze as he answered the old priest's question.

"It's because we're all seeking these men for our own reasons," he said.

"Ah, and each of you thinks your reason is the most important," the old priest surmised. He turned his eyes back to Sergeant Malero to hear his personal reason.

"I am a soldier, Padre," Malero said. "I am only following my orders."

"Ah, I see," the priest murmured, his knotty fingertips red now from the soldier's blood. He looked at Hardaway as if to hear his reason.

Hardaway shrugged and pointed at the Ranger.

"I'm with him, Padre," he said, as if shedding himself of any responsibility on the matter.

The priest looked again at the Ranger.

"I'm here to enforce the law, Padre," he said. "These men broke the law. I'm here to bring them to justice."

"They break the law in America, and you bring them to justice in *Méjico*." He paused, as if considering it.

"I have authority, given by your government in the Matamoros Agreement—says I'm granted right to pursue felons across the border when they are fleeing a crime."

The old priest gave him a doubtful look.

"Because you are authorized to kill men on both sides of the border does not make you justified in God's eyes," he said, approaching the issue from a whole other angle.

"I never said it does, Padre," the Ranger replied. "I'm hoping he justifies me himself when that time comes. He's the one saw it when it happened."

"Oh." The old priest straightened a little. "Then I will say no more on this," he said with a dismissive brush of his bloody hand. "The three wounded hombres are in the building behind the church. There are beds there where you can rest, since you are not *enemigos* and you can keep from killing each other."

"*Gracias*, Padre," the Ranger said. He looked at Sergeant Malero and said, "We're going on after the Traybos soon as we've rested ourselves and our horses. You want to ride with us, you're welcome."

"No, I will remain here until I am well enough to report to my regiment." He carefully touched the blood-crusted bullet graze atop his head. "It is my new superior's decision what happens next."

"I understand," the Ranger said, raising his sombrero, setting it back atop his head.

When the two stepped outside the infirmary door and turned the corner toward the adobe building behind it, Hardaway looked back over his shoulder and shook his head.

"Did he strike you as being hurt that bad?" he said.

"I don't know. I'm not a doctor," the Ranger said, walking on.

"His bark fell off awfully quick if you ask me," he said. "I'd think he'd be all up for getting revenge on the men who killed his soldiers."

"Some folks don't hold grudges like others," the Ranger said without looking around at him.

"Yeah, I suppose that's it," said Hardaway, but he stared at the Ranger with a curious look until they reached the open door of the rear building and walked inside.

Seeing the Ranger, Dallas Garand stood up with his rifle in both hands. His hat had been split a third of the way up its crown to accommodate his thickly bandaged head. His left eye had turned purple and swollen shut. His face was otherwise pale and haggard; his right eye was bloodshot and looked a little unfocused.

"Easy, men," he said sidelong to Folliard, DeSpain and Prew, who also stood holding their rifles, Prew leaning on his to take pressure off his bandaged foot. "Ranger," he said, "if you saw what happened along the trail and came here to gloat, I've got lots of good men lying dead back there."

"I wouldn't gloat about that, Garand," Sam said.

"What *are* you doing here?" DeSpain cut in. He eased down under a cold stare from Garand.

"I'll ask you that same question," Garand said. "I hope you didn't come here bringing wounded soldiers. If you did, they can still be killed, church house or no."

"We brought two of them here," Sam said. "They both died on the way." He nodded toward the window.

Garand let his hands relax around his rifle stock.

"Well . . . I suppose it's over anyway with the soldiers," he said. "We lost some good men, but by Godfrey, we showed that bunch."

"Showed them what?" Hardaway asked.

Garand gave him a dirty look; then he turned his swollen and bloodshot eyes back to the Ranger.

"It never would have happened if they had come upon us showing some respect."

"Really?" The Ranger gave him a skeptical look.

"You know how they get down here, these beaners," Garand said. "We would have had the Traybos' tails bobbed and braided by this morning if it hadn't been for soldiers poking in. One of them ran right out into the trail—couldn't keep from running him over. Then that damn sergeant and his huffy attitude . . ."

"Heh-heh-heh," DeSpain cut in, chuckling under his breath. "I spit a plug right twixt his damn horse's eyes."

"So I heard," the Ranger said. He asked Garand, "What's your plan now?"

"My plan is to go straight on, kill the sons a' bitches and get the money back," Garand replied. "We were getting ready to leave when you showed up, you and Fatcharack here."

Fatch Hardaway glared at him but held himself in check.

"What about you two?" Garand asked. "Don't think you're going to get ahead of us. This is still my show and I'm running it."

"No problem with me, Garand," the Ranger said. "You're in the lead. We won't try to pass you up."

"That's just fine. See that you don't," Garand said. He touched his battered hat brim, turned with his battered, bandaged men and left, Earl Prew thumping along on his rifle barrel behind the others.

"That son of a bitch," Hardaway said when the four

walked out of sight toward a small livery barn. "He still thinks he's cock of the walk." He leaned his rifle against the wall, sat down on a cot and leaned back and adjusted his gun belt. "What now?" he asked.

Sam walked a few feet to another empty cot and sat down. He took off his sombrero and leaned his rifle against the wall.

"Get yourself some rest," the Ranger said. "I'll wait until they leave and go grain and water our horses."

"*Gracias*, you do that, Ranger," Hardaway said sleepily, pulling his hat brim down over his eyes.

In the afternoon when the Ranger finished filing a thin, small X in both front shoes of Hardaway's buckskin, he set the horse's hoof down and patted its chest. Laying the flat bastard-cut file aside, he straightened and rolled down his shirtsleeves and buttoned them. He saddled Hardaway's horse alongside his own and led both animals to a hitch rail and spun their reins around it.

Having watched the Ranger mark the buckskin's shoes, an old Mexican liveryman scratched his bald head and stared curiously. He watched until Sam walked out of sight toward the adobe building where Hardaway lay sleeping out of the day's heat. At the open doorway, the Ranger leaned and watched the last of a long stream of trail dust rise and drift away on a hot breeze.

After another moment he turned and walked inside to Hardaway's cot. He planted a boot on the side of the cot and shook it until Hardaway sat up with his eyes blinking, his hat falling onto his lap.

"Jesus, Ranger, what?" Hardaway said, trying to get his mind working clearly.

"It's time to go," Sam said.

"Go? Go where?" Hardaway looked around, shoving his hair back out of his face. He saw the Ranger pick up a canteen from a table and hook its strap over his shoulder and pick up a cloth bag.

"Back on the trail," the Ranger said.

Hardaway yawned and wiped his face with his palms and tried to make sense of things.

"Damn, it'll soon be night out. I haven't had a bite to eat," he complained, sitting on the edge of the cot, shoving his hat back down on his head.

"I brought you a canteen of hot coffee and a bag of food the nuns fixed for you." He shook the canvas bag a little. "Get up. We're leaving before dark. You can eat on the trail."

"Well, hell yes," said Hardaway in a testy voice. "There's nothing I like better than eating in the saddle, washing dust and bugs down my gullet with Mexican sage coffee."

"Then you are in for a treat," the Ranger said with the thin trace of a grin.

"Can I ask why you're in such a hurry all of a sudden?" Hardaway said, standing, taking the offered cloth bag and the hot canteen.

"We've got a long ride to where we're headed," the Ranger said, picking up his rifle from against the wall and checking it.

Hardaway cocked his head sideways.

"Wait a minute. How do you know how far we're going? I'm the one leading you to the Traybos."

"We're not going after the Traybos tonight," the Ranger said, appearing tight-lipped about any further information.

"Oh? Well, just where the hell are we going tonight?" Hardaway asked.

"We're headed back to the ruins," the Ranger said. "Grab your rifle." He nodded toward Hardaway's Winchester leaning against the wall.

Hardaway walked to the rifle and picked it up. The Ranger watched him turn around with it hanging in his hand.

"Why?" he asked bluntly, a confused look on his face.

"Because that's where the sergeant is headed," said the Ranger.

"The sergeant is resting in the infirmary," Hardaway said.

"Huh-uh," the Ranger said. "He left here nearly a half hour ago. I timed it."

"What makes you think he's headed back to the ruins?" Hardaway asked. "And what do you care if he is?"

"He's headed there because that's where the bank money is," the Ranger said, walking toward the open doorway. "We're headed there for the same reason."

"Whoa, now," said Hardaway. "All that bank money is lying back there at the ruins? I don't believe it. The Traybos wouldn't have left there without it." He followed the Ranger out the open doorway and toward the horses.

"They don't know they left without it," the Ranger said over his shoulder. "I believe the sergeant switched the money on his captain before the Traybos made their getaway. That's why he didn't want to go with us and get revenge for losing all his men. That's also why he said he didn't see any money bags back at the ruins."

"Damn," said Hardaway, starting to realize the Ranger just might be right. "If he's been gone a half hour, maybe we best kick it up some, before we lose him."

"I don't want to follow him too close, take a chance on spooking him," the Ranger said, reaching the horses and unspinning his barb's reins. "But we won't lose him."

"Yeah, why's that?" Hardaway asked, unspinning his buckskin's reins.

"I filed an X on the front edge of his horse's shoes," the Ranger said. "He'll likely not see them unless he's looking awfully close."

Hardaway chuckled as he swung up into his saddle with his rifle and bag of food in one hand. He slid his rifle into its boot.

"That is damn slippery of you, Ranger," he said with a slight chuckle. "If the dumb bastard falls for it, shame on him. I reckon he deserves it." He leveled his hat as they put their horses forward on the dusty trail.

The Ranger didn't respond. He adjusted his sombrero and gazed out along the trail ahead.

Chapter 19

In the gray hour of dawn, Sergeant Malero had stepped
his horse quietly through strewn brick and stones and
gone directly to the clearing where he had met Torez
and the rest of the soldiers under the captain's com-
mand. Once through the clearing, he stopped and
stepped down from his saddle and led his horse to a
spot at the bottom of a crumbling adobe wall where he
had hastily buried the money in two brown woven grain
sacks he'd rummaged from the man in charge of the
feed supplies for their animals.

Laughing under his breath, he fell to his knees on
the ground and began scraping away with his bare
hands at the dirt and debris he had scattered atop the
hastily buried money. When his hands came upon the
feed sacks, he stopped cold for a moment as if surprised. Then he sighed, took a firm grip on each bag
and pulled them from under the loose dirt.

"Ah, there you are, my precious darlings," he said,
chuckling tearfully, as if with both pleasure and pain.
"You do not know how deeply I love you." He kissed

one of the sandy sacks, then spat dirt from his mouth. A string of saliva swung from his lips.

"And now we must hurry," he said to the sacks, still laughing to himself, his breath bated, sweat beading on his forehead even in the cool of morning. Standing, he staggered a little in place, lifted both sacks chest high and spoke to them as if they were alive and could hear and understand him. "I vow I will never leave you alone like this again," he whispered.

He lowered the sacks to his sides and started walking back to his horse, but then he stopped cold at the sight of the two armed figures standing in the morning gloom. Dropping the sacks on either side of him, he started to grab for his pistol standing on his hip beneath a holster flap.

"No, no, you do not want to grab your pistol, Sergeant," a voice called out, stopping him. The speaker stood shadowed beneath a wide hat brim in the silvery light. A shiny pistol hung down his side. "What you want to do is raise your hands before Iyo shoots a hole in you."

On the right of the man speaking, Malero saw a thin young Mexican aiming one of the French rifles at him.

Malero raised both hands slowly and cocked his head.

"Is that you, Carlos?" he said with surprise.

"*Sí*, it is I," said the Mexican. A large, dried bloodstain circled a bullet's large exit hole in the right shoulder of his tan uniform shirt. He motioned the young rifleman forward alongside him as the two stepped closer through scattered brick and stone. "I told my friend Iyo that you would be here *in time*, and *in time*, here you are."

"But, Carlos I—I thought you were dead," said Malero. "I saw you fall from your horse."

"Now, why did you think that, Sergeant Malero?" the soldier said mildly. "Just because you emptied your pistol at me?"

Malero tried a friendly laugh and spread his hands wide as if to give the man an embrace if he walked in close enough.

"Eh! What does it matter *why* I thought it?" Malero said through a wide grin. "The main thing is you are alive, and for that miracle I must thank God!"

"I thank God that your aim was bad," the soldier said, not sharing the sergeant's congenial attitude. "You shot my horse, my hat from my head and the man riding beside me, before a bullet finally struck me as I turned to flee from you."

"Ah, then it is a good thing you fled," said Malero. "Before I *mistakenly* killed you." He raised a finger, pointing out the positive side of the matter. "Always in battle there is confusion. We kill each other . . . but in the end we all see our mistake and we reconcile—"

"Lying in the dark, in the dirt, bleeding," Carlos said, cutting Malero short, "I asked myself, 'Why would my own sergeant want to kill me?'"

Malero shrugged and looked all around, as if baffled himself about the answer to such a question.

"Then it came to me," Carlos continued, tapping a finger to the side of his head. "It is because I gave to you those feed sacks." He nodded at the sacks on either side of Malero's feet. "At first I thought, 'Why does my sergeant want two large feed sacks? Like the rest of us he carries very little out here.' Then I decided you needed the sacks so you could switch the gringo money to them. You wanted me dead in case the matter of the money ever came up." He gestured toward the sacks of money on the ground. "Now I see that I was right."

"I always said, 'That Carlos, he is the smart one,'" said Malero, still trying to lighten the gravity of his situation.

Carlos looked at the young man beside him with a slow nod.

"Who did you say your friend is?" Malero asked, hoping to focus them on anything besides killing him—long enough for him to figure his next move.

"This is Iyo," said Carlos. "He found me in the dirt and saved my life." He patted a thick bandage unseen beneath his shirt.

"I see," said Malero, sounding serious and concerned. "You owe him much gratitude."

"I do," said Carlos. "Iyo also found his brother and his cousin lying dead at the water hole back along the trail the other day. They were good horse thieves—looking for a horse and a gun to steal for him, so he could ride across the border with them. But some heartless son of a *puta* they were robbing killed them both before Iyo even got the opportunity to prove himself."

"It is too bad." Malero shook his head in regret. "Yet, I must say, it is always better to already have yourself a horse and a gun when you arrive here. This trail is so

fast—*too fast* for some. And it is so *terribly* harsh and
brutal for those whose spirit is not yet prepared for how
quickly the world can turn on its heels when guns are
pointed and men's tempers—"

"Stop giving to us all of your malarky, Sergeant,"
Carlos interrupted, raising the cocked pistol in his
hand. "Give us instead the sacks of money lying at your
feet."

"Carlos, Carlos, my good soldier," said Malero, taking up a voice of authority. "As to this money, let me
explain something—"

All right. He was going for the holster flap, he
decided. That's all there was to it. He wasn't certain
whether the flap was fastened or loose. But it didn't
matter. There was no other move to make. "I must hold
on to this money and protect it, in case the people it
belongs to come looking for it—"

Sergeant Malero never got the chance to make his
move. The last thing he saw were two blasts of fire
from the rifle and the pistol in the two men's hands. He
hit the ground dead, before the echo of the gunshots
had rolled out of hearing.

Walking forward, Iyo stopped a few feet back from
the sacks of money. He flipped the empty cartridge
from the smoking French rifle, replaced it and held the
rifle at port arms, the way Carlos had shown him.

Carlos grabbed the sacks in either hand and held
them up with a squeal of delight. He turned a full circle, up on his toes. Then he stopped and faced Iyo with
a wide grin.

"What did I tell you? Eh, Iyo, *mi amigo*? Look at this. I was right! I was right!"

The thin Mexican watched him jump up and down on the balls of his feet. "No horse thieving for you! We are rich, you and me! Do you hear me? You are rich, Iyo!"

Iyo gave a modest smile and nodded dumbly. "*Sí*, I am rich now," he said.

At the sound of gunfire, the Ranger and Hardaway had reined their horses to a quick halt and sat gazing up the trail through the silvery morning light. They were close enough to the ruins that they saw birds rise from their perches in high treetops and bat away from the loud rolling echo.

"I can't say for sure about the pistol," Hardaway said in a hushed voice. "But that's one of the *federales'* rifles. I've heard enough of them lately that I can *guaran-damn-tee* it. The French ought to stick to making bubbly wine and women's drawers and leave everything else alone."

The Ranger just gave him a sidelong look, then gazed back up toward the ruins, stepped down from his barb and stooped and looked closely at the hoofprints in the dirt. He touched his gloved fingers to the mark of a shoe with the two small lines filed on it. The hooves turned off the trail and cut through a stand of tree, brush and cactus.

A shortcut to the ruins? Sam asked himself. It stood to reason that soldiers would know every path in and out.

"What do you think, Fatch?" the Ranger asked. "Is there one or more than one in there?" Standing, he gazed again toward the ruins, this time along a thin path through the tangle of cactus and woodland growth. Along the path he saw freshly tramped weeds and brittle broken brush.

"I'd say somebody got their clock stopped up ahead. But I don't want to guess how many's in there," Hardaway said. "A man draws lots of folks to him when he's got that kind of money at his reach and grab. Anyway, I'm still plumb dumbfounded that you ever figured what the sumbitch was up to."

Sam nodded to himself and stepped back into his saddle.

"Let's go in on this path and see where it leads us," he said.

"Suits me," said Hardaway. He drew his rifle from his saddle boot and laid it across his lap.

They rode onto the path quietly and followed it over a hundred yards before they heard a horse walking toward them loosely and loudly, with no apparent regard for being heard.

Stopping behind a large pine, the two waited until the rider came into sight. The Ranger's eyes took in the French rifle lying across his lap and the gun belt and flap holster draped over his thin shoulder. Behind the young, skinny rider, the two sacks of money were stacked one atop the other and tied down with stripes of tan blood-stained cloth, the color of the Mexican soldiers' uniforms.

"Hola," the Ranger called out suddenly.

He and Hardaway appeared so quickly, the young

man had no time to make a fast retreat. He froze; his horse stopped on its own, as surprised as its rider by their sudden appearance.

"Hola," Iyo replied warily. His eyes moved back and forth like well-oiled bearings. He knew he was in trouble, but he had no idea what kind or how bad it was.

"I'm Arizona Ranger Sam Burrack. We're searching for Sergeant Malero and those sacks of money you're carrying." He pointed as he spoke, seeing no need to beat around the bush about it.

"No hablo inglés . . . ," the young man said.

Before the Ranger could reply, Hardaway sidled his horse up quickly and called out, "You better learn to *hablar inglés* in two seconds, or I'll split your head like a melon." He started to lever a round into his rifle chamber, but the Ranger reached over quickly and clamped a hand over his, stopping him.

"Wait. Hold on, boss, *por favor*! I speak *inglés*! I am Iyo Julio Montoya."

"See how that went?" Hardaway said to the Ranger, relaxing his hands on his rifle.

The Ranger called out to the young Mexican, "Where is Sergeant Malero? How did you come by that money?"

"The sergeant is dead," said Iyo. "So is the soldier, Carlos, who killed him with me."

"Damn," Hardaway said quietly. "It's going easy enough so far. He must think you're a priest."

"Hush up, Fatch," the Ranger said sidelong. He said to Iyo, "The money you have is stolen. You can't keep it."

"Oh, but yes, I *can* keep it," the young man said, starting to speak faster. "I see how things work when it comes to money. The desperadoes who first stole it killed the people and took it from them. They come to *Méjico* and the soldiers take it from them. Then the sergeant takes it from the soldiers, and Carlos takes it from the sergeant." He paused. The Ranger saw a familiar look come into his eyes.

"Slow it down, Iyo. I see what's coming," he warned. He pulled his barb a step away from Hardaway, letting him know to keep his rifle out of play unless it became necessary.

But Iyo would have none of it.

"This money does not know who it belongs to," he continued, still talking faster, getting himself ready. "Now I take it from Carlos, and I keep it! Now it belongs to me!"

The Ranger saw his hand go behind his back. Iyo reached for the pistol he had stuck there instead of carrying it in the flap holster. His thin hand moved quick, quick enough for the Ranger to realize that he was no stranger to pulling a gun and firing it at a man without a second thought or hesitation.

As the big revolver swung around cocked and ready, the Ranger's Colt bucked once in his hand. With a sound of finality the shot sent Iyo flying backward from his saddle, over the sacks of money through a red mist of blood. Iyo's body rolling over the horse's rump spooked the animal—sent it high-stepping sideways so wildly that it lost its balance and fell onto its side. The ties holding the money sacks loosened as the horse flailed its hooves trying to right itself. The Ranger sprang forward on his barb, grabbed the horse by its bridle as it stood up and held it firmly, circling with it on the barb until the horse settled.

"Jumping Moses!" Hardaway shouted, settling his buckskin. "To start out easy, that sure took a foul and ugly turn."

The Ranger didn't comment. He only shook his head as he held the horse's reins and loosened the one sack left tied behind the saddle. Then he turned the horse loose to chuff and shake itself out and collect its shaky nerves. On the ground he picked up some stacks of money that had spilled out. Hardaway watched him with a crooked little grin as he picked the money up and stuffed it back into the sack.

Bent over to pick up the sacks, the Ranger stopped with his back to Hardaway.

"Let me ask you something, Fatch," he said quietly, suddenly frozen in place. "Are you going to shoot me in the back, or let me turn around and face you before you pull that trigger?"

"I don't want to shoot you at all, Ranger," Hardaway said, sounding sincere. "That's the gospel truth."

"But you will, for the money,' the Ranger said.

"Damn it, yeah, if I have to," Hardaway said, sounding unhappy with himself. "I was all right, until it spilled out and I got a good look at it."

The Ranger straightened and kept his back turned to him.

"Well, I expect you did the best you could," the Ranger said with resolve.

"I believe I did," Hardaway said. "I truly do."

"Let me ask you something else before we get started throwing down," the Ranger said.

"Go on and ask. But there ain't no throwing down to it, Ranger," Hardaway said. "Just stand there. I'm taking the money and I'm out of here—don't *make me* kill you and I won't."

The Ranger continued as if he hadn't heard him. "Was you ever going to *really* lead me to the Traybos?"

"That's a tough one," Hardaway said. "I was trying to, but I was glad every time we got sidetracked from it. I wrestled with it over and over. Now that it turns out like it has, I might admit to myself that I never was going to. Those ol' boys are just too damn good to go down this way. I've never jackpotted a pard in my life. Can you understand that?"

"I believe I can," the Ranger said.

"All right, move aside from that money," Hardaway said.

"Huh-uh," said the Ranger, "you're not taking it. It's going up the trail with me. I'll find the Traybos on my own some way, and I'll tell them if they want it, guess what they've got to do to get it."

"Jesus, Ranger," said Hardaway. "If you're not the most hardheaded, damnedest person—"

"Let's not call names and hurt each other's feelings," the Ranger said, cutting him off. "You know the game. You're either in or you're out."

"Don't do it!" Hardaway shouted, seeing Sam turn toward him, his right hand bringing up his big Colt, cocking it on the upswing.

Raising the rifle halfway to his shoulder, Hardaway hesitated at the last second. Instead of firing, he jerked his buckskin's reins hard as a bullet from the Ranger sliced through the air.

As the buckskin spun and bolted forward, another shot exploded from the Ranger's big Colt. Hardaway bowed low in his saddle and sent the horse thundering away through the brush. Standing near the dead Mexican, Sam raised his Colt again and fired another shot wildly in the air, as he had the shot before it.

He stood for a moment in the ringing silence; then he picked up both bags of money, walked over and tied them back atop the settled horse. As he led the horse over to his speckled barb, the barb chuffed and grumbled toward the other horse and stamped its hoof in disapproval.

The Ranger patted the barb, but said firmly, "Don't you start. It's time we get on out of here—see if we can't get ourselves some work done."

Chapter 20

Fatch Hardaway didn't slow his buckskin down until he reached a place where the trail wound upward and he could look back and down at the rise of dust he'd left looming in the air behind him. When he finally did stop and step down from his saddle, out of breath, he took down his canteen from his saddle horn, sat down on a rock and uncapped it.

That was close. Too close, he told himself.

He threw back a long thirsty swig from the canteen and swallowed it before he realized that instead of water, he'd drunk down a mouthful of last night's bitter leftover coffee, grounds and all.

"Damn it to hell!"

He threw the canteen away, stood up and spat several times. Still the bitter aftertaste lingered. He wiped his shirt cuff across his mouth and paced back and forth. All right, he told himself, the shoot-out with the Ranger had rattled him—no denying it. He looked at his right hand, saw it tremble a little. *Jesus* . . . He lowered his hand and looked all around as if concerned that someone might have seen him so thrown out of sorts.

But a miss was as good as a mile, he told himself, pacing again, keeping an eye on the lower end of his back trail. He didn't know what had come over him back there. He never should have figured the Ranger would give up the money just because he got the drop on him. Sam Burrack was not that kind of lawman. He had already seen enough to know that. The sight of all that money had overwhelmed him. Now he was left with nothing. No reward money—*huh-uh*—that was out of the picture now.

"Damn it!" he cursed, causing his buckskin's ears to pique at the sound of him railing aloud at himself. What in the living hell had he been thinking? Well . . . that was clear enough, he thought, settling down as he slowed his pacing and tried to do some clear thinking. He'd made a play for the money—big money, had he been fortunate enough to pull it off. He settled down some more and shrugged. He couldn't blame himself for trying. It would have been worth risking his life had it turned out well from him.

But since he did go for it, he should have had it already settled in his mind to kill the Ranger flat out, not pussyfoot around about it. That had been his problem. He should have shot the Ranger from the get-go when he had him in his sights. He took a deep calming breath and let it out. Now, if he left matters as they stood, he'd lose out on the reward money and the stolen bank money too. He couldn't do that. The only way he

could square things for himself and make something
on this deal was to go to the Traybos and take a chance
on them not killing him.

He'd have to face Wes and Ty Traybo straight up,
and tell them what the Ranger had said—that he was
coming to them with the stolen money and *guess what
they would have to do to get it from him.*

That was the deal, he decided. It wasn't the best plan
he ever had, but it was the only way he was going to
make up for losing out on the reward money. At least if
he took the deal to the Traybos, he might still get his
hands on a piece of the stolen bank money.

He took up his reins and stepped back up into his saddle. The Traybos would most likely kill the Ranger getting their money back, but Hardaway took some solace
in the fact that he wouldn't be the one doing the killing.
He had to admit, riding with the Ranger, he'd come to
respect him some, enough that he couldn't bring himself
to kill him when he had him cold. But once he brought
in the Traybos, the killing would be out of his hands.

Good enough . . .

Now that the Ranger wasn't riding with him, he knew
a shortcut off the main trail that would cut his time getting to the Traybos by nearly half. It was time to put the
Ranger out of his mind. After all, he was an outlaw,
damn it—what did the Ranger expect? Anyway, Ranger
Burrack knew the game, he told himself, nudging the
buckskin forward.

But damn it, he liked that Ranger. To tell the truth,
he felt bad about all this. *Easy,* he cautioned himself.
This was all about money, *big money*; and he'd never

seen it fail. Big money managed to outweigh bad feelings every time.

He rode on.

Pushing the buckskin hard throughout the day, knowing the big horse could take it, he only stopped twice along the meandering empty trail, each time to water himself and the horse at a runoff. He doubted if anybody could track him across some of the rough, rocky, overgrown terrain he had just crossed, but had the Ranger done so, Hardaway was certain he'd thrown him off by now.

The Ranger was good, but nobody was *that good*. He stopped for a moment and looked back over his shoulder across the rugged endless peaks and deep shade-blackened valleys he'd crossed as if in affirmation. Yep, he was off anybody's tracking ability.

So long, Ranger, he said to himself, finally satisfied that he was riding free and clear.

He smiled to himself and put the frothed and dirt-streaked buckskin forward on the last three miles to where his shortcut looped over and onto a long upper bend in the main trail.

It was afternoon when he reined his horse up at a crooked wooden hitch rail out in front of an adobe and scrap-wood hovel he remembered from one of his few preceding trips through here when he'd ridden with the Traybos. The hovel sat perched in a bowl of fine-stirring dust on a wide spot in the narrow hill trail. The rear of the building stood against a sheer wall of layered stone that stretched upward three hundred feet.

At the rail stood three filthy, fierce-looking horses and a brush-scarred supply donkey. Hardaway cocked his rifle across his lap, noting that one of the horses wore a scalp hanging from its saddle horn. Flies circled and whined over the scalp and a hanging machete streaked with black dried blood.

Hitching his buckskin next to the stinking animals, Hardaway swatted his hat through a greater cloud of flies and stepped onto a short-plank boardwalk. A goat bleated at him from the corner of the hovel. He stepped over a big gray shaggy dog lying stretched flat on its side, appearing from all outward signs to be dead. Yet as Hardaway continued on in through an open doorway, the dog raised its head three inches, looked at him, then let its head collapse back to the sun-bleached planks.

"Bienvenido, amigo," said an ancient Mexican as Hardaway stepped inside, relieved to be out of the harsh afternoon sunlight. With outstretched arms as thin as hickory kindling, the old man waved him farther in with long, knobby fingers.

"Gracias," Hardaway said, remembering the old man from past ventures. "I see you are still here."

"Where else would I be?" the old Mexican asked with a baffled expression. He shrugged his thin shoulders, then spread a single-toothed grin.

"You've got a point there," Hardaway said, looking all around as he walked to a low rickety bar and laid his rifle atop it. The tip of his rifle barrel pointed, not by coincidence, in the direction of the three horses' owners.

Without asking, the old Mexican stood a corked

bottle of mescal on the bar top; he stood a gray-filmed glass beside it and brushed away a nosy fly.

"We have beans, amigo," the old man said.

Hardaway shoved the glass aside and pulled the cork from the mescal bottle.

"Dump some on a plate," he replied. He wiped the dusty rim of the bottle and took a long drink, feeling eyes from the end of the bar staring at him.

As the old Mexican stepped away toward a side doorway leading to an outside *cocina,* Hardaway drew a wrist across his lips, stared down-bar at three bearded men in greasy fringed buckskin and wide sombreros.

"What?" he said flatly, his hand resting between the standing bottle and the prone Winchester.

The men continued to stare, their gun hands resting down their sides, near the butts of revolvers holstered there. Lying strewn along the floor against the bar sat bundles of ragged blankets and hides. A battered slouch hat lay tilted atop one of the bundles.

"We just was wondering, cousin," said one of the men, this one wearing a thin, wispy black beard, looking as filthy and as fierce as the horses standing out front. "How would you like to lie down with a woman awhile?"

Hardaway gave them a curious look, his head cocked slightly.

"Which one of you's a woman?" he asked.

The men looked taken aback for a moment. One started to snarl and reach for his gun, outraged. But the spokesman settled him with a look and waved a dirty hand back and forth in front of them.

"No, no, no, you've got us wrong, cousin," he said quickly. "We're none of us women."

"Thank God," said Hardaway. "I was worried." He eyed them with repulsion. Leaving his rifle hand in place on the bar top, he lifted the bottle with his left hand.

"We've got women here, fool," said the one who had taken offense. This one wore a thick red beard. He gestured a grimy hand at the bundles of blankets and hides on the dirt floor along the bar. In the shadowy light, Hardaway saw one of the bundles move a little and realized that the blankets and hides covered three women huddled together, their heads bowed as if they were seeking to turn invisible and disappear.

"We was thinking you might could stand a turn or two," the third man offered with a lewd grin. "They're every one fresh from the southern border, sweeter than plums."

"Slavers, huh?" said Hardaway, looking the men up and down again, not hiding his contempt.

"That's not a name we like hearing," said the third man.

"No offense," Hardaway said with a hint of sarcasm. "I meant to say, men of a *sporting nature*?"

"Yeah, that's us, all right," said the third man. Long dirty yellow hair hung past his shoulders; his beard was a tangle the color of dried sage.

Hardaway just stared at the three men.

The man with the thick red beard grabbed one of the women by her blanketed shoulder and dragged her to her feet.

"Stand up there, little princes, show this pilgrim what you've got covered up."

"Sit down," Hardaway said to the frightened girl before she could open her blanket. The girl stood trembling, not knowing what to do; a chain ran from her ankle to the girl next to her.

"How much for the three of them?" Hardaway asked. He lifted a thick leather wallet from inside his coat and dropped it on the bar.

The men looked at each other.

"For how long?" the one with the red beard asked.

"For good," Hardaway said. "How about a hundred a head, no haggling, no questions asked?"

"We can get more from the brothels across the border," said the man with the wispy black beard.

"You can feed them all the way there, hope none of them get snakebit or run off in the night," said Hardaway. "I'm talking three hundred right here and now."

"Three hundred *American*?" the man with the yellow beard ask.

"Is there any other kind?" said Hardaway.

"What are you going to do with them?" the red-bearded man asked with a suspicious look.

"What do you care?" Hardaway said with a serious look. "I might want to raise them like they're daughters of my own."

The three chuckled.

"I bet," said the one with the red beard.

"The fact is I own a place southeast of here, on this side of the border," Hardaway said. "I can always use new girls."

"Three hundred . . ." The three looked at one another. One fingered his black wispy beard.

"Hell yes, let's do 'er up," said the one with the red beard. "Give us the money."

"Give me the women," Hardaway countered.

The man gave the standing girl a shove and kicked at the blankets and hides on the floor, saying, "Get on down there. You girls have been boughten."

"Get going, *vamanos!*" The man with the black beard clapped his hands loudly at the women as they scurried down the bar and stopped near Hardaway and sank back to the dirt. A chain rattled from ankle to ankle.

"The money," the man with the red beard said firmly.

"The key," Hardaway said in the same tone. He picked up the wallet and held it ready to pitch down the bar top.

The man with the black beard pulled out a key and slid it along the bar. Hardaway caught it and slid his wallet down the bar in return.

The man with the red beard clamped a thick hand down on the sliding wallet, stopped it and picked it up with a grin. Hardaway tossed the key down to the young woman wearing the hat and whispered to her in Spanish, *"Sal de aquí rápidamente, pasa, llega a casa."*

"Llega a casa?" she asked, not believing the man who had bought them was telling them to go home.

"Sí, rápidamente!" said Hardaway, pulling them up, shoving them toward the front door.

"What the hell!" shouted the red-bearded man, jerking a thick stack of bills from the wallet. "These ain't American, they're Confederate! This stuff is older than my daddy's socks!"

Hardaway saw the women scurry out the front door, one with the key in her hand, not waiting until they unlocked their shackles.

Hardaway jerked his Winchester, cocked and ready, up from the bar with a wicked grin.

"Stop them women!" shouted the one with the black beard. "This Rebel money ain't worth nothing!"

"Stay where you are," Hardaway warned. "I'll kill the three of you."

"Like hell you will," said the one with the dirty yellow beard, stepping forward, his hand going to the butt of his gun.

"Come and get it." Without hesitation, Hardaway pulled the trigger. But the hammer only fell with a heart-stopping click.

Oh no! He levered the rifle quickly and tried again, but no empty shell flew out of the chamber and no fresh round moved into it. Hardaway pulled the trigger anyway, hoping against hope. It only clicked again.

"This son of a bitch ain't loaded!" shouted the one with the red beard. The three moved forward quick, not even drawing their guns.

"Beat his head till shit squirts out his ears," said the man with the red beard, flipping the leather wallet over his shoulder.

Damn you, Ranger! Hardaway shouted to himself as

realization set in. He looked all around, catching a glimpse of the old man walking in from the *cocina* with a steaming bowl of beans in his hand. Seeing what was going on, the old Mexican stopped and backed out of the doorway.

Chapter 21

Hardaway awakened with a drum pounding painfully inside his head and a hand trying to stave off the pain by pressing a cool wet cloth on his forehead. Before opening his eyes, he lay still for a moment recounting what had happened before the three slavers picked him up and slammed him down hard atop the bar. He'd seen the glistening blade of a boot knife raised above his chest. He'd heard gunshots. Then his thoughts had gotten jumbled. He'd felt something wet and warm splatter all over him. But that was as far as his recollection could take him.

He opened his eyes and saw the woman with the slouch hat sitting beside him on the edge of the wooden table where he lay. Sitting up slowly, he looked all around until his eyes came to rest on Carter Claypool sitting in a wooden chair, which was pushed back against the wall. He recognized his Winchester rifle sitting across Claypool's lap, beside Claypool's own rifle.

"You awake?" Claypool asked.

"Yeah, I'm awake," Hardaway said with a thick tongue. He rubbed his face and looked around. The bodies of the three slavers lay sprawled in a corner beneath the buzzing flies. "You killed them?" he said.

Claypool rocked his chair forward slowly and stood, both rifles in his hands. He didn't answer Hardaway. Instead he motioned the woman toward the open doorway and spoke to her in Spanish. The woman moved away and out the door, the chain no longer on her ankle. The other two women who'd been sitting huddled against the front wall rose and followed her. Claypool walked to the doorway and stared out, seeing the women help each other atop the slavers' horses. Two of the women rode double, the one behind leading the supply mule. The one in a hat kissed her palm and waved it toward the doorway. Claypool only nodded at her.

"Let me ask you something, Fatch," he said quietly, turning back to Hardaway. "Why did you stick your nose in, start a fight with that buzzard bait?" He gestured toward the bloody bodies of the slavers.

Holding his ribs on his left side, Hardaway shook his bowed head and shoved his hair back from his eyes.

"There's just something about a damn slaver always makes my skin crawl," he said. He raised his bloodshot eyes to Claypool, whose own battered face was healing right along. "I'm obliged you killed them before they killed me."

Claypool walked back to the chair and sat down and placed both rifles across his lap. He raised the leather wallet from his lap and looked it over, turning it back and forth.

"I see you're still trying to pass your Dixie dollars," he said.

"Yeah," Hardaway said, managing a crooked smile, his lower lip swollen and split. "I don't know why, though—call me sentimental, I guess. I've never had anybody fall for it." He paused and touched his finger-tips carefully beneath his swollen eye. "What're you doing here anyway?"

Claypool sat staring skeptically at him for a moment.

"I'm over here scouting out anybody who might've known about this shortcut and come looking to catch us by surprise." He continued staring and said, "Guess who I found."

"Huh-uh, you're wrong, Carter," said Hardaway. "I didn't bring the Ranger here. I admit I was riding with him, thinking very seriously about leading him on up, sticking him in your front yard. Fact is I couldn't do it."

Hardaway saw his own revolver stuck down in Claypool's waist beside the big Starr he'd taken from Folliard.

Claypool just gave him a questioning look.

"The Traybos and you never did anything to me," Hardaway continued. "I couldn't reconcile myself to doing it. I had too much respect for all of you."

"That's a real fine thing to say, Fatch," said Claypool. "But I'd be more moved hearing it if I hadn't seen the Ranger riding right behind you on my way here. It would be easy for me to think you two had this set up this way."

"What?" Hardaway snapped his eyes up; he glanced

toward the doorway as if he might see the Ranger standing there. "That can't be. I left a trail so light a mountain cur couldn't follow—"

"He's stuck to you like a burr," Claypool said, cutting him off. "I put him here in about an hour, more or less. So . . ." As he spoke he casually raised his short-barreled Colt from his fast-draw holster and rested its butt atop his thigh.

"You've got to be joking," Hardaway said, stunned.

"Tell me if this sounds like a joke," Claypool said, cocking the short-barreled Colt.

"Wait! Damn it!" said Hardaway, starting to talk faster. "I didn't bring him here! I came here to tell you he's coming and he's got the money!"

"What money?" Claypool asked, the Colt still cocked, the hammer ready to drop with a slight touch of his finger.

"The bank money from Maley. What money do you think?" said Hardaway.

Claypool grinned tightly.

"Nice try, Fatch," he said. "But I've seen the money. It's headed right up the trail—should be arriving along about now."

"No, you didn't see the money, Carter," Hardaway insisted. "You saw the sacks it's in. But you never saw the money, did you? Hell no, you didn't, because a Mexican sergeant switched it to feed sacks and buried it before you boys came and took it back."

Claypool considered it; his short Colt sagged a little in his hand. His thumb moved up and rested easily over the cocked hammer.

"I don't know why, but I about halfway believe you, Fatch," he said.

"It's the truth," Hardaway said. "The Ranger and I followed the sergeant back to the ruins. Another soldier killed him. Then a Mexican fellow killed the other soldier—the Ranger killed the Mexican. Anyway, I saw the money with my own eyes when some of it fell out of one of the sacks. I couldn't stand it. I made a play for it and the Ranger stopped me. He told me to tell the Traybos he's got the money. If they want it, guess what they've got to do to get it. I was coming to tell the Traybos." He gestured a hand toward the dead slavers. "Then all this . . ."

Claypool took a deep breath and let down the Colt's hammer.

"I don't think you could have made all that up," he said. "Not on the spur of the moment." He gestured toward a bowl sitting at the far end of the bar. "Your beans are getting cold."

Hardaway watched him stand up again, holding both rifles, and slip the short-barreled Colt into its low-cut holster.

"So, then," Hardaway said hesitantly, "you are not going to shoot me? I mean, I'm sitting there eating, all of a sudden—"

"I'm not going to shoot you, Fatch," said Claypool. "Not yet, at least. But you do not want me taking you to the Traybos to find this is all part of some shenanigan you've dreamed up." He raised a finger to emphasis his warning. "I will wear you out with a rake before I kill you."

Hardaway stood up sorely and walked to the bar, his hand clutching his left ribs.

"An observation, Carter," he said in a pained voice. "I'm not an old man by any means, but beatings have got to where they hurt lots worse than they used to."

"You're not telling me a thing," Claypool said. "I'm getting over one myself." He stood at the bar and watched as Hardaway ate hungrily in spite of his banged-up condition.

"I've got to ask," he said. "What are you doing riding with a lawman anyway?"

Hardaway shook his head and drew his wrist across his sore lips.

"That's a whole other story in itself," he said. "I killed a saloon owner named Lonnie Lyngrid—something you never want to do in Texas, by the way. It's worse than killing an ordained preacher."

"I've heard that." Claypool nodded.

"Anyway, I killed him, burned his salon down around him." He shrugged. "I figured that's the end of that, or so you would think."

"But no, ol' Lonnie had a rich family and they raised a stink, so I had to cut out down here. I took over a place called the Bad Cats Cantina. Not a bad business, but I got sick of dealing with whores and idiots day in, day out. I made a deal with the Ranger. He would check to see if I'd cooled off any. Which I had. In return I agreed to lead him to you boys."

"And you did," said Claypool.

"Not exactly," said Hardaway. "Although I admit I was wrestling with the notion."

Claypool shook his head with a disgusted look.

"You could have crawfished," he said. "Breaking your word to a lawman never meant much to anybody in our business."

"Crawfish?" said Hardaway. "Hell, I had him set up to be shot down in the street! But then he tells me Lonnie Lyngrid had a bounty on his head. So, instead of me getting hung for killing him, I've got a reward coming all the way from Ohio."

"All right," said Claypool, indicating he was with him so far.

"But here's the drawback," Hardaway continued. "I've got to have the Ranger attest to me having rightful claim on the money before Cleveland, Ohio, will send it to Cottonwood and I can get it." He paused, stuck a wooden spoonful of beans in his mouth and chewed, giving Claypool time to unravel it all out.

But Claypool only stared at him, appearing to not even try to understand.

"And you believed all that mess?" he asked.

Hardaway stopped chewing.

"The Ranger is not known to lie," he said. But a doubtful look spread across his face. "I mean, it sounded truthful enough."

"You're an outlaw, Hardaway," said Claypool. "You think a lawman cares any more about lying to one of us than we do about lying to one of them?"

"Jesus," said Hardaway. "Now I don't know what to believe."

"Maybe that's been a problem of yours," said Claypool. He shook his head and rapped a knuckle on the bar for a bottle of mescal. As the old Mexican appeared with the bottle and two brown-filmed shot glasses, Claypool related Hardaway's story to him in Spanish. The old man listened as he pulled the cork and laid it beside the bottle. When Claypool reached the end of the story, the old man cackled aloud, so fiercely that he slapped both hands onto the bar top, coughed and wheezed and grasped the bar for balance.

"All right, gawl-damn it, that's enough," Hardaway said, getting testy.

When the old man walked away, Hardaway simmered and said to Claypool, "You know, come to think of it, Burrack unloaded my rifle. That's what nearly got me killed here."

"There you have it," Claypool said with resolve.

Moments later, atop their horses, the two turned from the hitch rail and rode a half mile up a steep, narrow path. They sat behind the cover of rock and brush and looked back along the trail through a battered naval telescope Claypool carried in the bottom of his saddlebags.

"Here you go, Fatch," said Claypool. After staring down through the lens, he held the telescope over to Hardaway. "Watch the distant line of pine. You'll see Ranger Burrack moving along the trail as the trees thin out. What you won't see is any sacks of money."

Hardaway scanned the ground through the telescope for a few seconds until he spotted the Ranger in the circling lens, appearing no more than a few yards away. Hardaway jerked his head away from the lens and blinked as if clearing his eye.

"Son of a bitch!" he said. "There's no way he could keep on my tracks that well. Mine's not the only tracks down there."

"Yeah, but they might be the best," Claypool said. He swung down from his saddle and stepped back behind Hardaway's horse and stooped and looked at his hoofprints. "Did you ever have an X on your horse's front shoes?"

Hardaway turned in his saddle and stared back at him.

"No, hell no, *never*," he said.

"You do now," Claypool said.

"Jesus! You're joking!" said Hardaway, swinging down quickly from his saddle.

"I'm not *Jesus*, and I'm not *joking*," Claypool said as Hardaway stomped over from his horse. "Why do you keep asking me that? Do I look like a man prone to frivolity?"

Hardaway didn't answer. Instead he stooped down beside Claypool and studied the tracks, then cursed and stood up. His face reddened with embarrassment as realization set in.

"I'm a damn fool, Carter," he said. He collapsed the telescope between his palms and handed it to Claypool as Claypool stood up and dusted his knee.

Claypool only nodded without coming out and saying he agreed.

"It's an old manhunter's trick, Fatch," he said. "You're not the only man who's ever fell for it."

"Yeah, but he just told me he used it to track the Mexican sergeant back to the ruins," said Hardaway.

"Then you might have at least expected it," Claypool said.

"And I didn't," Hardaway said with self-contempt. "All right, he got me." He looked all around and spread his hands. "What do I do now? If I had pullers, I could yank the shoes, but then he'd know to follow unshod tracks."

Hardaway considered it.

"Wait here and shoot him when he rides into range," he said with finality.

"Like I said, he's *not* carrying sacks of money," said Claypool. "Did you see any money sacks on his horse? No, you didn't," he added before Hardaway could say anything. "Sending you up here with that message, he's set himself to ride into our midst without us being able to kill him. He's got sand, I'll give him that."

"So what do we do?" said Hardaway. "I suppose I could turn this horse loose and send it off in the wrong direction. Ride double with you the rest of the way?"

"No, I don't think so," said Claypool. "Besides, I've got some detectives dogging our back trail. I'm not going after them with you hanging on behind my saddle."

"Maybe I can help?" Hardaway said.

"Maybe you can at that," said Claypool. "We'll get rid of these detectives. Then we'll deal with the Ranger. First let's put some miles between him and us. If he wants into our neck of the woods so bad," he added, "let's let him in. If he's got our money, we'll get it from him and kill him." He gave Hardaway a grave look. "If it turns out you're lying and he doesn't have our money, I don't have to tell you where that puts you."

"You'll see I'm not lying, soon as we get to the Traybos," Hardaway said, the two of them turning, walking back to their horses.

Chapter 22

Three miles off the main trail, at the end of a path winding through the narrow jaws of a stone canyon, the Traybos, Baylor Rubens, the doctor and Rosetta had stepped down from their horses and into a cabin constructed of log, clay and stone. Allowing Ty to walk on his own, the doctor and the woman remained close at hand and followed him to a bed in a room off to the side. The doctor pulled fresh gauze and ties from his medical satchel as Wes stepped in behind them and tossed both of the trail-worn canvas sacks into a corner.

"I want to see you both out here when you're done," he said, nodding toward the other room. Then he turned and walked out.

In the front room he stepped quietly over to a corner cabinet built into the wall and reached inside. He glanced back at Rubens, who was down on his knees in front of the hearth.

Rubens had taken logs from a pile of firewood stacked against the wall, and he shoved them back deep into the heath's blackened mouth.

"We've never brought outsiders here before," he said

over his shoulder to Wes Traybo as Wes walked over
and stood back watching him start a fire.

"Are you questioning my judgment again, Baylor?"
Wes asked in a firm tone.

"Not questioning it," Baylor replied. "I'm just wondering what your thinking was behind doing it, is all."
He took a long hearth match from a wooden box, struck
it and held it under some dried kindling already nested
in the hearth.

"That's the same thing, Baylor," said Wes.

"I didn't mean it to be," Rubens said, straightening a
little, watching the fire take hold in the kindling and
flare up to feed on the dry pine bark. "But you have to
admit it's damn risky," he added.

"Don't worry about them being here," Wes said.
"There's a reason why it's not risky. We won't have to
worry about them ever telling anybody."

Rubens thought about it, his eyes staring into the
growing, spreading flames.

"You don't mean we're going to . . . ?" His words
trailed.

"Would you do that, if I asked you to?" Wes asked
quietly.

Rubens rubbed his palms nervously on his thighs.
He swallowed a dry knot in his throat, staring into the
flame.

"I—I think I need a drink, *real* bad," he said, instead
of answering.

"I figured you might say that," Wes said. "Turn
around. I've got something for you."

Rubens turned slowly, uncertain of what to expect.

But then his eyes widened at the sight of Wes standing before him holding out a full bottle of rye whiskey.

"Lord yes!" he said, grabbing the bottle from Wes' hand. "Much obliged, Wes. Thank you, Jesus," he said, lifting his eyes heavenward. He hurriedly pulled the cork, palmed it and raised the bottle high in a long, gurgling drink.

As he lowered the bottle, he let out a deep hiss and asked, "Will you be drinking with me? You deserve a good swig. We *all* do after this run." He glanced around, used to Bugs Trent being nearby.

"Don't mind if I do, Baylor," Wes said, taking the bottle.

"I mean no offense, questioning you just now," Rubens offered, taking the bottle back after Wes had taken a swig. "And I know you mean no harm to come to the doc and Rosetta."

"You're right. I mean them no harm," Wes said. He watched Rubens take another deep swig, lower the bottle and wipe a hand over his lips. He looked up curiously at Traybo.

"So . . . what did you mean, then?" he said.

"I meant, we won't be here if anybody shows up looking for us," Wes said. "There's too many people getting too close to our lair." He lowered his voice. "As soon as Ty's strength is up, we're shedding the place for good."

"For good?" Rubens looked up at him.

"Yep, for good," Wes said. "I'm thinking my brother and I might quit the business, move far away from here.

Maybe we'll pull together a ranch up in the north country."

Rubens gave him a despondent look.

"I don't know nothing but robbing," he said.

"Come with us, learn the cattle business," Wes said.

"I hate cattle something awful," said Rubens. "So does my horse." He pointed toward the other room. "Hell, Ty hates cattle. I've heard him say it."

"That's just one thing we can do, Rubens," Wes said. "It doesn't have to be a cattle ranch. It could be something else."

But the thought had stuck in Rubens' mind. He took another swig and gazed off in consideration.

"Cattle ranching," he murmured, shaking his head with a sad look on his weathered face. "I don't know how I'm going to tell my horse."

"Look at me, Baylor," Wes said. "You've ridden with us a long time. We've had the best of it—robbing banks, trains, anything else that suited us. We lived lives most men envy."

"Damn right we have." Rubens gave a proud grin.

"But we were never killers," Wes continued. "Now we are. We've crossed a line I never wanted to cross. It's time we back away from it and do something else. You're welcome to come along, whatever we do."

"If it's time to get out . . . I'll get out," he said. He tipped the bottle toward Wes as if in a toast. "Here's to what it was," he said. Then he took another long deep swig.

Rubens and Wes both looked around at Dr. Bernard

as the doctor stepped into the room. The woman followed him inside, shutting the door.

"Your brother, Ty, is doing much better," the doctor said. "Apparently running gunfights must agree with him."

"I might say the same for you, Doc," said Wes. He looked at the woman, who stopped and stood beside the doctor. "You too, Rosetta. As hostages go, I couldn't have done better."

The two just looked at him.

Wes drew the same leather pouch of gold coins he'd been carrying inside his coat. Then he drew another pouch he'd taken from a hiding place in the corner cabinet when he'd gotten Rubens a bottle of whiskey.

"These are for you," he said, stepping forward and holding the pouches out to them.

Rosetta took the pouch and held it to her bosom. The doctor started to speak, but Wes stopped him.

"Doctor, you've been tougher than a pine knot. You've saved my brother's life. You fought for us when the odds were stacked against us. But now it's time for you to go home. If you stick with us any longer, you'll lose your way out."

Dr. Bernard took a deep breath and let it out.

"Yes, I understand," he said. He gripped the pouch and hefted it in his hand. He started to protest that it was entirely too much, but Wes Traybo gave him a look that invited no argument on the matter.

Rosetta quickly put the pouch inside her clothes.

"*Gracias*, Wes Traybo," she said, "for hiring me to take care of your brother and for allowing me to return to my people. I am no longer a *puta*."

"You never were, far as I'm concerned," said Traybo. "You had to play the hand dealt to you." He turned to the doctor. "Now get out of here, both of you. Once you're out, forget your way back, for a few days anyway."

Rosetta turned toward the door to the room where Ty was resting in bed.

"I must say good-bye to Ty first," she said. She started to turn, but Wes stopped her.

"No," he said, knowing now that Ty was getting better, he would never want her to leave. "I'll tell him good-bye for you."

"Come, Rosetta, let's be on our way," the doctor said. He looked at Wes and nodded good-bye, then turned with his satchel on his shoulder and led the woman toward the front door.

Wes watched from the front window as the two departed toward the stone canyon. Before they rode out of sight, he saw the doctor stop his horse all of a sudden, jump down from his saddle and run to a pine standing beside the trail. The doctor bowed against the tree, resting one hand on it, and vomited profusely on the ground at his feet.

Wes smiled thinly to himself. He watched the doctor wipe his lips on a handkerchief on his way back to his horse, step up into his saddle and continue on.

"Tough as a pine knot," he repeated to himself.

When Wes turned around, he found Ty at the door to the other room staring at him.

"Rosetta and the doc are gone?" he asked, gazing past his brother, trying to see out the window.

"Yep, I sent them away," said Wes. "You don't need any more nursing. It'll spoil you."

"Yeah, but damn," said Ty, supporting himself against the doorjamb, "I never got to know her, not in the way I wanted to."

"Yes, you did," Wes said. "She did what needed doing, and you got to know her as much as you needed to. Anyway, she's got family waiting for her in Guatemala. There's no place for her with us." He walked back to where Rubens sat, watching everything, a glazed, whiskey look on his face.

"Are you going to hog that bottle, Baylor, or share some of it with your pards?" he said.

Riding at a quick clip, feeling pressed to put more miles between themselves and the Ranger, Claypool and Hardaway reached the main trail and turned onto it without slowing down. Doing so was a mistake, one that Claypool realized a second too late as the sound of rifle fire exploded on the hillside above them.

A barrage of bullets sliced through the air around them; before Claypool could get his rifle raised, his dun whinnied in pain and went down beneath him. At the same time, two bullets hit Claypool, one in his side and one in his chest. Beside him, Hardaway took a bullet that knocked him out of his saddle and sent him rolling off the edge of the trail. He caught himself and crawled back up and returned fire. But in the middle of the trail, Claypool was in big trouble.

A hard volley of rifle fire erupted as he struggled to his feet and tried to run to his downed horse. The horse lay center-trail on its side, screaming pitifully, flailing its hooves.

Another bullet hit Claypool as he dived atop the badly wounded animal and spread his arms wide as if to protect it. Blood spewed up from the horse's side and splattered down on man and animal alike.

"No, Charlie Smith!" Claypool shouted, seeing where the mud packing had fallen from the graze on the horse's rump from his run-in with the banditos at the water hole. "What have I go you into!" he shouted, hugging the horse, his rifle gone from his hands and lying fifteen feet away in the trail.

"Kill that son of a bitch!" Dallas Garand shouted from ten yards up the rocky hillside, having managed to track them there and lie waiting above them in ambush. Hardaway returned fire as the barrage of rifle fire filled the air again. But even as he fired, he saw Claypool buck and twist as bullet after bullet sliced into him. When he saw that neither Claypool nor his dun was reacting to the continued sting of hot lead slicing through them, he crawled backward down from the edge of the trail, leaving a smear of blood in the dirt.

On the hillside Garand stood in a haze of looming gun smoke and waved an arm back and forth to Fain Elliot and Artimus Folliard. Beside him stood L. C. McGuire.

"Stop firing. He's dead," Garand said. He took a fresh cigar out of his inside lapel pocket and stuck it in his mouth. He looked down at Claypool lying stretched out atop the dead horse. "You two get down there, finish off Hardaway." Under his breath, he said, "I knew that son of a bitch was with them." He turned to McGuire and said, "L.C., follow me."

He positioned his rifle back over his shoulder and walked up the hillside to where they had left their horses, Rio DeSpain holding the animals' reins in case they needed to make a fast getaway.

Elliot and Folliard stood up, looked at each other and started down the hillside through brush and over rock. They looked back and forth along the edge of the trail where they'd seen Hardaway firing at them.

"Come out, come out, *Fatcharack* Hardaway," Elliot called out in a dark laugh. "I will make your thumb into a watch fob."

"Speaking of thumbs," said Folliard, "Claypool's is all mine. He also took my Starr pistol. . . . I'm taking it back if it's on him."

"Suit yourself," said Elliot, stepping out onto the trail and walking across it, his rifle pointed at the far edge where they'd seen Hardaway. He called out, "If you make me track you down, it'll go harder on you." As Elliot approached the edge of the trail, Folliard veered away and walked to where Claypool lay sprawled facedown, the back of his bloody coat riddled with bullets.

He took Claypool by his wrist and turned him over, off the horse's side.

"There's my Starr," he said, seeing the big revolver stuck behind Claypool's belt. He grabbed the gun, held it up and looked it over with a proud smile on his still battered but healing face.

But suddenly his smile froze as bullet after bullet

from Claypool's short-barreled Colt ripped upward into his chest, pitching him backward. The fourth shot entered just beneath his cheek and sent a gout of blood and brain matter exploding in the air.

"What the hell are you doing?" Elliot called out, spinning toward the sound of gunfire, mistakenly thinking it was coming from Folliard's gun. But as he saw Folliard falling back beneath the upsurge of blood, he turned his rifle toward Claypool just in time to catch two bullets in his chest. As he spun, Hardaway's rifle barked from the edge of the trail; the bullet pounded Elliot a third time in the chest.

From up the hillside, Garand heard the short-barreled Colt. He and L. C. McGuire looked down and saw the two detectives lying dead and bloody in the middle of the trail.

"You can't kill these sons a' bitches!" he said as if in awe, his cigar falling from his lips. Without a moment of hesitation, he sprang the rest of the way up the hillside, McGuire right behind him, to where Rio DeSpain stood holding the horses.

"What's the deal?" DeSpain asked as Garand leaped atop his horse and jerked it toward the trail. McGuire shrugged and stepped up into his saddle, turning his horse behind Garand.

"They're dead—we're gone," Garand snapped. "That's the deal."

"Me and L.C. got you covered, Mr. Garand," DeSpain said, leaping up into his saddle, turning the other two horses loose.

Seeing Garand and his two men riding away atop the

hill, Hardaway struggled against the pain in his lower left side and pushed himself to his feet. He staggered past the body of Elliot, out around the dead horse and saw Claypool lying covered with blood, his short-barreled Colt in his hand, his eyes barely showing life.

"Damn it, Carter," said Hardaway, weaving in place. "I wouldn't have had this happen . . . for nothing."

Claypool made the slightest gesture with his eyes, letting Hardaway know he heard him.

"There just ain't nothing . . . I can do for you," Hardaway said. He sank down to the ground beside him, laid his bloody hand on Claypool's shoulder and patted it. "Go on, close your eyes now," he said quietly.

Chapter 23

The Ranger rode the last thirty yards with caution up from Hardaway's shortcut and onto the main trail. Having followed the X on Hardaway's horse's shoes, he knew it was a pretty good bet that Hardaway was involved in the rifle fire he'd heard. He had only stopped at the old Mexican's trailside hovel long enough to water the barb, but he'd noted the new set of tracks belonging to whoever had thrown in with Hardaway. He'd also seen the bodies of the three slavers, the old Mexican leading a team of donkeys dragging them to the edge of a tall cliff across the trail from his hovel.

The Ranger finished watering the barb and led the dusty animal across the trail and stood watching the old man.

"Qué ha sucedido aquí?" he asked.

"Ah, it was nothing," the old man replied in better English than the Ranger expected for such a remote place. He gave the Ranger the account of a *norteamericano*—a *tejano* perhaps—offering to buy women from three slavers with worthless money, of another *americano* arriving in time to save his life from the slavers, and killing the three of them with a short-barreled Colt. His memory on the matter was crisp and clear, yet when it came to recalling any names, his eyes glazed and appeared at a loss.

"The Traybo brothers' gang?" the Ranger said, testing.

"Traybos? *No hablo* Traybos," he replied, his English suddenly turning stiff and unmanageable.

In relating the story of the shooting to the Ranger, the old man stopped at intervals and stepped forward long enough to roll a slaver's body and watched it sail, bounce, flail, slide and twist into shapes heretofore unattainable to their human skeletal form. At the end of each gruesome exhibition, the old Mexican looked back at the Ranger with his one-toothed grin, his tired eyes sparkling with amusement, and continued his tale.

After the third body had made its descent, and the old man finished telling the Ranger what had happened, he saw a questioning look on the Ranger's face and shrugged his thin shoulders.

"This is hard ground and I have no shovel, no pick." He gestured out across the deep rocky chasm to where buzzards had begun rising into the sky almost before the bodies had landed and settled. "Besides, *los santos* teach us it is good to feed God's creatures, eh?"

"I can't argue against the teachings of the saints," the Ranger replied. Knowing he'd gotten all he was going to from the old man, Sam stepped into his saddle, turned the barb and rode on, stopping only now and then to make sure he was still following the X Hardaway's horse had left in its wake.

And he rode on, only quickening his barb's pace when the onslaught of rifle fire erupted less than two miles ahead of him.

Now each step of the barb shortened his distance yard by yard from the turn in the trail and the drift of rifle smoke looming above it. When he could smell the strong bite of burnt powder, he stopped and stepped down from his saddle and cocked his Winchester, the rifle already in his hand.

Leading the barb, he warily rounded the turn and saw Claypool's dead dun lying stretched out midtrail. As he proceeded closer, he saw Hardaway sitting, swaying slightly, his hand still resting on Claypool's bloody shoulder.

"Don't think I can't . . . see you coming, Ranger," Hardaway said painfully, his free hand gripping Claypool's Colt against his own bloody belly wound. "I could nail you from here. . . . Nothing you could do about it."

"Oh . . . ? What's stopping you?" the Ranger called out, moving slowly forward as he spoke, gaining what knowledge he could of the situation as he moved deeper into it.

"Gun's not loaded," Hardaway replied painfully.

"That's a stopper," the Ranger said. He walked into sight over the side of the dead dun and looked down at Hardaway. "Loaded or unloaded, lay it down, Fatch," he said in a warning tone, his rifle loosely pointed at Hardaway.

Hardaway sighed and opened his bloody hand; the

short-barreled Colt fell to the ground in the fork of his outstretched legs.

The Ranger moved in, looking all around. He stooped and picked up the Colt and checked it. He looked at Carter Claypool lying pale and dead, looking small, the breadth and depth of his personal magnitude gone out of him.

"You're not lying," he said to Hardaway, and he stuck the Colt down behind his gun belt.

"I could have . . . told you that too," said Hardaway, his free hand going back to his belly wound.

"Who gulched you?" Sam asked.

"Who do you think?" said Hardaway.

"Are we going to do it this way?" the Ranger said, eyeing him sharply.

"Garand and his gun monkeys," Hardaway said. "I caused it, leading you up here . . . causing Carter to get in a big hurry, you dogging us."

Sam just stared at him.

"I saw what you did . . . X-ing my horse's shoes. Real funny. Ha-ha," he said with sarcasm.

"You wasn't sticking to your part of the bargain, Fatch," the Ranger said.

"I would have," said Hardaway. "Sooner or later . . . most likely, maybe—"

"See what I was dealing with?" the Ranger said, cutting him off.

"It doesn't matter now," Hardaway said. "I expect I'm dead . . . before I can take you to them."

"How bad are you hit?" the Ranger said.

"Gut-shot," Hardaway said grimly. "What does that tell you?"

The Ranger shook his head in regret. But then he asked, "How are you feeling?"

Hardaway gave him a dark stare. "Is that you taking . . . some kind of cruel, sick revenge on me for me not—"

"No, Fatch." The Ranger cut him off again. "I mean how do you feel right this minute? Are you wishing you had died an hour ago?"

Hardaway still gave him the dark stare.

"No, I wish . . . I could sit awhile . . . get up and go on an hour from now," he said, crossly.

"Then you're not gut-shot," the Ranger said with a sense of relief that Hardaway did not yet share.

Hardaway sighed deeply and raised his hand from over the bloody wound.

"Here's my gut. . . . Here's the bullet hole," he said.

"You've got a bullet in your belly, Fatch," Sam said. "That doesn't mean you're gut-shot." He leaned his rifle against the dead dun's belly, reached out both hands and took Hardaway by his shoulder and started to pull him up.

"What the hell, Ranger?" Hardaway cried out painfully.

"I'm getting you on your feet. If this doesn't feel like a knife turning in your gut, you're not gut-shot."

"Jesus, please *no*!" Hardaway screamed. But up on his feet for a second, he took on a strange look of surprise and said, "Whoa, that didn't hurt nothing like I figured on."

"Now sit down," Sam said, giving him a little nudge back down onto the dead horse's side.

"Damn it, make up your mind!" Hardaway barked. "I said it's not as bad as I figured. . . . I didn't say it felt *good*!"

"Easy, Fatch," Sam said. "I can get you patched up some. But you're going to have to take me to the Traybos. The doctor from Maley is there, remember?"

"Lord God Almighty," Hardaway moaned, shaking his bowed head. "Had I known I was going through all this . . . I could have just drawn you a map . . . and stayed at the Bad Cats. . . ."

"What about that reward? Don't forget about that," the Ranger said, wanting to keep his spirits up until he got medical treatment.

"That was all . . . a made-up story," Hardaway said. "Everything you told me . . . was a damn lie."

"Huh-uh. I X'd your horse's shoes so I could follow you, and I unloaded your rifle so you couldn't shoot me in the back," Sam said quietly. "But I didn't lie about the reward. It's there waiting for you." He pushed himself to his feet and started to turn and walk to the barb.

"Think about this," he added, gesturing toward Claypool's body. "If you'd shot me in the back, or if I hadn't been able to follow your horse's tracks, where would you be right now?"

Hardaway shook his bowed head again.

"Obliged, Ranger," he said in a dejected tone. "Now I feel even more like an ass than I did."

An hour later the Ranger wrapped a cloth around Hard-away's wound to slow the bleeding and sat him on a rock while he dragged Carter Claypool's body to the side of the trail and covered it with stones. He lugged the bodies of Fain Elliot and Artimus Folliard to the edge of the trail and rolled them off. As they tumbled down into brush and rock, he recalled the cheerful look on the old Mexican's face when he'd performed the same act earlier that day, but with a steeper fall to better fuel his amusement.

"The horse will have to lie there for now," he told Hardaway when he walked back to where he sat, his hand resting on his bandaged wound. "I can't wear these horses out dragging it."

Hardaway looked sadly at the body of Charlie Smith lying center-trail.

"Carter Claypool loved that cayuse something fierce," he said reflectively. "There's no way of knowing it, but I believe if a horse can love a human, ol' Charlie Smith loved Claypool in return, no matter the tough life he put that animal through." He breathed deep and the Ranger thought he saw his eyes well up a little.

"How's your belly?" the Ranger asked, to break his sad train of thought.

"Hurts like hell," Hardaway said. He stood up, seeing the Ranger getting ready to leave. "Anyways," he added, nodding toward the stones covering Carter Claypool, "there lies one of the toughest, most loyal, bravest hombres to ever throw on a long rider's duster and take up the gun."

The Ranger only nodded, allowing him to finish his coarse eulogy for the departed.

"How much did you know about him?" he asked.

"Not much, really," said Hardaway. "He snuck off and fought the War of Secession when he was going on fifteen—lied about his age. I don't know which side he fought on. I always got a feeling it wouldn't have mattered which side, he just wanted to fight. He left the war and fought ever since. You've got to admire a man like that. He was not a man of peace, nor did he make any phony pretense at being one."

The Ranger watched and listened until Hardaway stopped talking, put on his hat and leveled it.

"Let's go, Fatch," he said. "Don't start trusting my doctoring skills more than I do."

They mounted their horses and rode on, upward toward a hill line only a few miles above them. When they got to a place where a thinner trail turned off between the walls of stone, they stopped at the sound of horses' hooves clopping along at a walk on the narrow trail winding toward them.

"Hold it up, Fatch," the Ranger said. He took Hardaway's horse by its bridle and led it aside out of sight behind the edge of a tall chimney rock of iron-stained sandstone.

Hardaway sat bowed and silent, as he had for the last few minutes, his left arm cradling his wounded stomach.

"Whoever it is, shoot them," he murmured. "Get me on up to the doctor."

"Shhh," the Ranger said, hushing him.

"Careful this ain't some of the Traybo Gang coming," Hardaway whispered quietly in a pained voice. "This stone valley . . . winds on ahead, right to their front door."

The Ranger just looked at him.

"We're there to the doctor," he said haltingly. "I figured I best tell you . . . in case I pass out."

"*Hola* the trail," the Ranger called out, turning, seeing the two riders come into sight. "I'm Arizona Ranger Sam Burrack," he followed up quickly, opening his duster so they could see his badge.

At first the two riders had stopped abruptly and appeared ready to bolt away. But when they noticed the badge, they eased a little.

"Ranger, we are happy to see you. I'm Dr. Dayton Bernard, from Maley. This is Rosetta, also from there," the young doctor called out. "Have you come searching for the two of us?"

"I'll be damned," said Hardaway, realizing if he'd waited one minute longer he would not have had to reveal the Traybos' hideout in order to get treatment from the doctor.

"We are searching for you both, Dr. Bernard," the Ranger said, nudging his barb closer, checking the trail behind the two. "But right now we're in sore need of your medical skill. I've got a man shot in the belly here."

"Gut-shot," Hardaway corrected in a pained voice.

As the doctor and Rosetta stepped their horses forward, the doctor looked at Hardaway's hand resting against his bandaged stomach.

"I doubt very much you would be sitting in that saddle if you were gut-shot, sir," he said. "But let's get you down from there and take a look." He took Hardaway's horse by its bridle and led it off the trail, through a stand of brush, into a small clearing.

Chapter 24

In the afternoon, the Ranger and the woman had both helped hold Hardaway down as the doctor sliced into his back near his spine and squeezed out a bullet that had entered his lower front side, circled beneath the skin and stopped against a small lateral muscle. As soon as the bullet was out and lying in the doctor's bloody hand, Hardaway relaxed on the blanket he lay on and let his folded trail glove fall from between his teeth.

"Obliged, Doctor," he groaned. "I thought . . . I was a goner."

"You might yet be," the doctor said. "If you don't keep this wound clean and the bandage properly changed for the next few days."

"Can I—can I ride right away?" Hardaway asked, already feeling better.

"If you feel strong enough and can stand the pain, of course you can," the doctor said matter-of-factly. He worked as he spoke. "I advise against it, but do as your body will allow. I prefer you take at least two or three days of bed rest, but . . ." He gestured a bloody hand at their surroundings.

"I'll take it easy, Doc," Hardaway said.

The Ranger moved back and sat watching from a few feet away. He took a cup of coffee the woman poured and handed it to him as the doctor began preparing a bandage for Hardaway's back. As the Ranger sipped his coffee, the woman kneeled on the blanket, grabbed the bandage from the doctor and took over the task of dressing the wound, front and rear.

Dr. Bernard stood up and stepped back as she worked.

"How did things go for her?" the Ranger asked, holding an open canteen up for Bernard. He tapped the canteen against the doctor's leg to get his attention.

Bernard turned to him. He reached for the canteen, poured water onto his bloody hands and washed them.

"She wasn't harmed," the doctor said, drying his hands on a bloodstained cloth hanging over his shoulder. "Neither of us were. We did as we were told, and caused the outlaws no trouble."

Sam watched him and listened closely, noting that the doctor kept his eyes averted from him as he spoke. He recognized an edginess in Bernard's voice, a reluctance to discuss the matter any further.

"If you and the woman are all right, I'll be riding on to the Traybos when we leave here," Sam said. "Is there anything you can tell me that might make my job easier?"

The doctor squatted down beside him and propped his forearms on his knees. He let his damp hands dangle, as if resting them.

"You're going to kill them, aren't you, Ranger Burrack?" he asked in a manner that indicated he already knew the answer.

"Not if I can keep from it," the Ranger said. "They weren't known as killers until this robbery in Maley."

"What happened in Maley was a terrible misfortune," said the doctor. "Wes Traybo told me about it. It's true Wes killed the detective posed as a bank teller. But the detective's shotgun went off and killed Widow Jenson."

A misfortune. . . . The Ranger looked at him, seeing the man struggle with something inside himself.

"And you believe Wes Traybo *because . . . ?*" he said, leaving the question hanging.

The doctor gave a slight chuff and shook his head.

"All right, I asked for that," he said. "I just don't think the Traybos are *that bad.* At any rate I don't think they deserve to be shot down like mad dogs."

"Neither do I," the Ranger said. "But would you rather they get a trial, be found guilty and hanged? Or maybe dragged out of their cells in the middle of the night—swung from an overhead timber until they choke to death, slowlike?"

The doctor breathed a slight sigh and considered the matter for a moment.

"Law is a gruesome, ugly business," he said quietly, still not making eye contact.

"I can't argue with that, Doctor," the Ranger said. "And I suppose it looks all the worse to a man whose business is saving lives."

The doctor only nodded, studying the small flames in the fire they'd made to boil water and make coffee.

"I don't know that I will be in this *business of saving lives* much longer, Ranger," he said.

"Oh?" Sam said. "That's too bad. The folks in Maley will hate to hear it. You appear most handy at what you do." He gestured toward Hardaway as the woman ran a wrapping of gauze around him, covering him from his lower belly up to his rib cage.

The doctor hesitated for a moment, then turned and looked directly at the Ranger.

"I won't lie to you, Ranger," he said. "Being held hostage by the Traybos caused something to happen to me. It's as if I wasn't a hostage at all, I was actually riding with them—a *member* of the gang, so to speak."

The Ranger only watched and listened.

"I—I found myself wanting to do my part, put my efforts into helping them elude the law." He paused, then said, "I found myself shooting it out with Mexican soldiers. I wounded some of them." He shook his head. "I hope to God I didn't kill any of them."

"You've been through a lot, Doctor," the Ranger said. "You and the woman both. The way I'm going to report this is that you and this woman were held hostage, that you both cared for a wounded outlaw and were then released. I met you on the trail back to the border and saw no reason not to send you on your way."

"And anything further that I feel like mentioning about it is up to me, eh, Ranger?" the doctor said.

"That's as fair as I can call it," the Ranger said. "Whatever you did, it was done for the purpose of saving your life and the woman's. You can't be prosecuted just because you did a good job of it."

The doctor started to speak, but the Ranger continued without allowing him to.

"You're not the first young man to look at men like the Traybo Gang and see something admirable, even *enviable*, in the way they live. But they are gunmen and thieves. You just met up with them on the edge of what they're turning into. Another year of robbing, a few more *misfortunes*, as you say, they won't be the same people. That's why I wanted to bring them in before it all got too far out of hand."

"You could be wrong," the doctor said. "After the killing they might see where this road is taking them. They might stop here and drop out of sight, live respectable lives, never be heard from again."

"They could," said the Ranger. "It's happened before. But the odds are against it, the longer they go unchecked. The law can't wait to see if they *might change*. The law has to act and act swiftly. What happened to the widow in Maley might have been caused by a detective's shotgun going off. But the fact is, the detective wouldn't have been there wielding a shotgun had it not been for the Traybos."

"I can suppose you've had lots of time alone to work all this out for yourself, Ranger," the doctor said, glancing at the big Colt on the Ranger's hip, at Carter Claypool's Colt shoved behind his gun belt. "So I doubt if anything I can say on the Traybos' behalf will make much difference to you."

"You're right—it won't," said the Ranger, gesturing toward Hardaway as the woman helped him put his shirt on over his bandages. "He's been saying much the same for them ever since we've been on their trail."

"Perhaps I have said too much," the doctor said.

"Perhaps I need some time alone myself to think about these things."

"Thinking never hurts, Dr. Bernard," the Ranger said wryly. "I'm sure that's something we both agree on." He stood and slung grounds from the empty coffee cup. "If we're all through here, Dr. Bernard," he said, "I'll help him into his saddle and we'll be on our way." He looked over at the woman and said to her, "Carter Claypool killed three slavers and set some women free. I understand they're headed home toward the southern Mexican border. If you take a cutoff down the trail, it'll put you at the trailside hovel. The women started from there. If you can ride, you'll catch up to them."

Rosetta grew excited. She swiped a loose strand of hair from her face.

"*Sí*, I can ride a *caballo* like a bird rides the wind, Ranger," she said, "'specially if I go home."

"Thank you, Ranger Burrack," said the doctor. "She most certainly rides. I'll see to it she gets to the hovel and that she's well on her way."

"Obliged, to both of you," Sam said, touching the brim of his sombrero, first toward Rosetta, then toward the doctor. "Go home, Doctor—find the good in yourself."

Hardaway, seeing the Ranger standing, struggled up himself, buttoning his shirt.

"I still hate doing this," he said, looking at the Ranger.

"So do I, Fatch," the Ranger replied. "Let's go."

In the afternoon, Rubens had walked out to the barn, his bottle of rye in his hand, to keep watch on the trail for Carter Claypool, who should have arrived hours ago. Wes Traybo stood looking out a window, seeing Rubens stagger only slightly as he walked through the barn door and closed it behind himself. His brother, Ty, sat on the side of his bed, holding a bowl of warm elk stew, eating it with a large spoon.

"I've never seen any man drink as much as Baylor can and still get around as well as he does," Wes said over his shoulder.

"He told me once that he hadn't been what you'd call dry-eyed sober in over fifteen years," Ty replied. He blew on the stew and sucked it from the spoon.

"I have no cause to doubt it," Wes said. "A man can stay drunk so long he's better off staying that way."

After he'd warmed stew for his brother, Wes picked up the canvas sacks of cash and laid them up on the foot of the bed. Now, as Rubens closed the barn door, Wes turned to the bags and began untying them.

"I told him this is our last job," he said to Ty.

"How'd he take it?" Ty asked.

"Not good, but better than I thought he would," said Wes, loosening the last tie-down on the side of the canvas sack.

"I don't know why he should take it bad," Ty said. "He'll come out of this with enough money to last him the rest of his life if he keeps an eye on it."

"He's not going to do that," said Wes. "I wonder now

how Carter's going to take it. He's a long rider through and through." He picked the first sack up by either end and turned it upside down.

"Shouldn't he be getting here by now?" Ty asked. He looked around in time to see piles of pinecones, chopped-up brush and foliage from the hills above the ruins and torn Mexican newspaper spill out onto the bed.

"What the . . . ?" Wes stood staring, stunned for a moment. Ty let his spoon fall from his hand into the bowl of stew and got up unsteadily beside his bed.

"Where's the money?" he asked, a strange puzzled look on his pale, haggard face.

"Hell of a question," said Wes. "I want to know that myself!" He hastily untied the other sack, held it upside down and shook it in the same manner, only harder.

"Oh no," Ty said, the truth sinking in as he saw the same contents spill onto his bed. "We've been jackpotted *bad*," he added.

Wes rummaged deep through the debris as if some sort of answer lay there.

"The captain and his soldiers got us," Ty said, already getting the picture in his mind. "They're the only ones who can—" His words stopped at the sound of a gunshot. The two froze for a second; then Ty scrambled for his guns standing in his holster, his belt hanging from the bed's short head post. As he followed Wes out of the room, barefoot, toward the front door, another shot rang out.

"It's coming from the barn!" Wes said, snatching his rifle from against a wall. "Baylor's out there. Let's get him covered."

Wes ran across the stretch of ground between the rear porch and the barn, looking around for any sign of gunmen among the rocks and brush behind the cabin. Ty hobbled along as fast as he could behind him. The two fell in beside the partly open door, their backs against the plank wall.

"Hold it," Wes said, seeing a drift of gun smoke wafting out through the door. The two caught the smell of burnt powder and stared at each other.

"Oh no," Ty said, a dark look coming to his face.

Wes threw the door open and the two walked inside, hearing nervous horses chuff and grumble and rustle around in their stalls.

At the end stall, their guns still out and pointed toward a stronger rise and smell of powder, they looked over the rail and saw Baylor Rubens' horse lying dead in the straw. Rubens was leaning back against the wall in the corner. His empty bottle was nestled in the straw on one side; his smoking Colt rested on his other side, near his right hand. Smoke curled upward from the gaping hole in his head. His slouch hat lay a few feet away, a bloody hole through the center of its crown.

"My God, brother," Ty said quietly as if not to disturb a sleeping man. "Baylor has killed himself, and his horse too."

"He all but come out and announced it to me," Wes said, rubbing his bowed forehead. "I just wasn't listening as close as I should have been."

"Wait a minute, brother Wes," said Ty. "You can't blame yourself for this. As he spoke, he uncocked his Colt and stuck it down in his trouser waist. "Baylor was his own man. If he took a notion to do this, he sure as hell didn't want anybody talking him out of it."

"I'm the leader, Ty," said Wes. He uncocked his Colt and holstered it. "I let him down, hitting him all at once about getting out of the business." He looked around and ran his fingers back through his hair. "I'm telling you, this job has been a bad deal coming out of the deck. We lost Bugs . . . lost our money. Now Baylor's blown his fool drunken head off. I don't know what's to happen next."

Almost before he got his words out of his mouth, he heard a calm voice speak to them from just inside the open door. They spun around in place, their hands gripping their gun butts.

"Don't do it," the Ranger said in the same calm tone. "I'm Arizona Ranger Sam Burrack. You're both under arrest for robbing the bank in Maley, Arizona Territory." He held his Winchester cocked and aimed at Wes Traybo's chest. "Both of you ease your hands up away from your guns. I will not say it again."

The brothers did as they were told, but Sam noted they did not move their hands very far from their weapons.

"Let me make sure I understand, Ranger," said Wes. "You come all this way, from Arizona Territory, just to arrest us, *outside* your jurisdiction."

"You heard it right. That's the deal," said Sam. "We have an agreement with the Mexican government called the Matamoros Agreement. You can read the whole thing while you're awaiting trial."

"That's real considerate of you, Ranger, but we're not going," Wes said. "You and I both know there's a posse of railroad detectives wanting our hides nailed and tanned. Like as not, they're close behind you right now."

"They won't bother prisoners of mine," the Ranger said.

"Easy enough to say, Ranger," said Ty. "But for all we know you'll turn us over to them and let them settle up with us the railroad way."

"Not while I've got the money they keep in the bank at Maley," he said.

The mention of the money struck a note with the Traybos. Sam saw it in their eyes.

"How is it that *you* have *our* money, Ranger?" said Wes.

The Ranger noted that Wes already knew the money was gone.

"I took it from the Mexican sergeant who resacked it and hid it at the ruins," Sam said. "You can ask Fatch Hardaway when he gets here. I rode on ahead when we heard the gunshots."

"We heard he was riding with you," said Ty. "Why's he riding behind you?"

"He took a bullet in his belly from that posse you're talking about. They ambushed him and Carter Claypool. Claypool's dead."

"You're lying, Ranger," said Wes. "Carter Claypool would eat that posse alive."

"Not this time," said the Ranger. He nodded toward Claypool's short-barreled Colt standing behind his belt.

Seeing it for the first time, Wes winced and appeared to let go of all the tight wires that held him together.

"Damn . . . ," he whispered.

"Claypool's dead. So's this one," Sam said, nodding toward the body in the stall. "I heard you talking from outside. That's Baylor Rubens," he added. "Your men are dead. It's time you call it a run."

The two looked at each other, the fire appearing to have left their eyes.

"What's the chance we won't hang, Ranger?" Wes asked.

"Slim," said the Ranger. "But it's worth a try. Neither one of you has to die here today. Who knows what happens tomorrow?"

"Can you swear to get us to Maley without the posse swinging us from a tree?"

"No," said the Ranger. "But you've got my word I'll try. If they kill either of you, they have to kill us all."

The brothers shot another glace at each other.

"Have you ever been a long rider, Ranger?" Wes asked, only half joking.

"Unbuckle your gun belt and let it fall, Wes," the Ranger said without reply.

"All right, what the hell?" said Wes. "Take us on in." He unbuckled his gun belt and let it drop to the straw floor. He raised his hands higher and relaxed. Ty raised his hands also, following suit, his mending shoulder only allowing him to lift his arm a few inches.

"Play your cards right, brother Ty," Wes said, "you could learn the trade of stonemasonry over the next ten to twenty years."

"I heard what happened, the detective's shotgun going off," the Ranger said. "A good lawyer can whittle some time down for you." As he spoke he stepped forward with two pairs of handcuffs he carried behind his belt. He picked up Wes' gun belt and looped it up over his shoulder. He raised the Colt from its holster, unloaded it and stuck it back in place.

"You sound like you're trying to help us, Ranger," Ty said. He gave a weak half grin.

"I'm not trying to help you, Ty," the Ranger said. "But I'm not trying to hurt you either." He slipped Ty's revolver from his waist, unloaded it and shoved it down behind his gun belt, beside Claypool's short-barreled Colt.

"Are you able to ride?" he asked Ty.

"Absolutely, I am," Ty replied.

With both brothers disarmed, Sam handcuffed them to a barn post while he saddled their horses. When he'd finished with the horses, he uncuffed the brothers from around the post, recuffed them and gestured them toward the barn door.

Following them from behind, he led their horses out of the barn toward the cabin.

"Stonemasonry, huh?" Ty chuffed and gave a short laugh. "Is that a kind way of saying I'll be working on a rock pile?"

"See, brother Ty, you've learned something about it already," Wes said.

Chapter 25

In the rocks on the hillside overlooking the Traybos' hideout, Rio DeSpain and L. C. McGuire lay huddled out of sight beside Dallas Garand, the three of them having followed the trail up to the stone canyon on their own, seeing all the many tracks headed on up into the canyon even though the main trail was gone. Once above the clearing in the rocks, they had rested silently, watching the cabin. When the two shots exploded, they'd started to make their move as the two brothers ran to the barn. But catching sight of the Ranger riding up toward the cabin at a quickened pace, Garand decided to wait and see if the Ranger might make their jobs any easier for them.

"Here they come, Mr. Garand," Rio DeSpain said, seeing the Traybo brothers swing open the larger barn door and walk into the afternoon sunlight. Behind them he saw the Ranger moving forward, leading the two horses.

"By thunder!" said Garand. "We've got the sons a' bitches now." He levered a round into his rifle chamber and aimed it down over the top of a rock.

"What about the Ranger, Mr. Garand?" DeSpain asked, also taking aim beside him.

"What about him?" Garand asked gruffly.

"Want us to kill him too?" McGuire asked.

Garand had to think about it for a moment, watching the three men and two horses cross the rocky dirt yard.

"To hell with him," he said. "If we don't kill him too, he'll be a thorn in my side the whole way to Maley. We'll kill him and blame the Traybos. Nobody has to ever know but us three."

Rio DeSpain turned, looked at McGuire and grinned.

"You mean, dead men tell no tales, now, do they, L.C.?" he said.

"None I've ever heard," said McGuire.

"Pay attention to what we're doing, both of you," said Garand. "We can't afford to mess this up."

"We've got it, Mr. Garand," said DeSpain, taking aim again as he spoke. "All that bank money is just lying inside that cabin, waiting for us to take it."

"And take it we certainly will, all the way back to Maley," said Garand. "I won't have you turning to thievery on me. I'm in charge and don't you forget it."

"We won't forget," said DeSpain. As he and McGuire took aim, afternoon sunlight glinted off their rifle barrels.

In the yard below, the Ranger caught a glimpse of the glistening metal that could only be one thing and stepped up his pace.

"Get inside, both of you, quick," he said.

The brothers stepped it up, but they gave each other a look, walking side by side.

"What's wrong, Ranger?" Wes asked. As he spoke, he reached his cuffed hands inside his shirt and slid out the two-shot derringer he carried secreted behind the top button of his trousers.

Before the Ranger could answer, Ty staggered and started melting down sideways. Wes jumped over to grab him.

"He's falling, Ranger!" he said.

The Ranger saw Wes reach out for his falling brother. But at the last second, instead of grabbing Ty, who suddenly righted himself, Wes spun around and knocked the Ranger's rifle barrel upward. The Ranger saw the derringer coming into play and ducked back from it as the first shot whizzed past his head.

"Shoot him, brother!" shouted Ty.

The derringer swung around ready to fire again, catching the Ranger off balance. Sam tried to right his rifle barrel for a quick shot, but he already knew he'd be too late. The barrel of the derringer gaped close to his face. But as Wes Traybo pulled the trigger the shot went wild; he slammed forward with a loud grunt as the sound of the rifle shot exploded from within the rocks on the hillside.

"Wes!" Ty shouted as another rifle shot resounded behind a spray of dirt kicking up at Ty's heels. Seeing his brother fall to the ground with a bullet hole spouting blood from his chest, the young gunman threw himself toward him. A third shot zipped past his back and kicked up more dirt.

The Ranger grabbed Ty and shoved him on toward

the cabin, knowing there was nothing to be done for Wes Traybo.

On the hillside, L. C. McGuire and Rio DeSpain took aim again. As they both fired, Ty Traybo flew forward onto the ground in front of the Ranger as they ran up the path to the back porch. The Ranger dived to the dirt and half rolled, half crawled around the corner of the cabin. He fired toward the hillside.

Garand watched with satisfaction as the Ranger's bullet hit the hillside twenty yards away. "Fine work, L.C.," he said. He saw the look on DeSpain's face. "You too, Rio," he added.

A strange look came upon Rio DeSpain's face as he levered a fresh round into his smoking rifle chamber.

DeSpain chuckled in the same dark tone Garand had heard the night on the trail when DeSpain had spat in the sergeant's horse's face. "That ain't nothing. Watch this," he repeated, also the same as he'd said that on the trail. "We're taking the money, and you'll tell no tales about it." Behind him L.C. gave a little laugh.

"No, Rio, please!" Garand shouted. "Don't shoot! The money's yours! You can have it!"

"Hell, we already know that," said DeSpain, rolling a wad of tobacco across his tongue, tucking it into his other cheek. He fired three shots into Garand as quickly as he could lever the rifle and pull its trigger.

In the dirt around the corner of the cabin, the Ranger heard the three quick shots, but he noticed that no bullets struck the ground anywhere near him. All he heard was one of the bullets scream as it ricocheted off a rock.

As he looked back and forth along the rocky hillside, he caught sight of Wes Traybo crawling toward the cabin, leaving a wide smear of blood in the dirt behind him. Sam had no idea what had just happened up on the hillside, but it didn't matter, he told himself. He'd given these two outlaws his word. If the posse killed either of them, they would have to kill them all. He couldn't let them die in the dirt without offering himself alongside them.

This is crazy. They just tried to kill you. You don't owe them a thing, he told himself as he scooted up the side of the cabin and levered a fresh round into his rifle chamber.

"I know it, but here goes," he murmured under his breath, and in a crouch, he rushed from behind the cover of the cabin and bounded across the rocky yard to where Wes Traybo lay crawling on his belly.

In the cover of standing rock and high brush at the edge of the clearing, Fatch Hardaway stood crouched, his left arm closed around his bandaged belly wound. With his rifle barrel, he reached forward and parted the brush slightly, enough to see the Ranger running across the backyard of the cabin toward Wes Traybo, who lay bleeding in the dirt.

"Damn it, Ranger, what the hell's wrong with you?" he asked under his breath. Farther up the path to the rear porch, he saw Ty Traybo spread flat on his belly, facedown. Looking up, he saw L. C. McGuire and Rio DeSpain—*Spanish Rivers, the rotten son of a bitch*— both riflemen working their way down the hillside from rock to rock. *Dallas Garand's men,* he told himself, having last seen the two riding away with Garand after killing Carter Claypool and his poor horse. "Damn near killing me too," he whispered aloud to himself.

He started to raise his rifle to his shoulder.

No, wait, he thought. As of right now, he reminded himself, he wasn't a part of this fight. He let the rifle lower slightly, knowing that the second he pulled the trigger he would be in this up to his chin, belly wound and all. If there was ever a fight he had no business getting involved in, this was it. He could back away, let them shoot each other up. . . . *What about the reward money?* he asked himself.

He let out a breath, considering it, wondering if, as Claypool had said, the Ranger had concocted the whole story as a way to set everybody up. He lowered the rifle again, seeing the two riflemen reach the rocks at the bottom of the hillside and begin firing at the Ranger, who had started dragging Wes Traybo to his feet, the two of them struggling up the path to the rear porch.

"See? *Damn it* to hell," he said to himself. "You never know who's lying and who's telling the truth." In the dirt yard, he saw a bullet from one of the two rifleman hit the Ranger and knock him away from Wes Traybo and off his feet. The Ranger's Winchester flew from his hand. Hardaway saw the Ranger struggle toward the rifle. He saw Wes Traybo down again and crawling almost aimlessly.

He winced and raised his rifle again as the riflemen stalked forward out into the open now, growing bolder, knowing they had this thing won.

"Don't do it, Fatch," he ordered himself, cocking the rifle, taking aim. "Don't do it! All you're going to get out of this is shot all to hell! And you're wounded already!"

Yeah, well, he thought, ignoring his own warning. "In for a penny, in for a pound, or however that goes," he said aloud, taking close aim. He squeezed the trigger and felt the rifle buck in his hands. Behind him his horse jerked back from the sound of the gunshot, then settled and shook out its mane. Hardaway levered a round and took aim again, seeing both riflemen turn and fire blindly at the smoke above his cover of brush.

The Ranger didn't waste a second. Seeing the riflemen turn their fire away from him toward the high brush, he struggled up into a crouch. He made it to his rifle and limped over to Wes Traybo, who was still trying to crawl to the cover of the cabin. Traybo left a dark trail of blood behind him. Blood ran down the Ranger's leg from a deep graze across his left hip.

"Let's try this again," he said to Traybo, dragging him forward, struggling to get him to his feet as he looped Wes' arm over his shoulder. He caught a glimpse of DeSpain turning back toward them, firing a shot that hit the ground close to Wes Traybo's bloody back. L. C. McGuire had moved across the rocky yard toward the smoke rising from the high brush.

Before DeSpain got relevered and aimed, Sam had

Wes up and staggering forward with him. They dropped out of sight behind a stack of wood on the rear porch as DeSpain fired again. His bullet thumped into the firewood.

"I'm coming now to kill yas. Here I come, you sons a' bitches!" he sang out loudly, adapting his words to the tune of an old familiar hill song.

"You're hit . . . too, Ranger. But you come for me?" Wes managed to say to the Ranger. "Why?" He gazed at the Ranger's face, looking puzzled.

"I gave my word," Sam said, jerking a bandanna from around his neck and jamming it into the gaping hole in the outlaw's chest.

"But we—we tried to . . . kill you," Wes said, his voice growing weaker.

"So I noticed," the Ranger said grimly. He placed Wes' bloody hand on the bandanna, hoping Wes could keep it there.

Wes gestured his fading eyes toward DeSpain walking across the yard, singing his crazy death song to them.

"They might . . . have just saved your life . . . shooting me," the wounded outlaw said.

"It's a thought," the Ranger said. He tried levering a round into his rifle and found he was out of bullets. He felt his empty holster and saw his big Colt lying in the dirt across the yard where he'd fallen. He grabbed the short-barreled Colt from his waist and loaded it quickly with bullets from his gun belt.

"I'm coming now to kill yas. Here I come, you sons a' bitches," DeSpain continued to sing, his voice sounding closer. Sam was able to clear hear him lever his rifle now after each shot. "I'll be riding six white horses when I come."

"I'm coming now to kill yas. I'm coming now to kill yas. I'm coming now to kill yas, when I—" His lyrics stopped beneath the loud bark of the short-barreled Colt. The Ranger had stepped out suddenly from behind the stack of wood, leveled the short-barreled Colt and fired. One bullet, one blast of orange-blue fire.

DeSpain's eyes flew wide open and stuck there; the Ranger stood with the short-barreled Colt curling smoke, still leveled at him. He watched a dark trickle of blood seep down from the bullet hole bored through the center of DeSpain's forehead. The detective's hat had sailed to the ground behind him, afloat on a red frothy mist.

The Ranger looked at Claypool's Colt, not recalling if he'd ever fired a gun—including his own—that fired so clean and smooth, and with such perfection. Looking at the gun, he felt like telling it, *Good job*. Instead he looked off toward L. C. McGuire, who was still working his way from rock to rock, firing into the high brush. Sam started to pick up his rifle and reload it, gauging the distance toward the stalking rifleman. But before he could do so, he saw L.C. stand up to move forward, only to be knocked backward a full flip as a shot resounded from the brush.

"There's that," he said quietly, seeing Hardaway's arm reach out of the brush and wave toward the cabin.

Stooping back down beside Wes Traybo, the Ranger looked at him, seeing him fading fast.

"You . . . got him?" Wes asked, barely speaking above a hoarse whisper now.

"I got him," Sam said.

"Good." Wes gave a faint smile at the smoking short-barreled Colt in the Ranger's hand. "Carter would have . . . liked that." He coughed up blood. "Are you sure . . . you never rode long . . . ?" he whispered.

"Never did," the Ranger replied.

"Too bad," said Wes. "I'll see you in hell . . . I reckon. . . ."

"Huh-uh." The Ranger shook his head. "I'll go a long ways to keep my word, but not that far."

Wes managed to give a chuckle. "That's a . . . good one," he said. He sighed and closed his eyes.

The Ranger stepped from behind the stack of wood, walked over, picked up his Colt and slipped it down in his holster. He looked at Claypool's short-barreled Colt in his hand.

"I'm glad I never stood in front of you," he said quietly to the gun as if it were a living thing. He reloaded it and shoved it down behind his gun belt. He was standing reloading his Winchester when Hardaway rode up on his horse at an easy walk, his arm still cradling his bandaged belly wound. He led the Ranger's speckled barb that he'd seen standing in the brush were Sam had left it.

"You're hit, Ranger," he said, noticing the blood on Sam's leg, a bloody cloth stuck against the deep graze at his hipbone.

"I've been hit worse," the Ranger replied. "How are you holding up, Fatcharack?"

Hardaway stopped his horse and gave him a cold stare.

"I mean *Fatch*," the Ranger said. "That just slipped out."

"All right," said Hardaway. "It's bad enough I'm in pain here. I don't need aggravation to boot."

"I understand," the Ranger said.

Hardaway looked over at the body of Ty Traybo facedown on the dirt. He winced and shook his head. He nodded toward the stack of wood on the porch.

"He's dead too," the Ranger said. "Baylor Rubens is lying dead in the barn. So's his horse."

"His horse is dead too?" said Hardaway.

"Yep," the Ranger said. "It looks like Rubens shot the horse, then shot himself."

"That sounds odd, but I can see Rubens doing it," said Hardaway. "He was always what you'd call *peculiar*. A good hand in a gunfight, though," he added. He swung down slowly from his saddle, looking pained as he stood on his feet. "We've got burying to do," he said.

"Are you able to handle a shovel?" the Ranger asked. "I don't want you getting your wound bleeding. I see the mood it put you in."

Hardaway cradled his wound. "To be honest with you, I really don't feel much like shoveling. But the Traybos were good men. They deserve something. So does Baylor Rubens." He gestured an arm toward the detectives. "These sons a' bitches, I couldn't care less. Let the wolves and coyotes eat them."

"Why don't you go inside, see what you can rustle up for us to eat?" the Ranger said. "I'll get everybody underground. We'll leave first thing come morning—give both of us time to heal over some."

"What happens tomorrow?" Hardway said, testing to see where he stood with the Ranger.

"Tomorrow we ride to Cottonwood, get you paid," said the Ranger.

"Are you picking up the bank money and riding through Maley on the way?" Hardaway asked.

"Yes, we are," said Sam, stepping over and shoving his rifle down into his saddle boot. "Can you control yourself, seeing all the money?"

"Yeah, I'm good now," said Hardaway. He sighed. "There was something about being around the Traybos, Carter Claypool, the whole bunch. It just got to me for a while—brought out the ol' long rider still in me. But I'm over it now. I own the Bad Cats Cantina, but myself—" He shook his head. "Hell, I'm not what you'd call a *bad cat* anymore."

Arizona Ranger Sam Burrack is back!
Don't miss a page of action from
America's most exciting Western author,
Ralph Cotton.

TWISTED HILLS

The Badlands, Arizona Territory

Under a blazing desert sun, Arizona Ranger Sam Burrack slid two warm and spent cartridge shells from his bone-handled Colt and replaced them with fresh rounds from his gun belt. A thin sliver of smoke still curled in the gun's cylinder. He closed the Colt's loading gate and held the gun upright as he looked all around the rocky, dissolute desert floor. A mile out, trail dust rose and drifted across a stretch of flatlands reaching toward the border.

"Looks like your pal Pres Kelso decided it's time to clear out of here," he said down to the wounded outlaw lying beneath the sole of his left boot.

"Preston Kelso . . . was never my *pal*, Ranger," the wounded man, Curtis Rudabell, replied in a pained and halting voice. "I only rode . . . with him this one time. He's a . . . son of a bitch. . . ."

So it was Pres Kelso . . . , Sam ascertained to himself. That was what he'd wanted to know. Looking at the outlaw's bloody chest, realizing Rudabell wasn't going anywhere, the Ranger lifted his boot off of his shoulder.

He stooped down beside him, picked up the smoking revolver sitting at Rudabell's side and held it in his free hand. He picked up a tobacco pouch made from a bull's scrotum, with Rudabell's initials carved on it. He tipped up the brim of his pearl gray sombrero and took a long breath. Twenty yards off lay the horse Rudabell had ridden to death.

"Feel free to take anything of mine you might need," Rudabell said with bitter sarcasm.

"Obliged," Sam said, his own sarcasm more veiled. As he spoke, he shoved the tobacco pouch behind his gun belt. He felt a few coins down inside the bag mixed with some chopped tobacco.

"Sons of Mother Nancy . . . I'm left for dead . . . ," Rudabell muttered under his failing breath. "Blast Kelso's eyes. . . ."

"I could have told you he's a runner," Sam said.

Rudabell clutched his bleeding chest.

"Yeah . . . but you *didn't* tell me though, did you?" the outlaw said bitterly, his voice weakening as he spoke. He stared at his gun in the Ranger's hand. "Tell the truth. . . . I nearly got you, didn't I, Ranger?"

"To tell the truth, Curtis," the Ranger said quietly, "no, you didn't. Fact is, you didn't even come close." He looked all around again, feeling the scalding heat of the sun pressing hard on his shoulders through his shirt, his riding duster. "Can I get you something . . . some water?" he asked.

Rudabell gave him a sour look. "Got any . . . whiskey?" he asked.

"Not a drop," Sam said.

"That . . . figures," said the dying outlaw. He reflected for a second, then said, "You reckon . . . there'll be whiskey aplenty in hell?"

"Never gave it much thought, Curtis," the Ranger said. "Seems like a tough place to go drinking." He stayed patient.

"I bet I've . . . drank in worse," Rudabell commented.

"Where's Pres headed in old Mex?" the Ranger asked. He knew the odds were long on the outlaw telling him anything, but it was worth a try.

"He's headed . . . to Cold Water, Ranger," Rudabell offered without hesitation.

"Agua Fría . . . ," the Ranger said.

"Yeah . . . that's right, Agua Fría . . . ," said Rudabell. He gave a deep, wheezing chuckle, his teeth smeared red with blood. "I hope you bust out and . . . follow him there."

"I intend to," Sam said, wanting to get as much information as he could from Rudabell before he died. "Why do you hope I follow him there?"

Rudabell didn't answer, his eyes drifting shut. Sam shook the outlaw by his shoulder.

"You'll see . . . ," said Rudabell, his eyes managing to reopen and focus on the Ranger. "My kind of people . . . have taken over Agua Fría." He gave a waning grin; his eyes closed again. "Ranger, guess what . . . ," he whispered. He managed to grip Sam's forearm, as if to hold on and keep from sliding off the edge of the earth.

"What?" the Ranger replied, letting him hold on, feeling his grip diminish with each passing second.

"There *is* whiskey in hell . . . I see it, plain as day . . . ," Rudabell said. He let out a breath, which stopped short and left his mouth agape.

Lucky you, Sam thought wryly.

He shook his head, reached out, touched the barrel of Rudabell's gun beneath the outlaw's beard-stubbled chin and tipped his gaping mouth shut. A trickle of blood seeped from the corner of Rudabell's lips and ran down his cheek toward his ear.

Sam stood up and looked off at the trail of dust roiling in the distance, seeing it disappear over a low rise of rocky ground. Lowering his Colt into its holster, he took off his sombrero and ran his fingers back through his damp hair. He shoved Rudabell's Smith & Wesson down behind his gun belt. On the ground lay a set of saddlebags stuffed with cash from the Clifton-American Mining Project.

Since he'd retrieved the money, he reasoned, maybe this was a good time to pull back and do some thinking.

For the past year, he'd heard of various thieves and killers taking refuge in and around the town of Agua Fría. It was time he checked things out there. Under the Matamoros Agreement, the Mexican government gave United States lawmen limited rights to cross the border in pursuit of felons in flight from American justice. But after what he'd just heard from Curtis Rudabell, which was nothing less than a dare, he wasn't going to follow Pres Kelso there. Not today.

He'd head there later—maybe a week, maybe longer.

And when he did go to Agua Fría, he wasn't going to be wearing a badge. *Huh-uh.* He got the feeling that wearing a badge would be the same as wearing a bull's-eye on his chest. He looked himself up and down, the pearl gray sombrero hanging in hand, the long duster. He looked over at his Appaloosa stallion, Black Pot; then he gazed back down at Curtis Rudabell.

"Obliged for the warning, Curtis," he said to the dead outlaw. He stooped enough to grip Rudabell by his shirt collar and drag him off toward a pile of rock.

Preston Kelso rode hard and straight, nonstop, until he reached the shelter of a rocky hill line. He wasn't sure if he had yet crossed the border, but when he swung his sweat-streaked bay around and looked back through the billowing dust, he saw no sign of being followed. *What the hell—?* Only a vast and empty stretch of desert floor lay behind him. Nothing moved on the arid rocky ground, save for the black shadow of a hawk circling high overhead.

"Ha . . . ," he chuffed to himself in surprise. So much for all the brave and relentless lawmen along the border.

He smiled to himself; but then his smile fell away quickly, as his fear subsided and his memory sharpened.

The money . . . !

He turned quickly in his saddle and looked down at his bay's sweaty dirt-streaked rump.

Damn it to hell . . . ! He let out a breath in exasperation, realizing Rudabell had been carrying the money— not just some of the money, but all of the money.

"Damn it to hell!" he repeated, this time out loud,

looking back again in the direction of the place where he and Rudabell had the running shootout with a lone lawman. "Curtis, you lousy dog," he murmured, "if you don't show up with that money, you'd better be deader than a cedar stump when I find you."

He jerked the bay's reins, turning the horse hard-handed, as if it were to blame. He slapped the long ends of the reins to the winded animal's side and spurred it forward at a run. The bay chuffed hard in protest, but shot forward, resuming the same fast pace beneath the scorching desert sun.

"You fall dead on me, cayuse," he warned, "and I'll eat your tenders and leave your carcass for the night feeders."

He gave a dark laugh and pushed the tired animal a full hour farther until they reached a water hole at the base of a low rocky hill line. After both horse and rider had drunk their fill, Kelso started to step up into his saddle when he heard the chilling sound of a snake rattling its warning from a pile of rocks less than five feet away. Instead of swinging the already frightened bay away from the sound, he instinctively turned, snatched his Colt up from its holster, and fired into the rocks, blindly. The bullet ricocheted three times off the rocks, whined back toward Kelso's head, and zipped past the bay's ear.

The horse, badly spooked by the sound of the snake followed by the blast of the Colt and the whining bullet, reared in panic and jerked free of Kelso's grip.

"Whoa!" Kelso shouted. But the bay bolted fast, its reins sliding through Kelso's hand before he could stop it.

Seeing the bay bounding away from the water hole and the hillside, out across the desert floor he'd just crossed, Kelso swung his smoking Colt up in anger. He fired two wild shots at the fleeing animal before he stopped himself and let his smoking Colt slump at his side.

"You're going to let me down too . . . ," he shouted at the animal, walking forward, seeing the bay slow to a halt less than a hundred yards away. The bay turned quarter-wise to him and stared back, its head lowered, its reins hanging to the ground. Kelso saw the horse scrape a front hoof on the rocky, sandy ground.

"Stay right there, you flea-bitten bag of bones," he murmured to himself. "I will beat you god-awful fierce." Even as he spoke, he closed the distance between himself and the bay with his left hand held out, as if offering it some sort of treat. The bay turned its stance a little more toward him, its muzzle pushed out in curiosity. A hot breeze lifted its dusty mane.

"That a boy," Kelso said, easing forward the last fifteen feet, his Colt still hanging in his right hand. He knew how much he needed the horse to get across mile after mile of rocky hills and long stretches of desert between here and Agua Fría. "Easy now, ole pal of mine . . . ," he whispered, taking the last few steps. "You know I wouldn't hurt you for the world."

The horse stood still, blowing and staring at him until Kelso got close enough to reach out for the dangling reins. But just as he made a grab for the reins, the bay spun sharply, bolted off twenty yards, stopped again and seemed to jeer at him.

"You lousy son of a—" Kelso gritted his teeth, jerked his Colt up and fired again before he could stop himself. Because he was weakened and winded, the impact of the shot knocked him off his feet. As the bay turned and loped away from the sound of the shot, Kelso staggered to his feet and bolted after it, weaving, screaming, cursing both the horse and himself. He fired another wild, reckless round as he ran. Again the gun's impact knocked him to the ground.

For a half mile the bay continued to play its mindless stop-and-go game with him. Kelso, falling with every shot fired, was gasping for breath and so engrossed in catching the horse, he neither saw nor heard the four unshod Indian ponies and their riders bound up behind him and sit watching him curiously from forty feet away. Still cursing the bay, Kelso staggered in place, winded and sweat-soaked, his mind bordering between sunstroke and hysteria.

"I've . . . got . . . you . . . now . . . ," he said, his breath heaving in his chest. He shoved fresh rounds into his Colt with shaking hands while the horse stood fifteen feet away, scraping its hoof on the arid sandy ground. "You . . . rotten . . . dirty . . . no good . . ." Kelso panted and wheezed and struggled to catch his breath as he finished reloading, lifted the heavy revolver with both hands and took aim.

On one of the Indian ponies behind him, a young Apache brave named Luka looked at an older warrior, Wallace Bad Man Gomez.

"This one shoots at his own horse . . . ?" Luca whispered sidelong to the older warrior.

Without taking his dark eyes off of the staggering, cursing white man in front of them, Gomez nodded his head and laid his hand on the stock of an old short-barreled flintlock rifle lying across his lap.

"I have seen them do even worse," he replied, referring to his days as scout for U.S. Cavalry's desert campaign. He stared intently at the staggering, cursing white man. "And they wonder why we want to kill them."

The others grunted in agreement.

Kelso, with his revolver cocked and ready, finally steadied himself and smiled a dry lip-cracking smile.

"I've got you now, you run-off son of a bitch," he murmured to himself. He started to squeeze the trigger; but he stopped and clenched both hands tight on the gun butt as a searing pain sliced through his back. The Colt's barrel tipped upward, and fired a blue-orange streak into the sky. Kelso staggered in place but remained upright. His eyes widened as he saw an arrow shaft suddenly sticking out of his chest, its chiseled stone point smeared red with his blood. His left hand turned loose of his Colt and felt the tip of the arrowhead as if to make sure it was real.

Oh no! Damn it . . . ! Kelso said to himself. No sooner had he realized that an arrow was stuck through him than another bloody arrow head appeared beside the first as if to reinforce his findings. "All day it's . . . been like this . . . ," he gasped to himself. Behind him he heard his bay's hooves pounding away across the desert flatland.

Son of a bitch . . .

He turned to face the four Apache, his gun still up in

his right hand, but weaving unsteadily. One of the arrows through his back had sliced one of his wide suspender straps. The strap flew loose so fast, it caused the other strap to fall off his shoulder. As he'd turned, his low-slung gun belt and loose trousers fell down around his boots. He faced the Apache in his dirty long-johns as a third arrow whistled in and sliced deep into his chest.

Kelso grunted with the impact of the arrow; his Colt fell from his hand. Scrambling, he managed to stoop down for the gun as he saw one of the Indians come charging toward him. He grabbed the gun and stood just in time to see pony and rider streak past him in a roil of sand. He felt a strong hand lift his hair, hat and all atop his head, and in the next second, the rider was gone, swinging his pony in a short, tight circle, letting out a war whoop.

Kelso turned and stared, feeling a dark, sharp burning across the top of his exposed head. He caught a glimpse of his hat brim fluttering to the ground a few feet away.

"Oh . . . my God," he said, his gun hand falling to his side, dropping the Colt to the ground. "I've been ruint." He stared in disbelief at the young warrior whooping and shouting, waving the crown of Kelso's hat back and forth in his hand—Kelso's hair and bloody skin hanging beneath it. Staring at his own stringy hair clasped in the warrior's hand, Kelso sank straight down to his knees; then he flopped forward onto his face in the hot, sandy dirt.

As the Apache sat their horses above Kelso, the older warrior, Gomez, saw one of the young warriors raise a battered French Gruen rifle to his shoulder and take aim on the center of Kelso's bloody back. He held up a hand toward the warrior, stopping him.

"Let this fool's shots be the last ones heard," he said. He shook his head in disgust. "Even his horse deserts him." He looked all around as he turned his horse and gestured for the others to do the same. The young warrior Luka held Kelso's bloody scalp and stringy hair out for the others to see.

"A good day for one of us is a good day for all of us," he said proudly. The warriors and their horses fell in alongside Gomez and rode away abreast, out across the flatlands.

In the preceding silence, two hours passed before Kelso opened his bleary eyes at the feel of the horse's hot, wet muzzle nudging the side of his neck. A layer of dust had gathered on the top of his raw, bloody skull. In a weakened state, as he tried to push himself up from the ground, he felt the dried blood and the points of the two ground-stuck arrows reluctant to turn him loose. Yet, as his memory returned to him through a fiery painful haze, he managed to struggle upward onto his haunches and look at the bay, who stood staring at him.

"I'll kill you . . . for this . . . ," he said painfully, reaching all around on the dirt for his Colt.

The bay only chuffed and blew and shook out its mane, as if taunting the man for the sudden loss of his hair. Kelso, realizing the Apache had taken both his handgun and rifle, gave a deep sigh and pulled himself up on the bay's front leg and leaned against its side. The horse stood quietly.

"I don't know . . . what else can . . . befall a man . . . ," he groaned, seeing the brim of his hat and its sliced-off crown lying in the dirt at his feet. He stooped, picked up the brim and pulled it carefully down over his raw-scalped head, drawing the string taught under his chin. He crawled up the horse's side. "I'm killing you . . . first chance I get," he whispered to the bay. Righting himself in his saddle as best he could with arrows still sticking through him, he managed to turn the horse and ride away.